From Shards
To Sea Glass

Michele Wilder

Steaming Kettle Publications

michelewilder.info

Scripture quotations: Authorized King James Version (public domain)

Hymn quotations: "It Is Well with My Soul", "Come, Ye Disconsolate" (public domain)

Cover photography: Michele Wilder

Interior design: Polgarus Studio

Chapter One

"Are you aware, Miss Wycoff, that your parents had a safe deposit box?"

Claire compressed her finger with a sweaty palm. "Why, no."

"I didn't think so." Mr. Buchannan swiveled from his desk to the file-laden credenza behind him. He reached for a small cardboard box with a large yellow envelope balancing on it and turned back to face her. "I'm glad my letter caught up to you. My secretary gave up trying to call you three weeks ago."

He set the box on his desk. "Your boyfriend called a few times and even stopped by once demanding to know the status of your parents' insurance policies." He paused. "He also asked if we knew your whereabouts."

Claire's eyes widened. She squeezed the next finger as her hands began to tremble.

"We told him nothing."

She exhaled slowly through tightened lips. "Thank you."

"Your father had given me explicit instructions that you not know about the existence of the safe deposit box unless both he and your mother were deceased."

She clenched her jaw, willing her eyes to stop pooling. *I'm not going to cry. I'm not!* An unbidden tear rolled down her cheek.

Mr. Buchannan's long brown finger pushed aside the name plate reading "Rufus Buchannan, Esquire" and nudged a tissue box toward her.

Claire swiped a tissue.

He tapped the yellow envelope. "This contains copies of the paperwork for your files and the four lump-sum checks. Again, I'm sorry for the delay in receiving these claims, but once we finally obtained the required proof that your parents' deaths were not a result of suicide or homicide, the insurance companies processed them rather quickly."

She blew her nose. "I understand."

"Would you like to look at the checks now?"

She shook her head.

"Very well." He set the envelope aside and unfolded the flaps on the box. "Here are the contents of the safe deposit box. Thankfully your father had left the keys with me."

Claire mopped her eyes with the soggy tissue.

"On top of the contents I found an envelope with instructions that this note be read to you before you receive the items. Would you like me to read it?"

Claire nodded.

He withdrew a 3x5 card from a small white envelope and cleared his throat. "'Our dear Claire, These items hold great meaning to your mother and me and represent special times or people from our past. Some things you know about. Others you don't. Pay particular attention to the riddle in the small brown box. If you choose to follow its lead back to your roots, please be extremely careful. We love you, Claire. You are the best daughter any parents could ever hope for. Love, Dad and Mom.'"

Claire swooshed two more tissues from the box and buried her face in them.

Mr. Buchannan tucked the card back into its envelope. "Do you want to look through the contents now?"

She shook her head.

Mr. Buchannan returned the white envelope to the box before reclosing the flaps and setting the yellow envelope back on top. "Do you have any questions, or is there anything else I can do for you?"

She wiped her nose. "No, you have been most helpful."

"It has been a privilege to be of service to you and, of course, to your parents the past several years," he said while rising with the box and envelope. "Again, my deepest condolences, Miss Wycoff."

Using the desk to steady herself, she rose and took them from his hands. "Thank you for all your help, Mr. Buchannan. You've been most kind."

As she left, she clutched the box to her chest. Other than the two pictures, she held in her arms the only tangible remnants of her parents' lives.

ᘓᘓᘓ

The next day, the clinking of dishes and hum of conversation faded into the background as Claire pushed down on one of the buckling folds of the crisp, newly-purchased map. *Out of Hyding on the coast of Maine.*

Starting at the northeastern-most point, she inched her finger down the jagged coastline of Maine. *Out of Hyding on the coast of Maine.* She read every tiny name. *Out of Hyding on the coast of Maine.* She scrutinized every island and pond and county and town.

Out of... Her finger stopped. "Hydeport," she whispered. *Could it be?* She traced the remainder of the coast to the New Hampshire border then slid her finger back under the name of the town. Hydeport. *It has to be it. Nothing else fits.*

Should she *move* there? Perhaps focusing on solving the strange riddle would give her purpose and direction again. How she craved a diversion from the continual turmoil warring within her! Would she let her parents down if she didn't go? Leaning back she picked up her teacup and sipped the last cold swig of the sweet, milky liquid.

Move to Maine? She suspended the cup below her lips.

Leaving the painful memories in Chicago tempted her, yet traveling by herself across the country to a place she had never been intimidated her.

No, it scared her!

But then...

Her hand shook as she clinked the cup back onto its saucer.

...Daniel would never think to look for her there.

She refolded the map. *Maybe I should go—and soon!* She stood and floated a ten-dollar bill onto the check before slipping her arms through her coat sleeves. *How can I be sure of what to do?* Grabbing the map and her purse, she headed toward the door. *If I just had some kind of confirmation…*

～～～

Philip's stomach growled. With an hour to kill before exhibitors could enter the convention center, he drove to the parking lot of a diner he had seen on his way to the hotel last night. As he pulled his jeep into a parking place in front of the sidewalk, a young woman with a long mass of brown curls walked toward him. *Wow!*

He followed her as she approached the corner of his dark-blue, SUV-style jeep. He shifted into park.

She glanced at the front of his jeep then stopped in her tracks and stared. She lifted her striking, aqua-colored eyes toward him.

Captivated he couldn't look away.

Her eyes widened then returned to the front of his jeep. She blinked several times before turning about and hurrying down the sidewalk.

Coming to his senses, Philip reached for the door latch and pushed at the door. "Grrr!" The keys jangled as he turned them and pulled them out of the ignition. His seatbelt zipped across him while he yanked the door latch again. After unfolding his 6'2" frame from the jeep, he stepped out then up onto the empty sidewalk. He scooched in front of the jeep and inspected it thoroughly before scrunching his eyebrows.

He stood again and scanned the parking lot.

She had disappeared.

Chapter Two

I can't believe I'm doing this.

Erin, the property manager, cut into her thoughts. "My, what a fabulous May morning this is!"

Claire wiped her clammy hands on the sides of her thighs. "Yes—yes, indeed."

"Again, I do apologize that this rental isn't closer to Hydeport, but I just can't think of anyplace else available that comes close to what you're looking for."

"This twenty-mile drive hasn't been terribly bad, I suppose." The doubt blanketing her mind threatened to smother the weak flames of determination and excitement that had flickered to life last week.

Claire covered a yawn. She had dragged her twenty-four-year-old body into a motel late last night and while looking for breakfast in a vending machine an hour ago had spotted the realty office across the highway.

If this cottage doesn't work, maybe I should toss this whole crazy idea into the wind and head back west this afternoon.

"Now Lone Spruce Cove, or the Cove as the locals call it, is just over a mile beyond the cottage," Erin continued. "It's a small town but has a main street full of fabulous shops and a lovely little harbor."

Oh, no! She's trying to sell me on the town. The cottage must be a shack!

"The Cove is pretty quiet most of the year, but as we get closer to Memorial Day weekend it will swell with tourists and weekenders. Many homes in the area are summer or weekend residences, but the owner of the estate where the cottage is located lives here all year round."

As they meandered up Route 1, the two-lane highway between Hydeport and Lone Spruce Cove, dense evergreens and spindly, budding trees edging the road blurred past. When houses, antique shops, or inns parted the trees, bursts of the brilliant-blue ocean beyond them mesmerized her. The encroaching trees, however, suffocated her, and she tugged at the damp edge of her V-neck shirt.

The car slowed and turned right at a pop of pink—a square, wooden sign dangling from an iron hanger. Carved into the sign the name "The English Rose" glistened in gold leaf. Below the name three pink roses protruded in raised relief.

They wound through a short evergreen tunnel before the passage opened. Claire sat erect in her seat. Erin stopped the car.

"How beautiful," Claire whispered. "It certainly isn't Lake Michigan."

The deep-sapphire ocean extended for miles and miles until it faded to light blue then to frosted whiteness where ocean and sky met. The morning sun dangled over the water on their left and doodled a shimmering line of gold on the ocean's surface. Boats skittered in all directions.

They crept on, stopping again where the driveway divided. Erin pointed. "This is the landlord's house." She ducked her head and leaned over to look out Claire's window. "I just love the colonial style. It was built in the early 1800's."

Claire's attention roamed over the immaculate grounds to the garnet-colored, wooden doors on the detached garage to the symmetrical, two-story house standing tall and proud at a right angle to the shore.

"Just look at that stone chimney and those cedar shakes."

Garnet trim glossed in contrast to weathered gray shakes that hung like rows of teeth on the garage and house. "They're lovely."

Erin pointed up. "I bet it's a fabulous view from that upper story!"

Large windows filled with small individual panes looked out at Claire with an empty stare. The sun glinted off a stained-glass window on the front door beside black iron hardware befitting a castle.

Claire leaned back. "I can't imagine living in such a place—though I certainly wouldn't mind it."

The car rolled on and, after veering to the left, stopped at the bottom of a short incline in front of a tiny, butter-colored cottage facing the landlord's house.

"This is darling—like something out of a storybook!"

"Isn't it? It was converted from an outbuilding several years back," Erin said as they got out of the car. "Originally intended to be used only seasonally, the owner recently converted it to be lived in year round."

Led by slate squares pressed into the grass, they stepped toward a white door set with a round, stained-glass window pieced in the same design as the sign by the road. Buds tipped stark bushes beneath the windowless area on the left and the large, square-paned window on the right.

Once over the threshold, Claire's eyes fell instinctively to the gray granite-tiled floor. The calming smell of lavender floated from a twisted wreath hanging on the hallway's pastel-blue walls. Golden morning light extended its welcome across the tiles from the end of the short hallway.

On Claire's right, a bed covered with a brocade bedspread filled the center of the mint-colored bedroom. The antique mirror on top of a tall white bureau reflected the morning light from the window topped with an open Roman shade.

Her curiosity lured her past the bedroom, the bathroom across from it, and the pocket door hiding the hallway closet to the open room at the back of the cottage.

"As you requested, it's fully furnished," Erin said gesturing toward the white-washed wooden table and two chairs nestled within the kitchenette on their left. She picked up a tumbler from an open shelf. "I love these green, Depression-glass dishes." She returned it and nodded toward the leftmost corner. "The heat source is that woodstove."

Claire caught an earthy whiff of leather from the white loveseat at her right. The sun's permeating warmth radiated through the large windows at the far right corner of the room. "The light in here is amazing."

"It is, and because of the cottage's angle, you would have plenty of sun for much of the day. Do you think your worktable and supplies will fit in that corner?"

"Yes, I believe they will."

The sunlight glittering off the ocean beckoned her, and she walked to the French doors and threw them open. She closed her eyes. While infusing her lungs with the invigorating mix of salt air and balsam, she implored the sun to caress her with its rays. The balm of the ocean's cadence soothed her brittle emotions.

She turned to Erin. "I'll take it."

～✺✺✺

Erin locked the front door. "The landlord travels often and is, in fact, away now. While our company takes care of showing the rental and the paperwork, you pay him directly each month."

Claire bit her lip. "Do I have to wait until he returns before moving in? I'm supposed to return the little rental trailer by tomorrow morning."

"Oh, no, we can sign the papers, and you can move in today." She pointed toward the main house. "Just drop your payment through the mail slot in the front door up there when you return today and then on the first of each month."

Once again, Claire followed Erin's finger. *Hmm.* She liked the idea of having an excuse to get close to that house.

～✺✺✺

As the sun vanished, Claire drove back up Route 1, tired but satisfied with the day's accomplishments. *I can't believe I actually moved here...and all because of a riddle that makes little sense.* What would her parents have thought of her?

"Every event happens for a purpose, Claire." She snorted believing her mother's words even less now than when she heard them years ago. *"God always has a good reason for allowing things to happen even though we may not know or understand why at the time."*

Claire doubted God had anything to do with her move to Maine and

8

scowled. What possible reason could God have in allowing her parents to die? Why had God changed her world to one full of guilt and fear and misery?

She tightened her grip on the steering wheel. Sweat trickled down her neck as anxiety's familiar hand constricted her breathing. She forced deep breaths into her lungs as she turned at the sign and crept along the tunneled driveway.

Loneliness, her constant companion, reminded her of its presence. Once again she convinced herself that only because of grief had she been distanced from her friends and her work.

As the headlights pierced the darkness, Daniel came to mind.

A shiver slithered up her spine.

A week before their deaths her parents had expressed their disapproval and advised her to end her relationship with him. She squeezed her quivering lips together as she parked in front of the cottage and turned off the ignition.

The painful memory of that night at the coffee shop tormented her once again. If she had yielded, she would be married to him right now. It would have been so much easier to have just given in and said "yes"—and yet…

Unstoppable tears coursed down her cheeks. *I need to snap out of this.* She licked the salty drops that slid onto her lips.

The sudden roar of a motor jumped her. She straightened her body and listened. Just as quickly the throaty sound stopped.

Sniffling, she opened her door. The headlights blinked out, and her dim dome light did little to scatter the surrounding darkness. Oh, why hadn't she turned on some lights earlier?

She wiped her eyes on her shaking hand and inhaled the cool, breezeless air before tilting her chin. *I will put the past behind me and move on. I must!*

After grabbing a box of food from the back seat, she unlocked and entered the cottage, wishing an outside light hung by the door. With her elbow she flipped on the light switch in the hallway then the one in the living area before setting the box on the table. She returned to the car and carted in the box of important items and an overnight bag.

On the final trip, she grabbed her purse and jacket and shut the car door. She glanced up at the moonless sky where stars twinkled on their velvety, black blanket. She had never seen so many before!

With only a faint glow from the back of the cottage cutting through the darkness, her eyes dared fall to the restless deep several hundred feet away where scattered lights winked on its onyx face. Who would be on the ocean at night?

She glanced up her driveway toward the landlord's dark house. Her payment! She shuddered. *There is no way I'm going up…*

Something swished through the grass behind her. She whipped her body around and strained to listen.

The grass rustled again.

She froze. "Who's there?"

Only the lilt of the ocean answered her.

She peered into the darkness. "Who's there?"

Nothing.

Gripping her purse, she rushed into the cottage, slamming the door behind her and clicking the lock. She threw the purse and jacket on the bedroom floor then scurried through the living area to latch the French doors.

She felt eyes on her through the curtainless windows. Fear prickled up her arms and neck.

She scrambled through the cottage looking for more lights. Finding only the one in the bathroom, she clicked it on before crossing the hall and grabbing the bedspread. After maneuvering the loveseat to face the wall, she wrapped the bedspread around her and hunched out of view.

Her senses stood alert.

Minutes passed.

Warmed by the bedspread and lulled by the rhythm of the ocean, her body relaxed. Her eyelids fell as exhaustion weighted them.

Sniff. Was that cigarette smoke?

"Dad, don't light that. No, don't do it."

She tried to open her eyelids, but they wouldn't budge.

"Dad, don't you know what it will do?" she slurred.

Chapter Three

Claire's body jerked at the caw of a blackbird outside the window. Her eyes flew open.

Where am I?

The sunlight bounced off the light-blue wall in front of her. A motor chugged in the distance. She shivered and ran her hands up and down her cold arms. The bedspread lay crumpled between the wall and the loveseat. *Ah, the cottage!*

She rubbed the back of her stiff neck then rotated her shoulders before turning around and kneeling to face the room. She blinked at the bright morning sunshine before noticing one window stood ajar. No wonder she felt so cold!

She stood and righted the loveseat before slamming the window shut and flicking off the three light switches. While clicking the one in the bathroom, she scolded her reflection. "Scaredy-cat!"

She found her delicate floral teacup and saucer snuggled at the top of a box and placed the cheerful set on the counter. She had purchased the set shortly after her parents' deaths and found comfort sipping tea from it.

She pulled her tea kettle from deeper in the box and rooted around further to find its lid. She had dropped it while packing, breaking the handle and denting the top so that the lid no longer fit. She filled the kettle with water then placed it on the burner, holding her hands close to warm them.

She looked in the meager box of food she brought from Chicago and scrunched her nose at not having milk to put into her tea. She should have picked up groceries in Hydeport yesterday.

After preparing her light breakfast, she pulled a chair in front of the French doors to watch a boat as it stopped by a bright orange floating marker. A man in yellow overalls pulled a large rectangular object from the water. Seagulls gathered over it looking for their own breakfast.

Eager to investigate her surroundings, she placed her teacup on the table before donning her coat and knit hat and stepping into the brisk morning air. She followed another slate path leading from the French doors and through the grassy lawn to the edge of the cliff that overlooked the small beach. She steadied herself as she zigzagged down the steep path.

Once on the beach, Claire crouched and scooped up a handful of the cold brown-sugar sand mixed with small pebbles. She wiggled her fingers and released the sand while admiring the flecks of mica as they glinted in the morning sun.

A wave surged onto the shore, startling her into standing.

The beach extended to her right for a few yards before turning into flat rocks that rose above her head, tapering as they jutted out and down into the surf. To her left the beach stretched for many yards to a similar area of flat rocks, though this rocky area did not reach as far into the water.

Claire thrust her hands into her pockets and sauntered to the end of the beach where several tall, thick, wooden poles protruded from the ground in ugly contrast to the otherwise attractive beach. With stringy seaweed and crusty-looking growths clinging to them, she wondered about their purpose as they marched in formation into the water.

A white boat with a wide orange stripe rumbled deeply as it rounded the bend, slowed, and propelled in front of her. A man sat behind a steering wheel while another man holding a pair of binoculars to his eyes stood beside him, facing the shore.

Without thinking, Claire waved her arm in wide swoops. The man lowered the binoculars, brought them to his eyes again, then lowered them a second time before waving to her and motioning to the driver to move on.

As she neared the far end of the beach, the cliff graduated high above her head. Hidden from view until she stood in front of it, a narrow path led straight from the beach to the top of the cliff. Shoeprints marked the path and the sand below it.

Claire kicked at some cigarette butts. "Ugh!" Maybe there *had* been someone lurking about last night. No, exhaustion had toyed with her nerves, and the darkness had supercharged her imagination.

No doubt someone in the family in the main house strolled on this beach and smoked.

She turned about. From her new vantage point, the cottage had disappeared from sight, but she could see the entire top level of both the side and front of the main house.

She ambled along and picked up small pieces of granite, agate, and quartz delighting in their colors and textures, and planning on their use in future mosaic projects. She placed them in her coat pocket.

An outgoing wave washed over a flat, egg-shaped rock made of pink granite and flecked with green minerals. She just had to have it!

She waited for the water to draw back again before bending and reaching over as far as she could to grab it. As her fingertips curled around the rock— whoosh! The water raced in faster and higher than she had expected toppling her backward and soaking her pants and shoes.

She scrambled to her feet. "Yikes!"

She backed onto the security of the dry sand before the icy fingers of another wave slid up to grab her. The beach had narrowed since she first stepped foot on it. That's right! Unlike Lake Michigan, tides ruled the ocean.

Clutching her hard-won prize, she dripped her way up the path toward the cottage.

Chapter Four

With his small body ensconced in an imposing chair across the desk, Mr. Gibbons, the bank manager, looked over reading glasses perched precariously close to the end of his nose. "Would you like a savings account as well, Miss?" His bushy mustache twitched in sync with his ears when he spoke.

Claire stifled a giggle. "Yes, I would like both, thank you."

He lifted one eyebrow as he checked a box on the form with his pen.

"Slowly spell your first and last names," he said in a monotone.

"C-l-a-i-r-e. W-y-c-o-f-f."

He stopped mid-scribble and narrowed his eyes. "Are you related to the Wycoffs north of the Cove?"

Claire snapped her head back. She knew her father's only sibling lived somewhere along the coast of Maine but had never been told where. "I—I couldn't tell you." She shifted in her chair.

He frowned. "*Humph.* I hope not." He looked back at the paper. "Telephone number?"

"I don't have a telephone."

"You don't have a telephone? When you get one, make sure you supply us the number."

"I won't be getting a phone."

"Who doesn't have a telephone?"

"I won't be making any calls, and I don't want to receive any." She couldn't tell him she feared her old boyfriend would find her and try to contact her. "If you need me, you can send me a letter."

He heaved a loud sigh. "Where do you live then?"

"I don't have a post office box yet, but when I get one I'll bring in the number. I live at..." She pulled a piece of paper from an envelope on her lap. "...747 Route 1, here in Lone Spruce Cove."

Mr. Gibbons' eyebrows shot up as he scratched down the address. "So, you live at The English Rose estate then."

"Well—I live in a cottage there."

He examined her face and hair. "Uh—huh."

Claire's face flushed. "I've rented the little yellow cottage on the estate through a respectable property management company out of Hydeport."

"Oh, of course...of course. Yes, it would be nice to live in a cottage there. Beautiful property." He twiddled his pen. "You won't find a better landlord in the entire area."

Claire scowled before glancing down at the paper in front of him then back at him hoping he would get the point she wanted to move on.

"Now with what amount of money do you want to open your accounts, Miss Wycoff? You must deposit a minimum of one-hundred dollars in each account."

She handed him a white envelope. "These checks are for the savings account, and this cash," she passed him a larger envelope, "is for the checking account."

He opened the envelope of cash and stiffened in his chair. His eyes grew large as he fingered through the checks in the other envelope.

"Well, now, Miss Wycoff." He cleared his throat. "Please sign these." His hands shook as he gave her his pen and pointed to where she needed to sign. "I'll get these accounts set up for you immediately, Miss Wycoff." He gathered the forms and money and hastened from the office.

Claire rolled her eyes.

By the end of the visit, she had been introduced to all the employees. Mr. Gibbons led her to the door and opened it for her. "Welcome to Lone Spruce Cove and to our bank. If there is *anything* I can do for you in *any* way at *any* time, do not hesitate to let me know."

Claire walked the short distance from the bank to the post office and entered the small, free-standing, brick building. A heavyset woman in her mid-60s sat behind the counter. Framing her heavily freckled face, faded natural-red hair stuck out in different directions. Her nametag read "Lorna."

"I'd like a post office box, please," Claire said.

"You must be new to town. Don't recognize you."

"I am."

"Needing a box. Let's see here." She opened a drawer beside her and licked her fingers before thumbing through several papers. She selected one and slid it toward Claire before slamming the drawer shut.

"So you're new here, huh? It's a nice little town. A lot goes on here for being so small. You'd be surprised how busy it gets here in the summertime."

Claire picked up a pen chained to the counter and worked her way down the form.

Lorna planted her elbows on the counter. "You're here right before the two big summer events we have. One's in June, and the other's in August. They're pretty popular. I have to make sure we have plenty of stamps available for all the postcards people send from here. You wouldn't believe how many postcards we mail out during the summer."

"Is that so?"

"How long have you been living here?"

"I moved here yesterday." Claire signed her name at the bottom of the form.

"Why have you come? Not many people actually move here."

"Well, why not move here?" Claire smiled as she slid the form back to Lorna and rummaged in her purse for her cash and identification.

Lorna's forefinger skimmed down the form. It stopped and tapped the address of the cottage. Her finger glided down the rest of the way until it reached her signature. She slid her finger under Claire's last name several times.

Lorna raised her head and squinted one of her dark-brown eyes. "You related to the Wycoffs north of town?"

Here we go again. "There are Wycoffs close to town? Do they spell their name as I do?"

"Exactly the same. In all my years at this post office, I have never seen or heard of anyone else with the name of Wycoff other than those in that family—which is fine with me. No offense, though, if you're related to them.

"I…"

"Yup, they're quite a family, those Wycoffs. Since Garry died in that accident—what a horrible accident it was with that machinery crushing him. Terrible! I'm still not so sure about those boys, though." She frowned. "Something's fishy about it. Then again, you must know all about it."

Claire shook her head.

"When was that now?" She studied the ceiling as if the answer were written there. "Around a year and a half ago, I think. Maybe it's been two years now. Let's see." She picked up a pen and counted on her fingers with it. "May…June…July…Yes, it will be two years this coming July. Since Garry died—Garry, the father, you know—that granite quarry has been doing poorly. It was actually doing poorly *before* he died. At least that's what was being said around town."

Claire stared at her.

"Anyway, the place just isn't the same now. Not anything like it was. It's a shame, all run down like it is. Of course I think the showroom is still open a few days a week, but not that many people go there anymore. It's not as respectable as it used to be."

Lorna's chair groaned as she spun around and reached for a set of keys dangling beside several others on a pegboard. She swung back again and handed them to Claire before snatching the receipt and pushing it on the counter toward her.

"When my husband and I needed to retile our bathroom—the main one, not the one upstairs by the guest room—we drove by the Wycoff place, but the showroom wasn't open. So, we just decided to go to Jensen's in Hydeport. We could have gone up to Augusta, but Hydeport is closer. Really Jensen's selection is not much different than what you'll find anywhere in Augusta."

After placing the keys in her purse, Claire scooped up the receipt, baffled at how Lorna's thoughts could tumble from one subject to the next. How could this woman say so much in such a short period of time while still processing transactions?

Two people carrying stacks of packages came in, distracting Lorna when they set them on the counter. Relieved, Claire saw this as her chance to get away.

"Thank you, Lorna, for setting up my post office box," she said as she turned and exited the building.

She returned to her car and slid behind the steering wheel but did not turn on the ignition. Could these Wycoffs north of town be her relatives? Mr. Gibbons acted strangely when he spoke of them, and Lorna did not speak well of them.

As suddenly as the wave crept up the beach earlier and had left her sodden in its wake, uneasiness swept over her leaving her mind saturated with apprehension.

Chapter Five

Claire eyed the convenience store across from the post office but decided to check out the town first before returning to choose from their undoubtedly expensive and limited selection of groceries.

She pulled away from the curb and swung left down a wide curve. A narrow road veered to the right and dropped down a short steep hill to a small parking lot situated beside docks. Boats bobbed in a postcard-perfect harbor.

For two blocks Route 1 changed into lantern-lined Main Street. Brick sidewalks led to shops housed in the lower portions of abutting two- to four-story brick buildings. With colorful awnings, window boxes, and ornate signs, each shop enticed with its own unique character.

At the end of Main Street on the harbor side, she passed a small white church with a tall steeple and stained-glass windows. A sheriff's deputy had parked his cruiser in front of it and stood with two men at the top of the steep flight of stairs. Two arched doors had been propped open.

Past the church the road forked. The road on the right hugged the harbor. Before it curved out of sight, it passed a grassy lawn surrounding a parking area separating the church from a small, stately structure graced with tall windows. "Public Library" had been carved into a slab of granite between its grand pillars and above its wooden double doors.

Claire's stomach rumbled. She continued up Route 1 for a short distance before turning around. There would be time for more exploring another day.

As she inched back through town, diffused sun glinted off something to her left. Below a blue metal hanger, a sign in the shape of a black teapot blew back and forth. Claire smiled at the name, Tea with Grace, accented in silver-gilt lettering and surrounded by painted forget-me-nots.

She swung into a parking space and walked across the street to the shop. Blue and purple-striped awnings shaded two large windows above long white window boxes teeming with blooming forget-me-nots. A sign in one of the windows read, "Today's Scone: Blueberry."

Mmm!

She pushed the brass latch on the blue door. Violin music and the smell of buttery blueberry scones greeted her. Cloud-diffused sunlight streamed through a wall of windows at the far end of the shop, bouncing off whitewashed brick walls and a high ceiling covered in squares of embossed tin tiles.

On her left lay a long wooden counter beside a rounded-glass case full of sweets and savories stacked on silver trays. Her stomach growled again.

"Just a minute, please. I'll be right with you." A middle-aged lady in a blue apron carrying a tray full of dishes disappeared through a swinging door on Claire's right.

Claire walked to one of the large antique display hutches in a small retail section by the swinging door and admired the delicate teacups and tins of tea. Brightly-colored kettles sat on a table beside the hutch. She reached for a vibrant green one.

"Don't those kettles have a nice shape? They came in yesterday." Wiping her hands on her apron, the lady had reappeared. "I love all the different colors too. I ordered dark pink ones as well, but for some reason they were shipped separately. I'm expecting them in this afternoon's delivery."

Claire replaced the kettle. "I desperately need a new one, and pink is my favorite color."

"Well, if the shipment comes in today and you will be around tomorrow, I would be more than happy to hold one for you. You can pick it up any time after we open."

"Yes, please do that. I'll come by tomorrow afternoon."

"May I help you with anything else?"

"I sure could use a pot of black tea and perhaps a blueberry scone with lemon curd."

"Absolutely!"

The round-figured lady led Claire to the table she had hoped for, the one at the center of the wall of windows, before heading to the kitchen for Claire's tea and scone. Claire sat and gazed out the window.

A tall fence separated the alley directly below her from a grassy lawn. A paved pathway wound its way through the grass to the parking lot and along the water. An elderly couple sat arm in arm on one of the many wooden benches placed along the path. Boats—from small rowboats to yachts—strained at their ropes along the dock. Other boats, moored to large balls and little floating platforms in the harbor, bounced about in the wind.

Breaking her from her thoughts, the lady approached the table and placed a teacup in front of her then poured steaming water from a teapot over the strainer resting on the cup's edges.

Claire bent toward the cup, closed her eyes, and breathed in the sweet grassy smell of the unfurling leaves.

"Does this smell good!"

The woman smiled revealing deep dimples in her rosy cheeks. "Milk or sugar?"

"Both please."

The woman with curly, shoulder-length, brown hair and large brown eyes moved with decorum as she placed things on the table. "Will you be visiting Lone Spruce Cove long?"

Claire poured milk from a miniature glass pitcher into the teacup. "Actually I just moved here yesterday. I've rented a cottage and am planning on staying for a while at least."

The woman positioned on the table a dish cradling a large blueberry scone drizzled with sugary glaze and two small dishes, one filled to the brim with fluffy clotted cream and the other with bright-yellow lemon curd.

"Oh, that's great! Welcome to the Cove! My name is Grace—Grace Hearst—and this is my tearoom," she said, sweeping her hand toward the front of the shop.

Everything about this woman put Claire at ease, and she couldn't help but like her.

"I'm Claire." She did not say her last name and hoped Grace would not ask her for it.

"Where have you moved from, Claire?"

"From Illinois—the Chicago area."

Grace's eyes sparkled. "Hey, I'm originally from the Midwest too—from northern Wisconsin. I met my husband in college and moved here as his bride."

After adding sugar to her tea, Claire took a needed sip and replaced the cup on its saucer.

"You'll find the Cove quite different from Chicago. For one thing, the people are much more reserved than people in the Midwest. It may take a while for them to warm up to you, but they will with time. It took me years to figure that out and get used to how people think especially in such a small town as this."

As hungry as she was, Claire enjoyed Grace's warm company and the camaraderie she felt toward her.

"Did you come here with your family then?"

Sadness filled her. "No, I have no parents or siblings…and I'm not married."

"No family?" Grace scowled. "So young!"

Claire lowered her eyes.

"And a pretty girl like you? Not married?"

Claire gave Grace a slight smile.

"I'm impressed you moved half way across the country by yourself. You must have a lot of gumption!"

If she only knew!

"Are you looking for work? I have Nan who bakes for me, but I'll certainly need some extra help around here soon. 'The season,'" she said making quotes in the air, "will be in full swing before long, and I'm sure the customers would like you."

Claire did not expect such kindness. "Thank you, that's very nice of you, but I have other work in mind."

"Oh?"

Claire felt obligated to explain. "After laying tile for several years, I branched out into creating mosaics as well. I really enjoy mosaic work and plan on designing assemblages to sell."

"How fascinating! I'd love to see some of your work sometime."

A couple entered the tearoom. "I must be off," she said. "Let's talk about this another time."

After her last sip of tea, Claire paid her bill and prepaid for the pink kettle. "I'll be in tomorrow, Grace. Thank you ahead of time for saving the kettle for me. It was so nice to meet you." After a merry response, Claire left the tearoom and headed home.

$$\sim\!\!\sim\!\!\sim$$

As she unpacked the few groceries, unrelenting drops of rain tapped loudly against the cottage windows. The damp, coastal air chilled her.

She touched the smooth white enamel of the cold woodstove in the corner and bit her lip.

Okay, I can do this. It's not the same. Nothing is going to happen.

Chapter Six

Claire bent in front of the woodstove and lifted the latch. The doors creaked as she opened them. She reached for the paper and kindling stuffed in a galvanized bucket and arranged them inside the dark opening. Her landlord had thought of everything.

Her landlord! That's right! She stood and moved the envelope of money from the counter to her purse. She could not forget to drop off that payment tomorrow.

On the windowsill by the woodstove above a tidy stack of wood sat a box of matches. She reached for them but hesitated. *It's going to get awfully cold tonight if I don't.*

She grabbed the box and knelt before the woodstove. Striking the match forced the smell of phosphorus into the air. She stared at the bright, flitting flame as it consumed the slender stick.

"Ouch!" She threw the match into the woodstove and licked her finger and thumb.

The match landed on the paper, sending smoke curling above it. A black hole with glowing edges widened its mouth before igniting the kindling crisscrossed above it.

The fire warmed her face, but the sweat on her brow didn't come from the blaze. She slammed the doors and secured the latch hoping to shut the flame's disturbing reminder from her thoughts.

To keep her mind occupied, she busied herself about the cottage.

After bouncing from a hotel to a furnished room to a hotel again during the past five months, she had little to unpack. She measured the windows for curtains before opening the box to her new worktable and setting it up in the window-filled corner. She organized her tools and jotted down things to purchase in Hydeport.

The heavy rain continued, and Claire's heart and mood mirrored the gloomy weather. Returning from her bedroom with an empty box, she eyed the last box sitting on the table. The time had come to look through it once again.

She opened the flaps and pulled out the envelope of legal papers and check stubs. Being an only child, Claire had received everything; though, of course, nothing remained of her parents' house.

Loneliness and guilt washed over her like waves over the sand.

She would gladly give all she had back just to see…just to talk to…just to hug her parents again. How she wished she had said "I love you" when she left them off.

Claire closed her eyes and wept.

Her stubbornness over their advice regarding Daniel had made their relationship tense that last week. She had not even said a proper goodbye to them the last time she saw them. How ridiculous her "I'll be back in a jiff" sounded each time she replayed that fateful day in her mind.

She set the envelope aside and wiped her wet eyes.

Sniffling, she took out the two precious, frameless pictures of her parents. She would not have them—and would not be alive today—if she had not been taking them on that secret errand, an errand she never completed, to get them matted and framed for her parents' thirtieth wedding anniversary.

In their wedding picture, Claire's handsome father stood tall above her mother with his arm encompassing her small waist. His aqua-blue eyes radiated from his tanned face as he flashed his mega-watt smile.

Her mother's long brown hair fell in curls over her simple white dress. She held a book with a small bouquet of tiny white roses on it. Claire recalled the stories of her father's relentless pursuit of the brown-eyed beauty, finally winning her heart in the end.

Claire placed the current picture over the wedding one. Despite the lines of age and the silver streaks in their hair, the years had treated them well. She ran her finger over their faces. *How I miss you two!*

She never doubted their love for each other, and they got along well despite their sharp disagreements from time to time about religion. Many times she had looked through the house for her mother only to hear her, locked in her sewing room, praying aloud and crying about her husband's and Claire's disinterest in church and God. The memories now haunted her.

Claire set the pictures down and wiped her wet cheeks with the back of her hand. She studied the items at the bottom of the box. Why did her parents not want her to have or even know about these things until after their deaths?

Chapter Seven

Claire swallowed the lump in her throat.

Reaching into the box she pulled out a narrow aluminum box. After lifting the lid she ran the back of her fingernail across the tops of small square acrylic capsules standing on their ends and labeled in her father's handwriting. Each capsule enclosed a gold or silver coin bearing a date from centuries past. She replaced the lid and set the collection aside.

Next, she took out an antique Bible, the book her mother held in the wedding picture. She brushed her hand over the soft green velvet and the centered brass plate etched with the words "Holy Bible," surrounded by flowers. Thin brass pieces edged the book, and a latch inscribed with more flowers surrounding the name "Claire," the name of her maternal great-grandmother, bound the pages.

She flicked open the latch with her thumb and for the first time opened the Bible and leafed through its pages.

A piece of paper floated to the floor. Bending to pick it up, she recognized her mother's handwriting. Beside peoples' names, her mother had written birthdates, wedding dates, and other dates that meant nothing to her. Claire's name had been written three times, and only one had a date beside it—her birth date.

One date, written beside her father's name and a day only a few months before her parents' wedding, had been crossed out with a heavy pen indentation. The shape of a heart with a zigzagging line down its center had been penned beside it.

She returned the paper and, after snapping the latch, placed the Bible on the table.

She then lifted out an antique leather ring box. She swung its pivoting hook aside and opened the lid to reveal a gold ring with an unusual, emerald-cut stone at the center. The stone had three distinct, graduating colors—deep rose pink, to a thin area of light green, ending with rich emerald green. Large triangular diamonds sat on either side.

She took it from the box and slid it onto her right hand. It spanned the bottom of her finger to the first joint. As she moved her hand in the light sending sparkles flittering on top of each facet, she could hear her father's voice.

"Claire, on your wedding day you'll receive something very special to me, a ring that was my mother's. She is not alive now, but I know she would want you to have it."

She admired it for a moment longer before taking it off, nestling it back into its box, and placing it on the table.

Lastly, she withdrew a small cardboard box.

A few days before her 18th birthday, she had retrieved it from the family mailbox. Addressed to her father, Samuel Wycoff, she had assumed it contained a birthday gift. After her birthday passed, she asked her father about the mysterious box. With a brusque wave of his hand, he dismissed her question saying it was for him from a family member and of no concern to her.

Other than knowing her father grew up somewhere along the coast of Maine and had one sibling, he never spoke of his family and refused to answer her questions about them.

No return address filled the upper corner. She rubbed her finger over the smudged postmark and its only readable letters—"aine."

She pulled the lid off the box and withdrew a piece of azure-blue granite flecked with black mica, sparkling quartz, and feldspar. Its unique and extraordinarily bright color fascinated her.

About the size of her fist, the rock warmed in her hand, and she shifted it to her other hand before lifting a tiny, oddly-shaped key from the same box.

She examined it and wondered what sort of lock it fit.

Lastly, she withdrew and unfolded a piece of paper before returning the key and granite to their box. Though she had it memorized, she read the unfamiliar handwriting once again hoping to see something new.

> *Out of Hyding on the coast of Maine,*
> *Under pieces on a level plane,*
> *Those worth their salt will find its mate,*
> *Place of old design and date,*
> *Blue surrounds yet blue releases,*
> *Your deed for wealth until it ceases.*

When she initially read the riddle, she thought it was some kind of corny joke, but because of its presence in the safe deposit box and her father's words, concluded it was important.

While refolding the riddle, she thought about Garry and his death, his boys, and the "Wycoffs north of town."

She returned everything to the larger box and tucked it into the back corner of the hall closet. *I wish I knew what it meant or what I'm even looking for, but, Dad, I'll try my hardest to find the answer to this riddle for you.*

She would not reveal to anyone, at least for a while, her possible relationship to the "Wycoffs north of town." After all, there must have been a reason why her father had kept his distance from them and why he had warned her about them.

Chapter Eight

After spending most of the day shopping in Hydeport, Claire meandered through the brick-laid streets of downtown and parked by the bay. Though the threat of rain lingered in the brisk air, she bought a sundae at an ice cream shop and returned to her car to watch the activity in the bustling harbor.

As she skimmed the warm, fudgy sauce from the dish and lifted the spoon to her lips, a car ferry glided across the surface of the steel-gray ocean. Despite its size, the choppy water tottered the vessel like a toy as it steadied its course toward a large island across the bay. She wondered what it would be like to be on an island—on a tiny piece of land isolated from the rest of the world by the encompassing ocean.

She licked her spoon and dropped it in the dish before setting them on the seat beside her. She would never set foot on a ferry, let alone an island!

With time passing quickly, she started the car and drove home. Remembering her payment, she parked in front of the landlord's garage and rummaged through her purse for a pen and paper. Finding only a pen, she reached into her pocket and jotted a note on the back of her ice cream receipt.

I'm so pleased with the cottage. It is just perfect, and I know I'll enjoy living here. Thank you for renting it.
I look forward to meeting you.
Please let me know if I can be of any help around the property.
Claire Wycoff

She stuffed the note beside the cash in the envelope, climbed out of her car, and walked up the pathway toward the front door. Patches of blue poked through the racing clouds offering hope of sunnier weather even though rain still showered in wispy threads from a dark cloud over the ocean.

As she walked past the first two windows, something looked different. Had the curtains on the lower level always been open?

She wedged between some bushes and peeked through the window closest to the front door. Bookshelves lined with books and topped with wooden toy schooners filled the wall opposite her. Vintage maps hung on green-painted walls on both ends of the room. A computer sat on a roll-top desk on the far right.

Brrrring! Claire jumped. A telephone on a table under the window rang. She stepped back from the window, then scurried around the bush and up the three front steps.

She pushed the doorbell and admired the stained-glass window on the front door. White glass surrounded a gray shield outlined in red. A black-hilted sword made of clear glass ran diagonally across the center of the shield while three pink roses wound up its blade.

After pressing the doorbell again, she peered through the sword's clear glass but saw no one. The telephone stopped ringing, but she then heard a voice.

She pushed open the flap on the mail slot but held it open after sliding the envelope through the oval hole. A woman's voice finished recording on the answering machine.

"…and I'll be there Friday. Can't wait to see you. Love you!"

Dropping the flap with a clunk, she turned about and hurried to her car.

Once at the cottage, Claire emptied her car of her purchases, lingering only to put perishables in the refrigerator. She looked at the clock on the stove then at the broken teakettle. *I hope the tearoom isn't closed yet.*

As she had the previous day, she drove into the Cove and turned around at the end of Main Street. After finding a parking space across the street but a few places past the tearoom, she hurried to the shop.

"May I help you?" A teenage girl wearing a neon yellow shirt beneath her blue apron stood behind the counter. Straight brown hair sprouted from a ponytail and cinnamon-colored freckles sprinkled her nose and cheeks.

Claire saw a clear two-handled bag with a pink teakettle behind the girl. "Yes, I'm Claire, and I believe you're holding that teakettle for me," she said, pointing behind the girl.

"Oh, you're Claire." She adjusted her blue apron. "Yes, we've been waiting for you." She glanced at a large clock on the wall. "You got here just in time. We're going to close soon." She grabbed the bag and handed it to Claire. "Don't leave though. Mom needs to talk to you. She said it's important."

Claire tilted her head. "Oh?"

"Do you mind waiting a minute? She's in the kitchen. I'll go get her." The girl bounded off and disappeared behind the swinging door.

Claire occupied herself at the front counter, first admiring her new kettle then looking at the treats behind the glass.

Grace emerged from the kitchen. "Claire, I'm so glad to see you. Sorry to make you wait. Do you mind having a seat for a minute?"

"Sure."

Grace led her to a table away from the few remaining customers. She gestured toward a chair before flipping up the sides of her apron and sitting in one beside it.

Claire held up her bag as she sat. "I love the kettle. Thank you for holding it for me."

"Not a problem." Then Grace's face sobered. "I have to tell you something important." She leaned toward Claire and lowered her voice. "It's about something that happened the other night."

Chapter Nine

Claire placed the bag on the table and curled her hair around the backs of her ears.

"My husband, Tim, is the pastor of the little white church just up the street." Grace pointed in the direction of the church. "I'm sure you've noticed it by now."

Claire nodded.

"This past Wednesday night the church was burglarized and vandalized."

"Oh, no! I'm sorry to hear that."

"The burglar broke in through a basement window and stole some speakers and a computer, but," she continued, "he didn't touch the petty cash box, the new large-screen monitor in the nursery, or the offering box at the back of the church."

"How strange!"

"The most bizarre thing is that he took a hammer to the floor of the vestibule and smashed the old mosaic to pieces damaging it beyond repair. I'm thankful he didn't swing at the stained-glass windows too." Drops of sweat formed on Grace's brow, and she picked up the edge of her apron and fanned her face.

"That's terrible, Grace. Do you have any idea why someone would do this?"

"No idea whatsoever."

"I certainly feel bad, but why are you telling me this?"

"Ah! This is where you come in." She flapped her apron with more intensity.

"I told my husband last night about meeting you and that you lay tile and do mosaic work. Would you be willing to take a look at the floor and consider working on a new mosaic design and laying the surrounding tile?"

So soon! Claire's mouth dropped open.

"It's really an eyesore, and because it's directly in the path of people entering the church, my husband would like to get it fixed as soon as possible. We know a few people who lay tile but no one who does mosaics."

"Why, yes—yes, of course. Thank you for asking me. I'd be more than happy to look at it. Can I see it tonight?"

"Well, my husband holds church services on Saturday nights at the jail up in Brockton and then at the Penobscot County jail." Grace stopped fanning her face. "Would you consider going to church tomorrow morning? The service starts at 10:30. After the service ends, you can take your time to look it over and talk about it with my husband."

Claire sat up in her chair. Though she had not been to a regular church service in years, she didn't want to disappoint her new friend or jeopardize this opportunity. "Ok, I'll come."

The redness in Grace's cheeks subsided as she rose. "Oh, that's great! I'm so relieved you're willing to consider the project."

Claire also stood and picked up her bag.

"Thank you, Claire. I'll see you tomorrow morning at church."

"You bet!"

Swinging her bag, Claire left the tearoom. Her head spun from the information. The prospect of working again and of being asked to create something important so soon after arriving in Lone Spruce Cove encouraged her.

Before crossing the street, she glanced left to check for any approaching cars. When she did, the glaring lights of a shop a few stores down from the tearoom caught her attention. *I wonder if they sell clocks. I need one for my bedroom.* Instead of crossing the street, she turned about and walked toward it.

Large windows bowing from the navy-trimmed, beige façade displayed colorful artwork, nautical home décor, and elegant handmade jewelry. In gold leaf the name, The Compass Rose Gallery and Gifts, hung above a dangling wooden compass rose painted in forest green.

Beyond the window dressing, quilts and artwork hung against brown-brick walls with oozing mortar joints. Vintage dressers abutted the walls, and a long antique butcher's counter ran down the center of the shop. Wide wooden planks worn smooth from thousands of footsteps lay on the floors.

The atmosphere and merchandise beckoned her, and although she saw no one inside, the "open" sign in the window welcomed her. She stepped onto the tiled stoop and depressed the thumb latch. While slowly pushing on the door, she admired the workmanship of the worn mosaic compass rose at her feet.

Classical piano music greeted her as she entered the shop, and she breathed the luring mixture of lavender, soap, and balsam. Mesmerized, she closed the door with a soft click.

She walked to a display of granite clocks on the left side of the butcher's counter, set her teakettle on the floor, and picked up a clock. She cradled the cold, heavy piece in her hands then tilted it toward the overhead light to examine its Roman numerals.

"No! Absolutely not!" a man's voice blurted.

Chapter Ten

Claire looked to the back of the store where the door to a fluorescent-lit room stood open.

"Oh, come on, Phil," a woman shot back. "I worked hard on this. Besides, as you can see the model is—"

"Turn that around! Look, you know I have a great appreciation for art, but you also know very well that I will not accept this. Why did you even bring it in?"

"Because I think it is one of my best works, that's why. You know this is what sells. It's trendy. It's expressive. It's—"

"…offensive to me! I will not put it in the shop."

"You *used* to promote and sell artwork like this."

"Yes, I did, Barbara, and I'm ashamed to admit it. I'm different now, and you of all people should know that."

"You certainly are different. It's pathetic! If it weren't such a profitable store for me, I wouldn't even bother bringing my things in here."

Claire pressed her lips together. *I shouldn't be listening to this.* She shifted her eyes toward the front door.

Commotion flurried before a petite woman bolted from the back room. She had short dyed blonde hair, bright-green glasses, and long swinging earrings that looked like oranges. She carried two large canvases and an oversized black bag. A detailed painting of a nude woman faced Claire.

Claire's feet cemented to the floor.

Barbara glared as she passed her and exited the shop, slamming the door and jingling the bell above it in her wake.

I need to leave too. While she reached to place the clock back, the piano music squelched and a man, whom she guessed to be around thirty, walked out of the room writing on a clipboard.

He stood tall with a green plaid shirt covering his broad shoulders. Thick, light-brown hair parted to the side above rectangular glasses.

Where have I seen him before?

Unable to take her eyes off him, she bent and grabbed the handles of her bag. As she righted herself, it crinkled under the teakettle's weight.

The man's head whipped up. His eyes traveled from her hair to her face, then widened. His body straightened.

Her cheeks burned.

Blinking repeatedly, he locked onto her eyes. His mouth parted as if he were going to speak.

Unable to blink, she began to tremble. "I…"

The front door burst open, sending the bell into a violent jangle.

"Where have you been? You were supposed to close an hour ago, you workaholic!" A husky, bearded man laughed as he barreled toward the back of the store down the aisle opposite Claire.

The bespectacled man's attention flicked between her and the newcomers.

"We've come to take you with us to make sure you don't get lost," joked a second man as he too ramrodded toward the back.

Claire took advantage of the distraction and dashed toward the door. A woman about to enter stepped aside and held it for her. "Thank you," Claire mumbled as she hastened past her and shot diagonally across the street to her car.

～✑✑～

Jolted from his shock, Philip's mind raced. *Could it be?* He looked over the heads of his hulking lobstermen friends. *When did she come in?* "I have a customer, you guys." Philip pushed past them. "I just noticed her standing there before you came blowing in here."

One of the men looked about him. "I don't see anyone."

I can't believe it. Philip rushed to the windows. The cloud cover darkened the evening, and the shop's lights hindered the view on the opposite side of the glass. *She slipped away.* "I didn't even say anything to her," he muttered as he flipped the "open" sign over.

"You're joshing us. You didn't have a customer."

"There was a woman in here, Jason," the woman said to her husband. "I held the door open for her when she left." She turned to Philip and wiggled her eyebrows. "She's a pretty one, Philip."

That's an understatement, Sasha. "I saw her last week—that same girl and just for a moment—in Chicago. I'm sure of it."

"Yeah, *sure* you did," Jason's brother, Carl, said.

"No, I'm serious. It has to be her."

Jason crossed his arms. "I think you're delirious from not having a decent lobster dinner for over two weeks."

Carl flicked his hand. "Ah, she'll be back."

"I sure hope so."

Jason tapped his fingers along his crossed arms. "Can we go now? Dinner is waiting and…"

"Hey," Carl cut in, "have you heard yet what happened at church?"

Chapter Eleven

After hanging the last curtain and returning her worktable to its place, Claire tucked away the tiny colorful tiles she had purchased earlier. The assemblage ideas would have to wait. Though she hadn't seen the vestibule and had no idea what the mosaic would be, she wanted the job, and the thought of it sent a flutter of excitement through her.

She picked up the Maine map from the loveseat and refolded it.

Seeing the Maine license plate that morning in Chicago had caught her by surprise and instantly bent her teetering indecision eastward. What must that man behind the steering wheel have thought of her when he saw her standing there fixated on his...

That's where!

Distracted by the riddle, the license plate, and the prospect of moving to Maine, she had garnered only a glimpse of the man in the driver's seat—but that glimpse had been a clear one. He had been handsome for sure, and, yes, the man today looked strikingly similar to him. She slapped the folded map on the arm of the loveseat. *There is no way they are the same person.*

She walked to her bedroom and set out her clothes for church. *Is it possible?* She considered returning to the shop to ask him if he had been in Chicago last week. *Out of the question!*

During their brief exchange today, something she thought impossible had happened. The man had stirred the shattered pieces of her heart—a heart so broken she had been convinced of her inability to ever be attracted enough to someone to want to give or receive love again.

Attracted to him? Foolishness!

However, as it had done in the store, heat raced through her body and flared her cheeks. She removed a hat from a round box and set it on the bureau. No, despite the store's allure, she would not go anywhere near it...or him.

Clunk! A door closed. She clicked off her bedroom light and rounded the end of the bed. She went to the window, pulled back a side of the Roman shade, and peeked out. Lights emanated from the windows of the landlord's house and dispelled the night's grim darkness with its warm glow.

Chapter Twelve

At 10:05, Claire placed the hat on her head and picked up the antique Bible from the kitchen table.

She walked to the French doors to close them. The fresh smell of grass rode on the breeze that blew in and toyed with her hair and skirt. Water droplets clung to the grass tips and glistened like diamonds in the bright morning sun.

A magnificent schooner with two tall masts and four billowing red sails pointed toward the Cove. She watched in fascination as the sails collapsed at the feet of their stately masts. How grand it would be to sail on such a ship and on such a fine morning as this!

Not wanting to arrive at church late nor wanting to be early, she drove to town and found a parking place at 10:20. Clutching the antique Bible, she secured her hat with the other hand as she approached the stairs.

Children ran past her, releasing energy before having to sit still. Unexpected tears welled up as memories flooded back to when she was a young girl playing with friends before church. She lifted her face to the wind and blinked several times as she stepped up the wide stairs.

"Claire! I'm so glad you came." Grace scooted down the steps so that they could climb together. "I'd like you to meet my husband, Tim," she said when they reached the top where a man with glasses and a receding hairline stood. "Tim, this is Claire."

"Good morning! It's nice to meet you, Claire," he said, extending his hand. "I've heard much about you the past few days. Welcome to the Cove and welcome to church."

His relaxed and approachable personality calmed her.

He ushered her into the vestibule. "As you can see this is a real mess."

"It certainly is!"

"I'm eager to discuss it with you, but I have to meet with a couple immediately after the service. Would you mind waiting around town after church for about a half hour and then come back so we can go over the details?"

Claire nodded while continuing to look at the floor. "Yes, that will be fine."

"Great! Thanks, Claire."

The tile along the outer edges of the square-shaped room lay chipped and cracked, and a round area approximately four feet in diameter at the center of the room lay bare down to the subflooring. Though the vestibule had been cleaned up since the vandalism took place, Grace had been right. What an eyesore!

Grace broke into her thoughts. "A few of us who attend here are shopkeepers, and we open our shops right after the service ends at noon. If my husband happens to preach long and I rush out of here without saying good-bye, you'll know why."

"I completely understand."

"Sorry to leave you, but the kids are probably running wild downstairs in children's church."

"Of course, go ahead. I can find a seat."

Grace smiled and headed off through the sanctuary.

Claire checked her watch—10:28. She passed through the sanctuary doors and looked for an empty section of seats.

She walked down the carpeted aisle separating two long rows of shiny wooden pews. Brightened by the sun, stained-glass windows filled the side and front walls with color. Left of the elevated lectern, a woman's hands floated over the keys of a shiny black piano, playing a song Claire recognized but could not remember the words to. Right of the lectern, an exit sign in bold red letters drew attention to the door below it.

Claire walked half-way down the aisle and sat in an empty pew on the right. A man and woman in front of her turned around and greeted her, but no one came to sit by her. Several rows down from her sat the woman and two bearded men who entered the shop last night.

Soon the congregation stood and sang.

When peace, like a river, attendeth my way,
When sorrows like sea billows roll...

She remembered this song!

Whatever my lot, Thou hast taught me to say,
It is well, it is well, with my soul.

A lone tear slid down her cheek. She read the words but could not sing.

Thankful the song ended and she could sit again, Claire clenched her teeth, unlatched her Bible, and sat prepared to ward off any other unexpected emotions.

~~~

Late, Philip slipped into a back pew. Despite getting up before dawn, he wasn't able to catch up on his paperwork at the shop before church. As usual, time had gotten away from him. At least he made it before the preaching started.

He scanned the crowd for visitors. On his right, toward the middle, a woman wearing a hat sat alone. Few women wore hats to church in Maine, and he smiled, impressed that someone had the guts and style to do it.

During the message, the woman in the hat turned her head to the side, distracting his attention from Pastor Tim.

It's her!

Could this mysterious and beautiful young woman be a Christian? *Slow down, boy, not everyone who goes to church is a Christian.* He of all people knew that.

This time he won't let her get away.

Chapter Thirteen

The Bible lay clasped beside Claire.

She pumped the foot of her crossed leg into the air. The walls of the church closed in on her as a bead of sweat trickled from her ear down her neck. Her chest tightened as sadness, anger, and fear vied to reign within her.

After Pastor Tim said the last "Amen," two young boys sprinted down the far aisle, pushed open the door below the exit sign, and ran outside. She grabbed the Bible as she stood and darted between the pews to follow them into the sunshine.

～♥♥～

Philip opened his eyes after the prayer then twisted his wrist. His watch read 12:03. The businessman part of him told him to get up and go open the shop.

Instead, he rose from his seat and stepped into the aisle. The woman in the hat also rose.

"Hey, Philip! Good to have you back." Two of his friends cut him off. "How did your gift shows go?"

He watched the woman rush to the far aisle.

"I know you have to open up, but what do you think about the vestibule?"

"Yeah, you missed all the excitement," the other friend continued. "Did you hear all the details?"

"Yes—yes, the Harrimans filled me in last night," Philip answered, looking past them then down at his watch again.

She opened the door and dashed under the exit sign.

Gone again!

⟡⟡⟡

Claire flew down the stairs and hurried to the forked path at the back of the church. She chose the path that led to the harbor where the amazing ship she had seen earlier dominated the entire end of a dock.

She had forgotten it was Mother's Day. As if that hadn't been difficult enough, Pastor Tim then had to preach a disturbing message. She dreaded having to return in a half hour.

She slumped on an empty bench to collect her disquieting thoughts and dropped the Bible onto her lap.

Pastor Tim said nothing in the morning's message that she had not already heard before—many times before. She understood the Bible passages about the need for forgiveness of sins and acceptance of God's gift of salvation, but had never applied them to herself or acted upon them as Pastor Tim said was so important.

She crossed her arms. She might do something wrong once in a while—but a sinner? *Humph!* She frowned at the walkway under her feet.

A conversation with her father flew like a bat from the back of her mind where she had sent it years ago.

"A few weeks before your mother and I got engaged, I prayed a prayer to become a Christian, you know," her father told her once. *"It wasn't a big deal to me. I mean, after all, I'm a pretty good guy, and repentance?—it's not like I've murdered anyone or anything."*

Claire had agreed with him.

"It was important to your mother, though, so I prayed. Yup, I was willing to do whatever it took for your beautiful mother to accept my marriage proposal."

Claire idolized her father, but compared to what she had been taught in church, this conversation had confused her. She had settled her thoughts about it by figuring he had done what was best, since he usually did what was good and right.

Over the years, she shoved God to the back of her mind. As she got older, she went to jobsites on Sunday mornings with her father instead of to church with her mother.

Claire bit her bottom lip. Was her father right? Was Pastor Tim right? What if *she* died having never become a Christian? What was the truth? She wished she had talked about these things with her mother, but she never did—and now she never will.

Claire's arms fell onto the Bible. She opened the clasp and thumbed through the thin pages to the paper with the people's names and dates on it. She touched the scribble over the date beside her father's name then she touched the sketch of the broken heart.

Her mother had figured it out.

She stuck the paper back in and snapped the clasp before closing her eyes. She raised her head toward the sun, bathing her face in its warmth trying not to see…trying not to believe…trying not to acknowledge her terrible and painful new thought. If Pastor Tim spoke truthfully this morning, if her father never really became a Christian and deceived her mother just so that she would marry him, then…

She shuddered. No, she could not think of him in—

"Pure delight!"

Chapter Fourteen

Claire jerked and popped her eyes open. She dropped her face from the warm sun toward the voice.

A man with his palms on his bent knees leaned close to her face. She had neither seen nor heard him approach.

"Sorry?"

The corners of his mouth flinched. "I said, 'Pure delight.'"

"Yes—yes," she said groping for a response. She looked past his ear toward the schooner. "The ship is magnificent." She twisted her sweaty hands together.

"I meant you," he said as his eyes swept over her. "You are purely delightful to look at, but I do agree the schooner is amazing as well."

No one had ever given her such a compliment and she liked it.

Nodding to the bench he asked, "May I?"

"Of course. Yes. Please sit down."

"So you like the schooner, huh?"

The strong scent of sandalwood drifted past her nose. "It's beautiful. I noticed it this morning as it headed into the Cove. The red sails are splendid."

"I like those as well. I had white sails on her for many years but changed to the red ones last year. I think it gives her more distinction."

Claire whirled to face him. "That's yours?"

The man beamed, his dark brown eyes piercing her. "She's mine."

"Wow!"

"Oh, forgive me. My name is Parker Hollenbeck."

She guessed him to be in his late 40's. Black hair with gray temples framed the swarthy skin on his chiseled, clean-shaven face. Chapped lips, his only imperfection, surrounded straight white teeth that shone in bright contrast to his skin.

"My name is Claire, Claire Wycoff."

"Claire... *Wycoff.*"

Though she expected it, he thankfully did not ask if she had relatives north of town.

Wycoff... Claire Wycoff.

He looked both ways down the sidewalk, then to her fingers unadorned by rings. "Are you with or waiting for somebody?"

"No, I'm alone. I have a meeting with someone at 12:30 and am just passing the time until then."

"Are you vacationing?"

"Actually I moved here a few days ago."

Ah! Parker could hardly contain the excitement that surged within him. He rubbed his hands before clasping them together. "Would you like a closer look at the schooner?"

Claire glanced at her watch. "It's 12:16."

"Ah! Plenty of time!"

"Are you sure?"

"A few minutes are all we need. Come!" He cupped her elbow with his fingertips and rose, prompting her to rise as well.

"Well, how can I resist then?"

She held on to the brim of her hat as he led her along the iron-fenced pathway to the harbor then through a short metal gate before conducting her down a long pier toward the schooner. With a dramatic swing of his arm, Parker said, "I present to you the *Lady Katherine.*"

"The *Lady Katherine?* And who is she named for?"

"Good question! One should never name a vessel after a wife or favored woman; so, after my great-grandfather had this 57-foot beauty built in the early 1920s, he wisely named her after his mother, Katherine Hollenbeck."

"A wise man indeed!"

Parker squinted one eye and gave her a lopsided grin. "Are you being sarcastic, Claire Wycoff?"

Claire snickered. "Maybe."

Parker boasted about the schooner's features including its modernized navigational equipment and luxuriously upgraded interior. He pointed out the newly refitted hull painted red to match the sails and the lacquered oak deck and masts that glowed in the sun.

"I'd love to show you below deck."

Claire looked at her watch. "I really must go, though I wish I could see and hear more. Thank you for telling me about her. She's stunning."

"And so are you." Her radiant aqua eyes melted him. "Give me your phone number."

"I don't have a phone number."

"You don't have a phone number?"

She shook her head.

He had been in Maine for three weekends already with no prospects. "Have dinner with me then—this Friday night. Don't say no."

She pressed her lips together.

"No trying to think up an excuse because I won't accept it. Come on. I want to get to know you better."

"All right then."

He licked his lips. "Let me pick you up. Where do you live?"

She shook her head. "I've only just met you. How about we drive separately? I'll meet you wherever you'd like to go."

He huffed in resignation. "Okay, go past the church and veer left. Follow Route 1 for about ten miles until you reach Silver Harbor. Just after you enter the town limits you'll see the Silver Harbor Inn on your right. The restaurant at the inn is the Chart and Sextant. Meet me there at 6:00. I'll make reservations for us."

"At 6:00 on Friday, then. I will be there. Goodbye, Parker. It was nice to meet you."

"You too, Claire. I'll be looking forward to Friday." He planted his feet on the dock, crossed his arms, and watched her until she disappeared from sight.

A smug smile stretched his lips. What luck! To find such a beauty…and with the last name of Wycoff too. *Am I good or what?*

✑✑✑

"What do you think, Grace?" An older gentleman and loyal customer sat at the coveted window table. He pointed toward the harbor as Grace refilled his mug with steaming coffee. Some coffee dribbled onto the table. "Who is Hollenbeck trying to woo this summer? I don't recognize the girl."

"*Tsk!* Is he back in town already?" She lifted the spout then glanced half-heartedly at the harbor before setting the pot on the table and reaching for a cloth in her apron pocket. "I suppose it is the middle of May. Oh, who knows—some pretty, naïve girl who is new to town, no doubt."

The gentleman continued looking out the window as he sipped his coffee. "Honestly, that man acts like a teenager every summer. He's getting too old for that. I wonder what sort of scandal he'll be the center of this year."

Grace wiped the coffee drips, then reached for an empty plate. "I'm sure he'll manage to…" She shot her head up then tensed the muscles under her eyes when she saw Claire's hat. "Oh, no!" she gasped.

"What?"

"I know that girl! She *is* new to town and she's a new friend of mine. I need to warn her about him."

"Well, if you're any kind of friend at all, you would."

Chapter Fifteen

Claire felt Parker's eyes on her as she followed the path back to the church. He had certainly been a welcome distraction from her inward struggles. Despite their age difference, she found him handsome and engaging, and his flattery sent her self-esteem soaring.

Why not go out with him? She had learned a lot from her experience with Daniel and would be wiser this time. Besides, it's not like she had anything planned this week.

She put thoughts of Parker aside as she walked beside the church and past a basement window covered by fresh boards. She rounded the front and climbed the steps. Pastor Tim and the girl she had seen behind the counter at the tearoom sat on the top step.

"Sorry to make you wait around town so long after the service," Pastor Tim said as he stood to his feet and brushed off his pants.

The dark thoughts conjured by his message snaked through her mind again. She tightened her fingers around the edge of the Bible in an attempt to dispel them. "Not a problem. I've been soaking up the sun and walking by the harbor."

"Ah, well, it's certainly a nice afternoon to be doing that." He turned to the girl who had also risen to her feet. "Have you met my daughter, Holly?"

"Hi, Holly." Claire smiled and gave her a quick nod. "We've seen each other at the tearoom but we haven't been formally introduced."

"Hi!" Holly said with a smile before tightening the ponytail that stuck out at an angle.

Pastor Tim opened the front doors outward and wedged chunks of wood under them, flooding the small room with natural light.

They talked at length about measurements and tiles and subflooring, and, drawing from her experience, Claire advised him what should be done.

"Do you want the project then?"

"Definitely!"

"That's great! We hoped you'd take the job."

"Now what sort of tiles would you like to use?"

"The building committee discussed using local elements if possible like granite tiles or even rocks," he said. "There's a granite quarry north of town. I think it has a small showroom if you'd like to check that out first. Otherwise, there are plenty of showrooms in Hydeport and Augusta."

Claire nodded.

"Please feel free to experiment with different textures and colors that you think would be suitable. You know more about this than we do, and we're open to any suggestions."

The freedom to come up with her own ideas excited her. "What about the mosaic?"

"We'd like the focal area to be round, and inside the circle we'd like an open Bible—a black Bible with white pages and a red ribbon marker down the center. On the pages of the Bible we'd like this entire verse with its reference." He withdrew a piece of paper from his shirt pocket and handed it to her. "Do you think you can do that?"

Claire read the Bible reference but did not know the verse it alluded to by heart.

"Yes, I can." She slipped the paper into her Bible. "I have the floor pictured in my mind already. I'll make a template true to scale this coming week and find samples so that you and the building committee can make a final decision on Saturday."

~~~

Over the remainder of the afternoon, Claire hunched over her worktable drafting the outer floor of the vestibule and designing the basic layout of the mosaic. She checked and rechecked her dimensions to ensure perfect angles and curves. She had never pieced words before but welcomed the challenge.

She dropped her pencil on the sketch and stretched her arms before rubbing the back of her neck. The sun had begun its descent turning the few clouds hanging above the dark-blue ocean various shades of orange and pink.

Knock. Knock. Knock.

Startled, she sat erect on her stool.

Knock. Knock.

She went to the front door, unlocked it, and opened it a crack. Peeking around the door, she lifted her eyes then drew in a quick breath.

The man she saw at the shop last night stood holding a piece of paper. His green eyes peered around the door at her then widened.

Heat flew up her cheeks. *He's even more handsome up close.*

Chapter Sixteen

It's her!

Philip released a slow breath. *Calm, remain calm.* The note fluttered in the breeze and reined in his befuddled thoughts. "We meet at last."

She opened the door wider, her striking eyes staring at him, then stood motionless.

"Only this time I know your name—that is if you're Claire Wycoff." He flicked the note with his fingertips.

She swallowed. "I am."

He hoped his voice sounded calmer than he felt. "I'm Philip England, and, well, welcome to The English Rose estate."

"Thank you."

He looked at the note then turned it over. "If it helps," he said returning his gaze to her, "I like fudge sundaes with extra whipped cream and nuts too."

Claire's lips curled into a sheepish grin, and she opened the door all the way.

"I hope the cottage is to your satisfaction."

"Yes, it's better than anything I could have hoped for."

"Good! I'm glad to hear that." He folded the paper. "Um, is there anything you need?"

"No, no, I'm—everything is just fine, thank you."

Philip didn't just want to leave things at that and go home. *Think!* He wanted to talk with her more. Things had to be said. Questions had to be asked.

"Do you have time for a little tour of the property?" *Lame!* But he couldn't think of anything else. "Since you'll be here for a while—well, I hope you'll be here for a while—you might as well know about your surroundings."

Her shoulders relaxed. "I'd like that. Hold on, and I'll get my sweater and shoes. Would you like to come in?"

"No, that's fine. I'll wait out here."

She closed the door with a quiet click. *She had better not run away from me again.* He filled his lungs with air before releasing it slowly. He crammed her note into his shirt pocket, and thrust his hand into his pants pocket to fiddle with his jackknife.

She's my tenant! She lives in my back yard!

He ran his fingers through his thick hair. *Okay. Whoa! I'm not using my head here.* He determined not to allow his attraction to obscure his judgment.

Claire emerged from the cottage with smoother curls and cheeks that had calmed to light pink. Her sweater matched her eyes.

"You have an awesome view of the ocean. You must love living here," she said.

"I do and try not to take it for granted."

〰〰〰

Claire's hands shook as she closed the door behind her, but at least taking the time to comb through her hair had calmed the pounding in her chest.

"I'll take you around my house first," Philip said gesturing up her driveway with his left hand. *No wedding band at least.* They walked up the incline.

"Do you live alone?"

"Yes, at this time I do."

Her spirit sank at the prospect of him being engaged.

"The home and property have been in my family for five generations, and I'm blessed to own it now."

When they crested the driveway, Claire stopped. "The jeep! You really *are* him!"

Philip grinned. "Ah, so you recognized me—as I did you."

"And that Maine license plate."

"So it was the license plate that captured your attention. I didn't think it was the smattering of bugs on my grill that shocked you."

She giggled. "I can only imagine what must have been going through your mind when you saw me standing there."

Philip lifted his eyebrows and smiled but didn't answer.

"I guess I should explain."

Walking again, they followed a path that led to a long grassy-edged beach that, unlike hers, had no cliff. A wooden ocean kayak stretched upside down on the grass between bushes heavy with buds.

"This sounds crazy, I know, but I had been in the diner that morning trying to decide if I should move to Maine or not. Then when you pulled up right in front of me it was as if I had been dunked in ice water. When I saw that license plate I just knew I should move."

"Well, that makes sense."

"Does it really?"

"I think it does."

His words released some of the remaining fragments of doubt she harbored.

He continued. "And I was in Chicago on business which also makes sense, but what *doesn't* make sense is a little over a week later our paths have not only crossed again but have become entwined."

"It *is* bizarre."

"I'm sure God has a reason in it all."

That's what her mother would have said! Not wanting to talk about God or her mother, Claire changed the subject. "So this is your beach. It looks like you use it often." Two dark-red Adirondack chairs sunk into the sand around a well-used fire pit ringed with rocks.

"Not as often as I'd like to." He pointed to their left. "Despite that rocky outcropping separating our beaches, feel free to walk here if you'd like. My property ends at that tree line where those two large boulders are. The beach beyond that belongs to my neighbors, the Soames. They don't mind if I'm on their beach, but I usually stay off it."

They retraced their steps, then walked up the driveway a short distance past his jeep before Philip stopped.

"The property extends from that little evergreen forest behind my house, down to the highway, then east beyond the cottage to those woods there. Paths, some winding all the way to the highway, cut through the woods between my property and the neighbors' on both sides. Other than the path between my house and the Soames, I haven't been through the woods for quite a while."

"Will you tell me about the name—The English Rose?" she asked as they ambled back toward the cottage.

"My mother is from England, and my father met her while stationed there in the Air Force. They thought it ironic that his last name was England, and, well, that she was from there. They fell in love, married, and eventually moved here to take over the estate from my grandparents.

"Since my mother loves roses, especially the fragrant wild pink ones that dot the property, my father called her his "English Rose." In her honor he named the estate The English Rose. Late in life they had my two siblings and me. The three roses on the sign hanging by the road and on her family's crest on the stained-glass panel in the front door represent us."

"Oh, I love that story!"

They rounded the cottage to the path leading down to the beach. "Have you been down here yet?" Philip descended the path first and extended his hand to help her down. She didn't need his help, but grasped it anyway. His hand, so much larger than hers, felt warm and strong. Once she set foot on the sand, he let go.

"Yes, the beach and ocean drew me soon after moving in. It feels like my own little beach."

"Well, East Beach, as we've always called it, can be your private beach if you want. I own up to that extension of rocks," he indicated with a nod. "It's unlikely you'll ever find me here. I never liked the cliff, and the weir is ugly."

"Weir? Are those wooden poles weirs? What are they used for?"

They strolled toward the stakes. "A weir is a trap. Small poles are affixed horizontally between those large thick vertical ones. Then brush is woven like a net around the small poles to close in the holes. Over a few months, seaweed and other marine life grow over the brush filling in the gaps."

Claire tried to visualize his explanation.

"See how the land curves there? In theory, as the tide rolls in, the fish get trapped in the bowl-like area between that rock extension and the weir. Once the tide falls, the concentration of fish provides an easy harvest."

"I think I understand."

"When my grandfather was a teenager, he read about Maine's fishing industry in school and decided to build his own weir to catch herring. My great-grandfather gave him permission as long as he did all the work, paid for it himself, and gathered in his herring on a regular basis. However, his finances and enthusiasm for the project dissipated, and he abandoned the idea soon after placing these poles."

He shook his head. "I really should take them down someday."

～✇✇～

When they reached the far end of the beach, Philip stopped in front of the narrow path that snaked up the cliff. "This leads to one of those paths through the woods I was telling you about." He kicked at a cigarette butt. "Do you smoke, Claire?"

"No! I thought maybe you did. There were footprints here the other day too, but..." She looked about her then up the path. "...they must have washed away in the rain."

"I don't smoke, and, like I said, I've not been on this beach for quite some time." *Who's been trespassing?*

"I'm relieved to hear you don't because I'm..."

"Yes?"

She wrung her hands. "Nothing."

They turned about and headed back toward the cottage. *Maybe she feels unsafe.* "I'll keep a better eye out down here from now on."

They both fell silent.

Towering over her, Philip stopped and turned toward her. "Claire..."

She faced him and lifted her head. Not even the shadows of the sinking sun could cloak her beauty.

The time had come to stop talking about the property.

Chapter Seventeen

Philip cleared his throat. "I'm sorry about last night."

"Sorry? About what?"

"I didn't know you were there. I should have flipped the sign and locked the door before my meeting with Barbara—the woman you saw. I don't know how long you were standing there or what you heard, but I fear you overheard a most unpleasant conversation." The memory still irritated him, and he hoped Claire could not sense it in his voice.

"Oh, it's nothing."

"Well, I regret you heard it. I was just so surprised to see you standing there. Then, when my rambunctious friends stormed in, no doubt you felt unwelcome. I feel badly about it all. I looked for you after you left but couldn't see where you had gone."

"Please don't feel the need to apologize. I shouldn't have lingered, but the shop—*everything* in the shop…" She looked away. "…attracted me."

"Thank you for being so gracious and understanding. I hope you'll stop by again."

"Do you own the shop?"

"I do."

"How can I resist such a place? Of course I'll stop by again, maybe even this week."

"I'd be honored if you did."

They turned around and started heading back. Philip opened his mouth to ask her about herself, but she spoke first.

"Tell me about your shop. How long have you owned it?"

"My great-grandparents opened it as a mercantile in the late 1800s. My grandparents inherited it then passed it on to my parents who ran it for forty years. My family has always been involved in the arts and has been one of the largest supporters of local artists in this entire coastal region. With each change in ownership, the shop became less of a mercantile and more of a gift shop and gallery."

He adjusted his glasses. "I've worked there my whole life. After going to college in accounting and marketing, I became the buyer of all the merchandise. Gradually I took on more and more responsibilities as the work became too much for my aging parents.

"My siblings didn't want the daily task of running a brick and mortar and gladly left the store to me. I spend much time and effort sourcing local craftspeople and artists. I then sell their products in the shop and represent them at select trade and gift shows all over the United States."

"That's why you were in Chicago."

"Yes."

"You sound like a busy guy. How do you do it all?"

"Well, I wouldn't be able to without having a couple of amazing people working for me."

When they got to the end of the beach, Philip sat down on a smooth rock at the base of the border between their beaches and patted a rock beside him.

"Enough about me. Please, sit for just a minute and tell me about yourself, Claire. All I know is your name and that you're from Chicago. What brings you to the Cove? Do you have family or friends here?"

∼∼∼

Claire sat on the flattened rock. Within moments, the coldness of it seeped through the material of her clothing. She tugged her sweater across her and tucked her fingers beneath her arms.

Philip bent his long legs in front of him and wrapped his arms around his knees grasping his wrist with his hand. He gave her his full attention—something she was not used to.

"Well, I am from a suburb of Chicago. I'm an only child. My parents…"

She traced the cold sand with her finger while swallowing the huge lump in her throat. "My parents…" Her lashes attempted to keep pace with the inundation of tears. *I can't cry in front of him.* She quickly swiped at a rolling drop.

She expected Philip to ridicule her, but he sat as still as a foggy morning.

"My parents were killed in an accident five months ago." She wiped her other cheek with the sleeve of her sweater and sniffled. "I would have been killed too if I had been with them that day."

"I'm so sorry, Claire." He released his wrist and combed the sand beneath his knees with his long fingers. "I can't imagine the pain you must have gone through—what you must still be going through. Please accept my sincerest condolences."

What? No criticism? "Thank you." Feeling more secure, she continued. "Today has just been a little difficult—you know, the first Mother's Day without my mom."

"Of course. That's understandable."

He didn't mock me! She paused and breathed deeply. "I guess you can say I am here on a truth-finding mission."

How could she tell him about the riddle and the blue granite when she didn't understand their significance herself? How could she tell him about the disturbing thoughts and memories conjured by Pastor Tim's message this morning? Philip may be kind, but she could not risk—she could not bear—any mockery from him.

"I'm seeking the truth about several different things and hope to find them by living here. I don't know anyone here other than those like yourself whom I've just met." She paused. "I hope we can be friends. I—I really could use some friends."

"Yes, yes, of course."

His amiable attentiveness gave her the resolve to continue.

"My mother is a…was a nurse, and my father was a plumber. When my mother worked, I would go with my father to jobsites. During high school while other girls painted their nails and hung out at the mall, I learned to tile floors and walls and would work alongside my father whenever I could.

"A few years ago, someone introduced me to mosaics, and liking their beauty and diversity, I turned my focus to them. When not on jobsites, I designed mosaics for chairs and mailboxes and ornaments and enjoyed quite a following."

Her voice softened. "Then my parents' accident happened. I lost everything including the desire to work or even design these past five months."

She peeked over at Philip from the corner of her eye. He only nodded while raking through the sand.

"But," she said slapping the sides of her legs, "it's time to create again. I've finally set up the new work table and tools and supplies I bought two months ago, and I'm going to start living again." She brightened. "In fact, I don't know if you've heard about the church in town being burgled and the mosaic in the vestibule being vandalized."

"Yes, I know about that."

"Well, the pastor, Tim and his wife, Grace, do you know them?"

"Yes."

"They asked me if I would re-lay the tile and design a new mosaic, and I've accepted the challenge. In fact, I've been working on it all afternoon. I'm just not sure what to use for the piecework. The building committee wants me to source local materials."

"You could always use these." Philip opened his sand-covered hand. She reached over and plucked from his palm three pieces of what looked like colorful, sugared gumdrops.

"What are these?"

"Pieces of sea glass—or beach glass as some people call them."

"Sea glass?"

"Years ago people discarded things over cliffs and the sides of ships. The wave action would break things made of glass, like bottles, dishes, lamps, into shards against rocks and the ocean floor. After years of tumbling in the rough surf, the worthless shards would become pitted and smoothed and rounded into pretty glass treasures—such as these."

"How beautiful!"

"If I find a piece with sharp edges or that's clear, such as this one," he said picking up a piece by his foot, "I usually toss it back so it'll get roughened up more." He threw the piece over her head into the water.

"Past the Goldsteins' house over there used to be the Cove's town dump where people would simply toss their trash over the cliff into the ocean. Of course, it's no longer there and has been cleaned up, but because of it, I've found a fabulous amount of beautiful sea glass and pieces of pottery—not to mention other treasures—on these beaches over the years."

Claire studied the purple, brown, and dark green pieces Philip found and rubbed them between her fingers.

"They look like gemstones. These would be gorgeous in the mosaic."

Philip stood and brushed the sand off his clothes. Claire did the same. Her mind raced to projects she could use sea glass in. Wanting to find her own piece, she scanned the ground.

"When I was a boy I *did* think they were gemstones and picked them up by the pocketful. I admit I still can't resist searching the beach whenever I have the opportunity."

"Look!" Claire bent down and picked up a frosted white piece the size of a quarter.

"Good for you! Once your eyes are trained, the glass is easy to spot."

"I wish it weren't getting dark now that I've just learned about this."

"It's exciting to find a special treasure that's complete or even partially complete such as the top of a perfume bottle, a marble, a piece of pottery, or even part of a bottle with an embossed picture or words in it. My favorite pieces to find are red—though those are rare finds—deep purple, and cobalt."

Such endless possibilities these pieces offered! Plans formed in her mind to search the beach on a regular basis. "Oh, it would be exciting to find a rare piece."

"Would you like to see my collection of favorites sometime?"

"Yes, I would love that!"

"I have several jars full of glass. If you'd like, I'll bring them to you. You can go through them at your leisure and see if there are any pieces you can use for the vestibule. They aren't doing me any good sitting there in my garage, and you can use any and all pieces you wish."

"That would be fabulous. I can definitely see using these in the mosaic. Thank you."

The sun had sunk below the horizon, and as its last few rays spoked into the sky, darkness loomed.

"I suppose it's time I head to the house." He rubbed his sandy hands together. "Claire…"

He said her name with such seriousness. Concerned, she pulled her eyes from the beach.

"May I ask you one more question?"

"Of course."

"Please, not that I think you won't be honest with me, but I'm going to trust you for a truthful answer because this is very important to me."

His lead-in troubled her. "Okay."

"I came into church late this morning and saw you there. I wanted to speak with you, but you left too quickly afterwards. Besides, I had to open the store."

Ugh! Someone did *notice my fast exit!*

"Are you a Christian?"

She turned her head and looked out over the ocean. Could he read her mind? Could her heart be so transparent that he could see the battle raging there? No one had ever asked her that question before. A cold, heavy weight fell on her chest.

"No," she whispered.

～ン～

Philip thrust his hands in his pockets and indented the sand repeatedly with the toe of his shoe. The moment he saw her yesterday, he just *knew* she was the one who—oh, how could he have been wrong? "Thank you for being honest. I respect you for that."

"Why did you want to know?"

He shifted from one foot to the other. She had been honest with him and deserved a truthful answer. He just couldn't give her a complete one.

"Well, because I saw you at church and thought perhaps you were." He made no attempt to mask the disappointment in his voice. "I'm sorry to hear you're not. Being a Christian and living right is very important to me, and I hope someday you'll find the truth and become one."

Her jaw tightened, and she pressed her lips into a thin line.

"I need to go. It was nice to meet you, Claire. I know that we'll become friends with time. Good night." Without waiting for an answer, he turned around and strode away.

✺✺✺

"Good night," she whispered.

As she watched him disappear over the rocks, she felt as if a tall, thick wall had sprung up between them. *I did as you asked, Philip. I told you the truth.* Her fluctuating emotions and inward struggles resurfaced as she grappled with his question. Loneliness seized the opportunity to slide its cold arms about her.

If only I could have peace!

She clutched the pieces of sea glass to her chest and wept.

Chapter Eighteen

Claire pounded a second nail through the white corkboard, then jumped off the loveseat and stood back to make sure she hadn't nailed it askew. Satisfied, she grabbed some thumbtacks and the sketches of future mosaic projects and affixed them down the right half of the corkboard.

Up the left side she tacked the riddle, a blank piece of paper for ideas and notes, and a large circle cut out of the Maine map. She shoved a tack into the center of the circle—Hydeport. Surely whatever she was looking for lies within a two hundred mile radius of the town.

She returned the unused thumbtacks to their box before picking up the tiny key. She turned it about in her hands and ran her fingers over the embossed leaves on it before sliding the filigreed end onto a long, gold chain she purchased in Hydeport. She secured the chain about her neck and tucked the key under her shirt.

Claire skirted the template lying on the floor and sat on her stool. The afternoon sun streamed through the mounds of colorful sea glass piled high on her worktable, and she felt as if she were guarding a treasure trove of glistening gemstones. Late Monday morning she discovered industrial-sized, glass jars on her doorstep. True to his word and without being seen or heard, Philip had left his sea glass for her—all 22 jars organized by color! For two days she sorted out the pieces she would use in the vestibule.

Ready for the meeting the day after tomorrow, she curled her finger under her lip and reviewed the true-to-scale template made of taped grocery bags.

She decided to use unglazed dark-gray granite flecked with black mica from the walls to the mosaic's outer rim. The colorful four-inch outer rim would then be pieced with purple, aqua, green, and cobalt sea glass from Philip's collection. More dark-gray granite would surround the Bible's black-granite cover and dull white-tiled pages.

Leaving her stool, she knelt by the template and leaned on one splayed hand. She hovered her other hand above a piece of luminous red sea glass. She picked the piece up and repositioned it within the penciled confines of the ribbon border. If she spread the red pieces out it could work, but more would look much better.

She leaned back and rested her palms on her knees.

Designed in flowing, semi-scripted typography, she re-read the Bible verse she would piece with tiny, black tiles—*Jesus saith unto him, I am the way, the truth, and the life: no man cometh unto the Father, but by me." John 14:6.* After working on it all week, she had it memorized.

She sighed.

Its meaning burned in her heart.

❧❦❧

Other than the rhythmic lapping of the waves by her feet, stillness shrouded the early morning. The storms that rumbled through during the night had moved out to sea, drawing behind them wisps of fog that hung like gauzy curtains above the glassy ocean.

As Claire reached for another piece of sea glass, she curled fog-dampened hair around one of her ears. The storms and low tide left many beautiful pieces for her to find—though no red ones.

A quiet plop in the water broke the tranquility, and movement on her left in the ever-widening gap between fog and ocean caught her eye.

Philip dipped a paddle in the water as he glided from the rocky protrusion then between the two farthest weir posts. Sitting low in the kayak, his red shirt, wet from the fog, clung to his muscular chest and arms.

The pieces of her heart stirred once again.

"Morning," she said.

He did not acknowledge her as he slid past and vanished beyond the rocks between their beaches. Did he not hear her?

If he had, he had chosen to ignore her.

~ ~ ~

Leaving the property for the first time since Sunday, Claire backed her car up the short incline then drove past Philip's empty driveway. Realizing she would have to thank him for the jars of sea glass another time, she set out in search of the Wycoff showroom, hoping to return with samples to organize before getting ready for dinner with Parker.

She steered through town and after veering left, drove a short distance before turning up the first road north, assuming it would lead her to "the quarry north of town." For miles she passed endless evergreens on the hilly, twisting two-lane road.

She sped past a wide, dirt driveway noticing too late a huge chunk of granite carved with the name "Wycoff." She made a U-turn, drove back, and inched up the driveway to a large open area.

On her left, closed off by a metal gate, the driveway curved and disappeared around a hill. In front of her, pieces of rusty machinery stood beside flat granite slabs resting against slanted wooden frames. On her right, a rusty pickup truck sat in front of a small rundown building.

After parking beside the truck, she got out and walked to the door. Other than the lamenting coo of a mourning dove sitting on a telephone line, she heard nothing.

She twisted the knob. Locked. She rapped on the door. "Hello! Anyone here?"

She cupped her hands around her eyes and peered into the darkened showroom through a large window on her left. Dust blanketed piles of papers on a desk, and dirt coated the strewn boxes and tile samples on the showroom floor.

"Who are you?"

Claire jumped and dropped her hands at the gruff voice. She saw the reflection of a tall, stocky bearded man standing close behind her. *Where did he come from?*

She turned to face him and stepped aside. He had scraggly brown hair and sported a red flannel shirt and dirty jeans. She guessed him to be around her age.

"I'm—I'm Claire."

Scowling, he stepped closer to her and cross his arms. "What do you want?"

As a car whizzed past, she looked over his shoulder at the thick trees blocking her view of the road. Though she had worked on many construction sites in the past, never before had she felt so isolated.

Chapter Nineteen

She twisted her hands together. "I'm—I'm looking for locally-sourced tile. I was told there was a showroom here and thought I'd come to see the selection."

"Yeah, right," he said. "*You're* looking for tile. Why are you looking for tile?"

She furrowed her brow. "What does it matter why I am looking for tile?"

The man narrowed his eyes into long slits and stepped again, positioning himself inches in front of her. He reeked of sweat and cigarettes.

She moved back another step.

"The showroom is closed," he snarled.

She took another step back but stumbled on the uneven ground. She reached for the building to keep from falling.

Grabbing her, the man sunk his fingertips deep into her arms before righting her.

She writhed when he didn't release his grasp. "Let me go!"

He tightened his grip.

Filled with dread, she stopped struggling and lifted her eyes to his steel ones as they lanced into her.

"You'll have to look for our granite in Hydeport showrooms. We don't sell from here to the public anymore." His eerie calmness sent chills up her spine. "Leave and don't come here ever again."

Claire trembled. "I will. I *will* leave. Just please let go of my arms." Her voice quavered and her arms throbbed where his fingers dug into her.

She felt helpless as another car zoomed past on the highway.

"We don't want anyone getting hurt around here, now do we? Quarries are dangerous, so stay away." He sneered before freeing her with a slight shove.

She bolted to her car, got in, and locked the doors as he stood with his arms akimbo watching her. She backed up and, after turning, accelerated out of the parking lot, leaving a cloud of dust behind her. Her eyes welled up, and she shook all over as she drove toward the Cove.

What a horrible man! And to think I might be related to him. Ugh!

After driving into town and parking across from the Compass Rose, she sat behind the wheel and dabbed her eyes with a tissue. While rubbing her arms, she took deep breaths to calm her shaking before getting out.

Despite his disappointment in her before they parted last Sunday and his lack of response this morning, Claire hoped as she crossed the street that talking with Philip would calm her.

The bell jingled happily as she entered and walked over to an older lady behind the cash register. "Is Philip here today?"

"He was earlier, but he's gone for the rest of the afternoon. Is there something I can help you with?"

"I was just wondering if I could speak with him, that's all." When the clerk squinted one eye, she felt the need to explain. "I'm Claire and rent the cottage on his estate."

"Oh...you're Claire!" A smile spread across her face. "We've been expecting you. Philip told us about you Monday. He described you in detail, and I should have known it was you."

Claire's eyebrows shot up. *In detail?*

"I'm Marie. Philip asked my coworker, Emma, and me to make a special effort to ensure you felt welcome whenever you came in, so if you have any needs or questions, please ask."

Claire warmed at Philip's effort. "Thank you. I *do* feel welcome. I guess I'll look around a little bit then."

"Certainly! Take your time and enjoy."

Claire's shaking had subsided, and even in Philip's absence, she felt calmer. As she wandered around, she kept an eye on the door, hoping he would change his mind and return.

The shop's quality wares and colorful displays proved Philip's prowess as a merchandiser. Shelves and tables and baskets overflowed with items created in ways she had never known possible and in textures and scents that captivated and pleased.

Claire dangled from her finger a sachet in the shape of a miniature, plaid shirt—complete with tiny pocket and buttons—hanging on a Lilliputian-sized hanger. She sniffed its heady balsam scent.

Marie popped up beside her. "Those are made by a lady who lives in Silver Harbor. Aren't they sweet?"

"They're darling. They smell so good and are obviously well made."

"Philip searches high and low for things and won't even consider them unless they are the best in quality and workmanship. Many people want to sell their items here, but he is very picky. The nice thing is that once he finds someone, he does all he can to help them succeed."

Claire returned the sachet to its basket.

"He also helps organize two festivals every summer. They're quite successful for the vendors and give them yet another opportunity to sell their wares. Yes, Philip is a shrewd businessman for his age, not to mention just an all-around great person."

Claire remembered her father's suggestion of what type of man to marry—"*Claire, he should be a hard-working, business-minded man who will love you and take care of you.*" Claire shook her head back and forth. *Marriage? What am I thinking?*

Marie huffed. "Well, I don't care what you think. I've known him for a lot longer than you have, and he *is*."

Heat raced up Claire's face. "Oh, yes—yes, I believe you." She rested her hands on her hot cheeks. "I wasn't disagreeing with you. I was thinking about something else."

Marie squinched her eyes.

"I'm sorry."

"Philip is a young man of impeccable character and is more like a son to me than an employer. I'll defend him no matter who says what about him or who does anything against him. Don't ever forget that."

Claire's mouth dropped open. "I understand completely, Marie. I'm sure he is well-deserving of your loyalty. Believe me, I can't imagine doing anything to ever compromise his character."

"Well, good! I'm glad to hear that. Now please excuse me."

Claire finished looking through the rest of the shop and stopped at the counter before leaving. "Thank you, Marie, for taking the time to tell me about the shop—and about Philip. I'm sure I failed to see everything and will be back soon."

"Stop by anytime, Claire."

◦◦◦

Claire stood in front of the mirror and smoothed a wrinkle on her sleeveless emerald-green dress. She had purchased it to wear on a special date with Daniel, but he didn't like it and had told her to change into something different. She slipped her arms into the coordinating black sweater embellished with sparkling emerald-green beads before urging some straggling curls to join the others that fell in loose rings down her back.

After clasping in her small gold earrings and strapping on her black high-heeled shoes, she scanned her reflection one more time.

If only Daniel could see her now.

No! She stood straight and stuck her chin out. No more thinking of Daniel. Parker would occupy all her thoughts now. However, she knew quite well that up until late this afternoon her thoughts over the past week had tipped more in Philip's direction than Parker's. *Okay, so Parker won't occupy all my thoughts.*

With trembling fingers, she fidgeted with her earrings again before grabbing her purse and making her way to the car. Never before had she gone out with someone whom she knew so little about.

She backed up her driveway. A light blue sedan sat next to Philip's sport utility jeep. Neither vehicle had been there when she came home earlier. As she motored past, she saw a tall slim woman with long blonde hair. Philip, carrying a floral overnight bag in one hand, circled his arm around her shoulders as they climbed the front steps.

"Oh, no," Claire whispered. That must be the woman whose telephone message she overheard while slipping her payment into Philip's mail slot.

Was he married and didn't wear a wedding band? Was this a girlfriend or a fiancée?

Why, of course he had someone special in his life. Why wouldn't he? He was a decent, successful, handsome man.

Why should she be concerned about him and his life anyway?

He's my landlord—and that's all.

She snorted as she drove past. *So he likes blondes, huh?—tall, slim blondes.* No wonder he had ignored her this morning.

Chapter Twenty

As Claire drove through the Cove, she determined to enjoy her evening with Parker Hollenbeck no matter what. She cast a wary glance up the road leading to the Wycoff quarry as she drove past, then rubbed her upper arm. Before long, a large sign in silver letters announced the town limits of Silver Harbor and its incorporation date of 1826.

On her immediate right appeared a grand three-story house with equally-sized additions bumping out on either side. Striped awnings and stately chimneys accented the sage-colored complex. Lights prematurely illuminated trees and pathways on manicured grounds as well as on a large sign reading "Silver Harbor Inn."

She pulled into the parking lot and stopped beside Parker who leaned with arms and ankles crossed against a silver sports car. He beamed when he saw her. As she got out of her car, he righted himself and straightened his tie. "You came!"

"Of course, I came! I said I would, didn't I?"

He slowly looked her up and down. "You look ravishing!"

"Why, thank you. And you certainly look handsome."

He shut her car door and rested his hand on the small of her back. "I wasn't sure if you were the kind of girl to stand a guy up or not. I've been looking forward to this all week and didn't want to be disappointed at the end of my long drive from Boston."

Claire's mind flashed to the slim blonde and Philip's arm around her shoulders. She leaned closer to Parker and gave him her warmest smile.

Parker led her past the inn to the addition on the left. He opened a leaded glass door beside a spotlighted sign reading "Chart and Sextant" and guided her into a round room with a resplendent chandelier hanging from its high ceiling. Large odd-looking maps conformed to the curves of the walls. Antique, brass sextants fastened among the maps glistened under the chandelier.

A middle-aged woman in a black dress stood at a dimly-lit lectern. "Good evening, Mr. Hollenbeck. Your table is waiting."

She directed a cool glance at Claire before leading them through a room with floor-to-ceiling windows on two of its walls. Heads rose and eyes followed them as they walked by intimate, candlelit tables set with crisp white linens. They halted at a small table at the center of a large window that offered a sweeping view of the ocean.

"I've never been to such a fine restaurant. This is wonderful."

"It's the best in the area. I come here often."

After looking over their menus, a waiter approached and directed his attention to Claire. She opened her mouth to order the Atlantic salmon, but Parker spoke first. "We'll both take the stuffed lobster tails with new potatoes and seasoned asparagus." He winked at her as he grabbed her menu and handed both to the waiter. "You wouldn't know what to order. Trust me—the stuffed lobster tails won't disappoint you."

"Very well. I'll trust you then."

"Good…good. That's what I like to hear." He sipped some water. "Well, I might as well tell you about myself. No doubt you're curious."

"Okay."

"I'm a defense attorney in Boston—and a good one too. I represent the affluent, but, if a situation or someone interests me enough, I make myself available to them as well—even here in Maine where I'm also a member of the bar." He leaned toward her. "You don't need an attorney, do you?"

Amused, Claire shook her head. "No, not at the moment."

Gazing often behind her, Parker told her about the partners in his law firm and boasted about a few of the recent cases he won. After the meal came, he divulged some of his famous clients.

Disliking the lobster tail, Claire mixed the meat with her potatoes to get it down. "So, if you live and work in Boston, what's your connection to Maine then?"

"My family's estate, the second home I share with my brother and sisters, is just east of the Cove. I'm not always able to get away from the city, but whenever I can, I spend weekends and holidays there."

"Tell me more about it."

He wiped his mouth with the linen napkin. "The estate has been in my family for generations. The mansion sits on a rocky point that juts into the ocean offering a magnificent view of the harbor. You'll see. I'll take you there sometime. You'll also be impressed to know that Lone Spruce Cove is named after my family's property."

"Really?"

"A towering spruce tree stands on that point, though the original spruce uprooted during a storm as did its successor."

As darkness descended beyond the window, Claire's eyes glazed while he described the estate and the history of his family. With their empty dessert plates cleared, they lingered over espresso.

"Unfortunately, I have to return to Boston tomorrow. I have a trial coming up over the next two weeks and won't be back until Memorial Day weekend."

The flickering candlelight cast deep shadows on his face and shimmered off his graying temples. His brown eyes looked black and cold—so unlike Philip's green ones.

"You're beautiful, Claire." He reached over and caressed her hand as it grasped the handle of the espresso cup. "It will be hard not seeing you for two weeks."

She slowly pulled away from his hand and lifted the cup to her lips. She fixed her eyes on him over the rim and tried to decide if she really wanted to see him again. At least he appeared to be more mature and composed compared to Daniel.

She thought it strange that someone of his age and status did not already have a family. "You're not married? You don't have children?"

For a mere second he narrowed his eyes. The muscle in his jaw twitched before one side of his mouth curled into a priggish grin.

He pulled his hand back across the table. "Do you really think I'd ask you out if I were married?"

Her eyes flittered to her cup. "Well, no."

He held his left hand in front of his chest and wiggled his ring finger then pointed at her. "Ah, you think I'm old, is that it?"

"Of course not. It's just that—"

"Yes, I am a few years older," he cut in, "but age doesn't matter to two people who enjoy each other's company, now does it?"

"I didn't mean to insult you. It's just hard to believe that you're not already married."

"I'll take that as a compliment then, and to answer your question—just because I'm a little older than you doesn't mean I've experienced everything most men my age have experienced. Okay?"

"Okay."

He loved naïve young women.

"Do *you* have any children, my dear Claire?"

Claire's mouth fell open. "Of course I don't! I've never been married!"

The warm light of the candle's quivering flame chased the shadows that dared cross her face, further enhancing her beauty. The challenging hint of spirit in her passive innocence made him feel youthful and alive and strengthened his resolve to have her. "I've only seen one other person with eyes the topaz color of yours." He would insist she wear a topaz necklace when introduced into his social circles. "It's hard to believe *you're* not married. No one has ever asked you?"

Chapter Twenty-one

Heat flared before permeating every part of Claire's body. A bead of sweat trickled down the back of her neck. "I was asked once."

"Oh? I'm not surprised. And why did you reject—ah, what was his name?"

She squirmed and grasped the edges of her sweater. "Daniel."

"What happened? No doubt you broke Daniel's heart."

"I—I don't want to talk about it." Her right elbow caught as she pulled her arm out of the sweater. Parker reached over and held the sleeve while she freed her arm. As she reached to pull her other arm out, he brushed his hand over the blue, nickel-sized lesions.

"How did you get those bruises?"

"Oh, it's nothing."

"Nothing? Those look like finger imprints." He gently twisted her arm. "There's the fifth mark from a thumb." He ran his fingers over the same pattern on her other arm.

She pulled away from his touch and reached for her espresso cup.

"Come on. Who did this to you?"

She hesitated wishing—sweating or not—she had kept her sweater on.

"Don't forget I'm an attorney and have seen bruises like this before. Who grabbed you, Claire, and why?"

Unable to avoid his questions, she sipped some espresso as if she could gain strength from it before describing her trip to the Wycoff quarry, the unpleasant man she encountered, and his catching her from falling but not letting go.

While she spoke, Parker leaned back and drummed his fingers on the table, his eyes roving often beyond her. "I'm glad he was there for you!"

"What?"

"Obviously he kept you from falling. You could have injured yourself, you know."

"But don't you understand what I just said?"

"Of course I do, and I'm relieved no one actually tried to harm you. Don't you see? You surprised him. He surprised you. You stumbled backwards, and he rescued you from falling. No doubt he didn't realize his own strength…or how delicate a creature you are."

Her thoughts muddled; she now doubted her fears. "Do you think this man was one of the Wycoffs? Do you know them?"

"Oh, yes. Sounds like Hugh. Jake, the younger brother, never wears a beard. Both are a little hot-headed, but they're harmless, despite what people might say about them."

Harmless? She would not have attached that description to Hugh Wycoff!

"Are you related to them—to the Wycoffs?"

"I'm not sure."

He nodded then creased his brows. "Why in the world were you trying to get granite tile anyway?"

She told him of her past work, of meeting Grace, and the project at the church.

"It bothers me that you do menial work."

Menial work! "It's not menial! Tiling takes precision and skill, and a mosaic is an art form."

"Well, tiling floors isn't fit for an attractive young woman. You shouldn't accept any other tiling projects after this one. Maybe you should focus on doing mosaics only."

"I do intend to work on mosaic assemblages after the vestibule is done. I even have a little studio set up where I live."

"You must meet my sisters. They're both artists, and I'm sure they can advise you as you transition to devoting your time to your artwork. They can also introduce you into the right circles both here and in the Boston area."

"I'd appreciate that."

As they stood, Parker helped Claire with her sweater. "Let's see. Memorial Day weekend is in two weeks. My family traditionally sets sail on Memorial Day. Why don't you join us? You can meet my sisters and enjoy a sail on the schooner at the same time."

How could she turn down such an opportunity? "I would love that!" They confirmed the details as they walked out of the dining room.

On their way out of the restaurant Claire stopped in front of a large map beside the leaded door. "These maps are so strange. I've never seen anything like them."

He swept his hand around the room. "Each of these is a nautical navigational chart of either a section of Maine's coastal region or one of the state's island groupings. They offer navigational aids and detail water depths and topographical features along the coastline and seafloor."

"To keep from danger?"

"Precisely! See, like here." He pointed to the chart. "These islands are southwest of the Cove and east of Hydeport. Here is Lone Spruce Cove, and down here is Hydeport."

"I see."

"This particular cluster of islands is known locally as the 'Spice Chest,' since all of the islands from here to over here are named after a spice or herb or seasoning."

Claire ran her finger over the chart. "Basil Isle and look here—Cinnamon Stick Island. It does look like a cinnamon stick."

Parker slid his finger over some markings by a large island. "These indicate the island's coastal details. These numbers are water depths. This marker here," he said tapping the chart, "shows that rocks lie below the surface of the water and pose a danger."

"Fascinating," Claire said looking at the chart with new understanding. "Have you ever sailed between these islands?"

"The 'Spice Chest' islands? Oh, yes, many times, but usually I just go around them either straight into Hydeport or out to sea. It's been a while since I've actually sailed between them, but perhaps if the weather allows us we could do it on Memorial Day if you want to," he said with a wink.

✺✺

Claire followed Parker's sports car until, about a mile from the Cove, it pulled off and headed toward the ocean.

It had been a nice enough evening. She felt as if she knew more about him than he did about her, but she didn't mind. What *did* bother her was his defense of Hugh Wycoff and his attitude toward her tiling.

Despite that, however, she looked forward to meeting and networking with his sisters and sailing on that gorgeous schooner on Memorial Day. *Guess that answers my question about whether I should see him again.*

She turned onto the estate's driveway. As she emerged from the trees, darkness cloaked the area. Then her headlights reflected off Philip's jeep and the light-blue sedan.

Claire huffed. *So the blonde is still here.*

Chapter Twenty-two

Waking early, Claire wandered her beach hoping to find red sea glass for the ribbon. Finding several pieces, though no red ones, she meandered back to the rocks between her beach and Philip's.

When voices drifted over the barrier, Claire crawled up the rocks to snoop.

The blonde grabbed Philip's arms. "Oh yeah? I'll show you!" She pushed him backwards into the water then let go. "Take it back."

His arms flailed as he struggled to keep himself aright. "Ugh!"

Hopping about in the water, he raced up the sand and grabbed her arms. Claire repositioned herself for a better look as he wrapped his bare ankle around the blonde's to trip her, but she jumped away from his attempt and pushed him back again into the water.

Philip yelped. "This is freezing! My ankles are going numb."

Her laugh floated in the breeze. "I don't care. You deserve it after that comment. Take it back."

"I'm stronger than you, and you know it! I can *pull* you into the water if I want to."

"If you even try to pull me in and I happen to fall down, I promise you you'll go down with me."

They both laughed. "Okay, okay. I give up," he said. "That water is frigid!" They strode to the dry sand. Claire peeked between two rocks.

"You take it back?"

"Oh, I can barely walk now. Yes, yes, yes. I take it back." They laughed again as Philip sat and began rubbing his ankles and feet.

Claire backed down the rocks and scrambled up the cliff to the cottage.

Humph! Some Christian! He talks about how important being truthful and living right is, and then he has this woman stay with him—overnight!

Claire stomped to the cottage. Slamming the French door behind her, she tossed her new finds onto the kitchen table, scattering the glass across it and onto the floor.

Eager to leave, she grabbed her purse and got into her car. Thankfully she had an excuse to go to Hydeport to look for tile samples before her meeting with Pastor Tim and the committee at 1:00.

The tires kicked up rocks as she backed up the incline. Out of the corner of her eye she saw Philip and the woman strolling in the grass toward the main house. The woman gave Philip a shove at the same time he looked toward Claire. He waved his arm, motioning for her to stop.

I don't think so, Philip. Just like you didn't see me yesterday, I don't see you. She pressed her foot on the gas pedal shooting a billow of dust into the air.

⁂

Claire had just enough time to buy stamps before the meeting. "Good afternoon, Lorna." Her voice echoed in the empty lobby.

Lorna's chair complained as she straightened from resting her chin on her knuckles. "What'll it be today, Claire?"

"A book of stamps, please."

"Let's see. What have we here?" Lorna slapped her stamp folder on the counter. "How are things going with you? Is it working well staying out there with Philip England?"

"Well, if you're asking if staying at the cottage is working out, yes." She tented her fingers and bumped them together. "But, I'm certainly not staying *with* Philip. I haven't nor ever intend to set one foot in his house. Some blonde woman is doing that this weekend."

Lorna's hands stopped. She raised an eyebrow. "Really?"

"I'll take the ones with the roses on them," Claire said pointing to a book of stamps.

"That will be $8.80."

Claire rummaged for money in her purse.

"So, now, who's staying with Philip? Some blonde, you say?"

"I don't know and don't care." Claire slapped nine dollars on the counter beside Lorna's open hand.

"I can't imagine who this could be." Judging by the look on Lorna's face, Claire knew she wouldn't be afraid to ask around. Claire held out her hand and wiggled her fingers as Lorna took her time to make change.

Brightening, Lorna said, "I hear you'll be working on the church vestibule."

"Yes. In fact…" Claire glanced at her watch. "…I'm going to be late for a meeting to present the new design to Pastor Tim and the building committee."

Lorna dropped the two dimes and stamp book into her palm.

"I'm sure you'll do a fine job. I hear a lot of nice things about you, Claire." A corner of Lorna's mouth turned up. "News travels fast around here, you know."

Chapter Twenty-three

Pastor Tim, two men, and two women conversed among themselves as Claire arrived at the top of the steps carrying the template. Pastor Tim introduced her to the others which included Jason and Sasha Harriman whom she had seen at the Compass Rose.

Claire had returned to her car to retrieve the tile samples and sea glass when Philip appeared beside her. "Claire, it's good to see you! I've hardly seen you all week."

Claire bristled. "You've been busy, of course."

He reached for the box she held. "Here, let me take that. I'm here for the meeting too and can take it up for you."

She wanted to refuse, but because of its weight, she conceded and dropped it in his hands.

"Whoa, this is heavy!"

She grabbed the last box, shut the door, and they climbed the steps.

"I see you found the jars of sea glass. You're going to use some in the project, aren't you?"

His kind, easy conversation irritated her. Did he really think she didn't notice what had been going on at his house? "You'll have to wait and find out with the others," she clipped as they reached the top and she placed her box on the floor.

He shrugged before setting his box beside hers. "Okay."

Misery knotted her stomach. Gossiping about him with Lorna didn't make her feel any better, in fact, she felt worse. The edges of the template darkened from her wet hands as she positioned it on the floor. *Somehow I have to get through this meeting.*

She handed out the samples and described what she would use where. "The sea glass has been generously donated by Philip," she said gesturing toward him, "and there is plenty to use around the circle's outer edge in these colors."

People whispered and nodded their approval.

"I really want to use red sea glass in the ribbon, but I'm short several pieces." She held up the biggest red piece. The frosted whiteness on its exterior had disappeared in her sweaty grasp. "Please spread the word that if anyone has any they'd like to donate for the project, it would be appreciated."

"I'll make an announcement about it tomorrow," Pastor Tim offered.

Claire stated her price for her time and materials and asked for full accessibility to the church. She estimated the project to take a good month or more to complete.

"Thank you, Claire," Pastor Tim said before directing his words toward the others. "Let's all think about this tonight then discuss it and vote on it after the service tomorrow."

He turned back to Claire, "Will you come to church tomorrow? We can then ask you any other questions and give you our final answer."

Feeling as if she could burst into tears at any moment, she gave Pastor Tim a slow nod.

∽ఠ∽

Philip scratched his head. *Is she tearing up? What is her problem?* The engaging young woman he spoke with last Sunday night had turned into a completely different person.

As he talked with the Harrimans, he watched her gather her things and leave in silence.

∽ఠ∽

I can't believe I'm doing this—again! Claire curled her fingers around the edge of her mother's Bible and trudged up the stairs at 10:29, hoping no one would have time to say anything to her.

Sasha Harriman zipped over to her. "Claire, your vision for the floor sounds fantastic! I can't wait until it's done."

Claire gave her a weak smile. "Thank you."

Claire ignored Philip as she passed the back pew. *He has a lot of gall to come here after the past two days!* Neither vehicle had been parked outside his house when she left for church. Of course the blonde probably knew better than to make an appearance here.

Spotting an empty pew, she sat down on the end. Grace hurried toward her from the front. "Come see me this week," she whispered on her way to the back.

Before long, the song leader motioned for the congregation to stand and started the first hymn.

> *Come, ye disconsolate, where'er ye languish;*
> *Come to the mercy seat, fervently kneel.*
> *Here bring your wounded hearts, here tell your anguish;*
> *Earth has no sorrow that Heav'n cannot heal.*

As she sang the words, her voice cracked then wobbled to a whisper before falling silent by the end of the song. Tears dripped down her cheeks. Though she pined for peace and an end to her inner torment, a defensive wall stood between her hurting heart and a God who she did not know if she wanted or needed.

As she sat, she dreaded the message. "Today I'm going to talk about sin," Pastor Tim started.

Sin! Claire clenched her jaw. *Who wants to hear about that?* She glanced at the door under the exit sign and crossed her arms.

As her Bible lay clasped beside her, Pastor Tim pointed to scripture about things she had had no part of—murder and adultery—to things she had never thought of: coveting, gossip, lacking faith in God.

She fidgeted as her envy of the blonde and comments to Lorna gnawed at her. She grabbed a hymnal and setting it on her lap flicked the cover to cool her face.

"….in Jesus name, Amen," Pastor Tim concluded.

Finally! She returned the hymnal to its holder and engaged in conversation with a lady across the aisle before trooping to the church's entrance to wait.

Pastor Tim entered the vestibule, followed by the committee members. "We unanimously agree to your design and terms and will get a key to you today."

Claire forced a smile and addressed each member—each member except for Philip. "Thank you—all of you. I will do my very best." Clutching the Bible to her chest she left as quickly as she could.

Chapter Twenty-four

Philip knocked on the cottage door.

Claire opened it and darted him an icy look. "Hello, Philip."

He searched her face but couldn't read it. "I just want you to know your ideas for the vestibule are awesome, and I can hardly wait to see the end result. The sea glass colors around the circle and for the ribbon will look great."

"Thank you."

He held up a key between his fingers. "This opens the front door of the church. Don't hesitate to ask any of us if you need anything else."

Claire took it from him.

"Also, I'll be leaving within the hour for a gift show in Virginia. I'll be gone until next weekend at the earliest. Will you please keep an eye out around the place while I'm gone?"

Her voice hovered just above a whisper. "Of course."

Philip scrunched his brows. "Claire, I sense there's a problem between us. You don't seem at all like the same person I spoke with last Sunday. Have I said or done something to disturb you?"

Her face reddened as anger flashed in her eyes. "How, after a message like we had this morning, could you ask me if something is disturbing me?"

"What are you talking about?"

"Here…last week…you spoke to me about truth. You told me how important it is to be a Christian and to do right, yet you don't live it. You say one thing but live totally the opposite when you don't think anyone is looking!"

Philip stared at her while he searched his mind. What had he done to deserve such a serious accusation? "I have no idea what you're referring to."

"Oh, really? No idea?" Her voice quavered and tears of fury squeezed out the corners of her eyes. She hugged her arms in front of her. "You have a woman spend the weekend with you—overnight—and you have *no idea?*"

He flexed his jaw and stared at her in an attempt to remain calm. "And who else did you talk to about this woman?" He didn't wait for her reply. "Lorna, perhaps?"

She turned her head away from him.

That explains Lorna's half-cocked smile, sly eyes, and strange comment about him being "busy night and day" when he passed her on the sidewalk earlier.

Defiance replaced the exasperation in her voice. "It happened to come up while I was at the post office yesterday."

"What exactly did you say when it 'happened to come up'?"

"That a blonde woman stayed the weekend at your house."

Philip ran his fingers through his hair before spreading them on his hips. "Claire, you've crossed the line."

"What do you mean by that?"

"In case you haven't figured it out yet, there is no bigger gossip in this entire town than Lorna. If she can spread dirt about someone—anyone, even her own mother—she will deliciously do so disregarding how hurtful or inaccurate the information is.

"Next, what goes on at my house and in my life is *my* business and need not be blurted out to the entire town. We live far enough away so that we each have privacy, yet close enough so that we can't help but know what's going on in each other's lives. You *must* respect my privacy and not get involved in my life, and I will in turn respect yours and not get involved in your life."

Claire stared at him as if he had struck her.

"Do you understand this, Claire?"

"Yes," she whispered.

"Finally, I assure you I listened very intently to this morning's message.

Being a Christian is more important to me than anything else in the entire world, despite what you think. I'm certainly not perfect and have plenty of faults, but I desire and try my hardest to do what is right."

He took a breath and expelled it slowly hoping to steady his anger.

"Regarding the blonde who stayed overnight at my house this weekend, she had traveled up from Concord, New Hampshire, to visit me before driving on to visit our parents today in Augusta. Her name is Julie, and she is my sister."

Claire sucked in a breath. "I—I—never…"

"Goodbye, Claire."

≈≈≈

The following morning Claire knew quite well Philip was not home, but like a fool she kept expecting him to round the extension of rocks in his kayak. She kicked at a broken shell, sending it and a spray of sand into the water.

The few times she fell asleep last night, nightmares afflicted her, and she had awoken soaked in sweat.

She had dreamed of Philip, hammer in hand, shattering her finished mosaic, sending sea glass flying with each angry blow. Then, with hammer raised, he came after her. She tried to find her way out of the church but couldn't. Each time she entered a room or turned a corner, Philip waited for her as church members cheered him on, pointing accusatory fingers at her.

Then she had dreamed of being alone at night in a boat. It had only one light, and the loudness of the chugging motor deafened her. A monstrous wave crashed over the boat, darkening the light and washing her into the cold water. She called and cried in the dark swells, but no one heard her or came to her rescue.

A chill shot through her, and she rubbed her hands up and down her arms, testing the tenderness of her bruises with a few light squeezes. She hoped an early morning walk would clear her troubled mind before heading into town to start on the vestibule, but both clarity and comfort eluded her.

She bent and picked up a piece of glass—this one so rough it looked like a chunk of frosted ice. She wondered what it had once been a part of and how long it had been on its difficult journey to reach its beautiful state.

The white boat with the wide orange stripe that she had seen before glided around the bend. The same man with binoculars covering his eyes faced the shore. Claire waved to him as she had done before, and he waved back, this time without dropping the binoculars as they passed by.

She turned around at the end of the beach. New cigarette butts littered the ground, and fresh shoeprints impressing the path and beach disappeared into the wet sand by the water. She dismissed their existence.

Too many other more important things occupied her thoughts.

Chapter Twenty-five

After tossing her last tool into the box, Claire snapped the lid and pushed it into a corner. Before yanking its cord, she rubbed her stiff hands in front of the hot work light as plumes of vapor spiraled from between her lips. With the subflooring and preparatory work complete, she felt justified in stopping early. Well, early compared to the past four days.

Though the days' physical exertion offered reprieve, edging down the dark driveway each night plunged her heart and mind back into desolation. After locking the church, she smoothed her hair and brushed as much dust as possible from her clothes. The tearoom should still be open for a little bit longer. No doubt going there would lift her spirits and help her through the night.

"I was wondering when you would come by." Grace sat by Claire. "Holly, honey, please close up while I sit with Claire for a moment then go clean up the kitchen."

"Okay, Mom." Holly turned and left.

Claire glanced around the empty tearoom. "I shouldn't have come so late. I'm sorry. I'll eat this quickly."

"Ah, take your time. I'm happy to sit for a minute." Grace eyed her dusty clothes. "So how's the project going? I hear it's going to be beautiful. I'll *try* not giving in to temptation and peeking before the final unveiling, but it will be hard. I love your idea of using sea glass."

Claire wrapped her hands around her teacup. "Thanks. Everyone's positive feedback has meant a lot." She stared as if she could see through the milky liquid. "This project is good for me. I need the diversion."

Ah! Grace had sensed something bothered her. "Diversion? From what?"

As if awoken from an open-eyed sleep, Claire shook her head. "Oh, nothing." Between sips and nibbles, Claire described her progress during the past five days.

"My, you work fast! It'll be done in no time. Good thing too. People won't like using the side door now that the vestibule has been closed off." She chuckled. "And if someone's late, we'll all get to see who they are and when they came in!"

A faint smile crossed Claire's lips.

"Did you hear another place, the entrance to the library in Estherson, a town west of Hydeport, was torn up last weekend?"

"You're kidding!"

"Nope! Apparently, the robber stole a few artifacts and shattered the stoop outside the front doors. The police are pretty sure it's the same person who broke into the church."

"When did this happen?"

"The police think it was last Sunday night. Deliberately breaking up a beautiful old mosaic 'just because' doesn't make any sense." She brightened as an idea came to mind. "Hey, maybe you can do the work for them too."

"Oh, Grace, I couldn't possibly think of another big project right now." Claire spread lemon curd on a piece of scone. "I've never pieced words before, and, to be honest with you, I'm anxious about the Bible verse turning out right. Hopefully I'll feel more confident once I start." She popped the morsel into her mouth.

"Oh, you'll do just fine," Grace said patting Claire's arm. "So…what do you think of that verse anyway? You know, the actual words and their meaning?"

Claire chewed for longer than Grace thought possible before swallowing. "That's a good question. What's your opinion?" She stuffed the rest of the scone into her mouth.

"It's an important verse for sure. Everyone who steps on that floor will know who the source of all truth and the only way to heaven is." Compassion filled Grace's heart as Claire's expression and body language revealed an internal struggle. Her voice softened. "Claire, are you a Christian?"

Claire swallowed hard before draining her teacup. "Do you know you're the second person in two weeks to ask me that? No, I'm not." She clunked the cup down on its saucer. "I know what it means, and I know what needs to be done." She wiped her mouth and tossed the napkin on her empty plate. "I'm just having a hard time with the sin aspect and trying to decide whether I really need to become one, that's all. I need to think about it more."

"I understand." Grace smoothed her apron, hoping in fact she would give it more thought. "How is it going living at the cottage?"

Claire straightened the used utensils. "The cottage is wonderful in every way. I love having a studio area. The view of the ocean is magnificent. The pink teapot is perfect in the kitchenette, by the way. You'll have to come and visit sometime. I know I'm not home much now, but once the project is completed, please drop by—anytime."

"I'll do that. It's hard for me to get away, but I'll do it for sure sometime soon. I've always wanted to see Julie's cottage."

"*Julie's* cottage?"

"Yes, you know, Philip's sister. Didn't he tell you about her?"

"Well, not exactly…at least not regarding the cottage."

"Julie transformed an ugly outbuilding into that adorable cottage. She even did most of the work herself. She had planned on living there but got married and moved to New Hampshire soon after finishing it. It sat empty for years until Philip recently made it fit for all-season living and rented it out to you—the first person to ever live there."

"Oh."

"You must have found it peculiar that this tough, masculine guy had such a feminine-looking cottage on his property."

"I never really gave it much thought."

Grace paused, hoping her suspicions weren't true. "Speaking of Julie, did you meet her last weekend?"

Claire aligned the handle on her empty teacup with that of the little cream pitcher. "No."

"Well, I'm not sure if you've heard, but some terrible rumors have been spreading around town this past week about Philip."

Claire changed her position and picked at pieces of dust on her leg.

"Some people have been saying he entertains women every weekend." She watched Claire closely. "I even overheard some accusations about you."

Claire's head whipped up. "But I've never set foot in his house! And—and he certainly hasn't been in the cottage since I've been there! I've…we've…" She pushed her lips together.

Grace shrugged. "I'm just telling you what's being said. The most popular rumor is that he's having an affair with a blonde he met at one of his gift shows."

Claire hung her head.

"Philip is one of the most honorable people I know. Though we're all capable of wrongdoing and these rumors could be true, when I heard them, I knew in my heart they weren't."

Claire reached for her napkin and wiped the sweat that glistened on her upper lip.

"My husband has spoken with Philip several times this week, and he has emphatically denied the allegations. I don't know all the details, but my husband did tell me Julie, who was sporting a new hair color, visited him briefly last weekend. Someone must have seen her and started a rumor."

Claire's demeanor frosted, and her cheeks flushed to a deep crimson. She slapped her hands on the sides of her legs and stood. "Well, it will pass."

That's all you have to say? Disappointed, Grace stood. "True, but it has tarnished Philip's sterling reputation and thrown darts at his character and Christian testimony."

"I'm sure he'll be able to deal with it." Claire pushed her chair in. "I need to get home."

I've gone this far, so I might as well finish. Grace put her hand on Claire's arm. "One more thing, please, before you go."

Chapter Twenty-six

Claire felt like putting her hands on her ears and running from the tearoom screaming. Instead she crossed her arms and stood as still as a gravestone.

"Now, I don't want you to think I'm meddling, but I know the people in this town pretty well. As a friend, I want to warn you about someone because I don't think anyone else will."

You're too late, Grace. I already know how mean the Wycoff brothers are. She twiddled her fingers against her arm. "Okay, I'm listening."

"A few Sundays back I saw you on the docks talking with Parker Hollenbeck."

"What about him?"

"He may be handsome, wealthy, and influential, but he's a snake, Claire. Trust me on this."

Tsk! Claire's sigh echoed off the tin ceiling. She snatched her purse and charged to the cash register. Grace followed.

"He's a smooth talker. He flatters and charms people into his tangled webs."

Claire stopped at the front counter and rummaged through her purse. She dug out some bills and snapped her wallet before giving Grace her attention.

"Listen to me, Claire. Many times—too many times—he has slithered out of the Cove leaving in his wake a stream of broken hearts, broken lives, and scandals. I don't want to see you caught in one of his schemes and hurt."

Claire plunked the cash on the counter. "Thanks for the warning. Keep the change."

Grace opened her mouth as if she were going to say something further but closed it again.

Claire took her silence as a cue she could finally leave.

ひひひ

The noxious mix of profound guilt and obstinate disbelief churned Claire's stomach as she opened the door to the empty post office, a place she had avoided all week.

Desperate to ease her mind, Claire justified her association with Parker. She craved not only his attention and praise but also the opportunities he offered. She held her head high. *Besides, I'm a mature woman and can make my own decisions about Parker Hollenbeck.* Surely he couldn't be as troublesome as Grace said.

She entered the room lined with windowed post office boxes. Her keys jangled as she inserted the key and opened the brass door. Vertically-placed envelopes and ads as well as a small package filled the narrow space.

The knowledgeable Lorna did not return the package that bore only her name, city, state, and zip code. The return address read "Oberhaus, Ulanski, Cameron, and Hollenbeck" with an address in Boston.

After slapping the little door closed, she walked over and stood at a high wooden table and tore open the package. She pulled out a red velvet box and read the neat, pointed script handwritten on a small notecard.

> *My Dearest Claire,*
>
> *I loved our delightful evening together and hope there will be many more to come.*
>
> *I'm looking forward to seeing you again on Memorial Day for our sail.*
>
> *Meet me on the dock at 8:00 a.m.*
>
> *Warmest Regards, Parker*

She lifted the box's lid and withdrew a gold bangle bracelet molded into a delicate intertwining rope design. She slipped it onto her wrist. Its cold embrace contrasted to the warmth of the gold's glow in the light radiating from above.

He's spoiled me already, and we hardly know each other.

However, while running her fingers over the twisted rope design, Grace's warning whispered in her mind.

Her breath quickened as her imagination ran. She felt as if her wrist had been tied to one of Parker's tangled webs. Eager for release, she yanked the bracelet off and thrust it back into the box before snapping the lid shut.

She shoved the box and its notecard back into the package. *Is he really the man you say he is, Grace?*

Chapter Twenty-seven

Glass bounced from her pockets onto the kitchen table. Many churchgoers had handed her their precious red pieces of sea glass today, excited to have a part in the project. She made a pile, but set one piece aside.

A little boy had approached her before the service and opened his chubby hand revealing a tiny piece of rounded, red sea glass. "I found this all by myself." He looked from it to her then back to it again as he rubbed it with his fingers.

Claire scooched beside him. "You're kidding? You found this all by yourself? What a beauty!" She extended her hand, but he hesitated. "You don't have to give it to me if you don't want to."

"I'm not giving it to you. I'm giving it to God," he clarified.

"Of course you are. I know it's not for me. I'll be sure to put it in the mosaic where everyone will see it when they come through the door," she promised.

"You won't lose it?"

She unzipped her pocket and patted it with one hand. "You have my word. I'll take good care of it."

He looked at the piece one more time before dropping it into her pocket and running off.

The little boy had touched her heart. Despite its small size, she determined to include not just his but every piece of red sea glass given by these people.

As early evening approached, she hoped spending time on the beach, breathing the salt air and pacing her heart to the rhythm of the ocean, would give her peace. With the tide low, she poked around the exposed bases of the weir poles and completed a thorough search of her beach.

Still restless and with Philip not yet home, she crossed the rock border and roamed his beach as well. Obviously he had not combed it lately, for she found many pretty pieces—though no red ones. She approached the large boulders, the "gateway" as she thought of them, going onto the neighbor's beach. *Why not?*

Past the small forest that separated the two properties, a manicured lawn broken only by flat stepping stones carpeted the ground from the edge of the beach up to a grand house.

Claire dropped her head to scour the ground when movement out of the corner of her right eye startled her into losing her grip on the bag of glass. An older gentleman sitting on a weathered wooden bench not far from her met her gaze and jumped.

"Who are you?" he demanded.

"My name is Claire." She bent and picked up her bag.

He narrowed his eyes. "Why are you on my beach?"

"I'm sorry, sir. I should have been content to stay on my own beach."

"What do you mean your 'own beach'? I've never seen you before."

"I rent the cottage." She pointed toward the England estate. "Julie's cottage."

"Ahhhh….I see." The gentleman softened. "So Philip finally rented out that little dollhouse did he? And you're the lucky tenant, aye?" He patted the bench beside him. "Come, Claire. Come sit with me."

Finding the man affable, Claire approached the bench and sat at an angle so that they could face each other.

"Julie put a lot of work into that little house. For some reason she thought she'd never get married. I told her she would, but she wouldn't listen to me." He chuckled.

He held out his gnarled hand to shake hers. "I'm Harvard Soames, by the way. My wife, Maggie, is in the house," he said, nodding in its direction. "She doesn't care much for being out in the evenings anymore." He paused and eyed her lap where her left hand rested on the bag. "So, *Miss* Claire, you're not from around here I take it."

"No, I just moved from the Chicago area."

"Chicago, huh? You moved here all by yourself?"

She nodded.

"It's amazing what you young people do these days—just up and move here and move there with all that independence and confidence. Do you have a reason for coming to the Cove?"

"I do, Mr. Soames." She certainly didn't feel independent and confident but sat straight so he wouldn't think otherwise. "There are several reasons why I've come."

"Go on," he urged.

"I'm seeking answers to some unsolved…" She struggled to find the right words. "…matters in my family's past." The bag crumpled as she contorted it. "I'm also trying to come to terms with—with certain conflicts I'm grappling with. I'm seeking hope and—and purpose and direction in my life and…" Her voice hushed. "…and in my heart."

∿∿∿

As Mr. Soames studied her troubled expression and sensed the anguish in her words, compassion swelled within him—something he had not felt toward anyone for quite some time. He had been around the block enough times to know this girl wasn't flighty or trying to hoodwink him. He regarded her for a moment before deciding his curiosity about her family would have to wait.

"And what is it that brings you to my beach this evening?"

She told him about the vandalism at the church, her working on the mosaic, and the sea glass to be used in it. He gave her his undivided attention as if it were the first time he had heard the information.

"I need more red sea glass for the ribbon on the Bible and hoped to find some today with the tide out so far. Philip said you allowed him to stroll your beach, so I assumed that meant I could as well."

"I think the last time Philip 'strolled my beach' was fifteen years ago!" He chuckled again. "I like you, Claire. You sound like a sensible, spunky, hard-working young woman. Yes, feel free to come here any time you want to. I'll tell Maggie about you so if she sees you she'll know who you are."

"Thank you, Mr. Soames." Claire smiled.

Ha! I got a smile out of her!

"The tide is rolling in quickly. I suppose I should get going."

An idea sprung in his mind. He rested his wrinkled hand on her arm to stop her from rising. "Are you and Philip friends?"

Pain flittered across her face. "We've spoken about it."

"I've known him all his life. Oh, he was a rascal when he was a boy! He'd always wander over here and get into everything—rearranging our beach furniture and taking wood from our driftwood pile to build his little ships with. He grew up to be a fine young man, though, and I think of him as a son." *Yes, the son I never had.*

"I've only heard well of him."

"He made some unpopular decisions a while back. As a result, he's been treated poorly and hurt badly by people who he thought were his friends. You know, even this past week I heard some nasty rumors about him. I don't believe them though."

Claire pressed on the glass in her bag.

"He knows a lot of people and a lot of people know him, but I think he considers only a handful to be friends. I think, Claire, you have the potential to be a good friend to him."

Claire's eyes filled with water. "I *want* to be, but in the short time I've been here I've already managed to—to fail him miserably. I don't deserve his friendship."

"Bah! I find that hard to believe!"

She wiped a tear before it rolled down her cheek. "Mr. Soames, do—do you think he is the sort of man who is willing to forgive others? You know, if they asked him and desperately wanted his forgiveness?"

Mr. Soames cocked his head. Was she asking about the people he was referring to or about herself? He couldn't imagine this lovely young woman doing anything worthy of forgiveness.

"If you had asked me this, say, five or six years ago, I'd say 'no.' Oh, Philip was always basically good, but he had a mind of his own driven by his own ambitions, whatever they happened to be at the time."

He pointed a crooked finger in the air. "But, several years ago he changed. After watching him for a while, I asked him what happened to him. He told me he had become a Christian and encouraged me to be one as well. Of course, I don't have much time or need for religion, but I kept watching him to see if he would go back to his old self. And, you know what?"

She sniffed. "What?"

"He *has* changed—permanently changed—from the person he used to be. He's developed an unusual moral strength and an amazing sense of character, and he always seems so calm and peaceful."

He paused for a moment to reflect then nodded his head. "Yes, I believe he would be forgiving. I have a great deal of respect for Philip, and my respect is hard to earn."

As they sat in silence for a few minutes, seagulls flew overhead, announcing their arrival to those already bobbing on the ocean's surface.

Mr. Soames rose from the bench and stretched out his hand. "I'm feeling a little chilled from the night air and should get inside. It has been nice to meet you, Miss Claire, and I hope to see more of you."

She thrust her bag into her pocket and clasped his hand then patted the top of it with the other one. "I hope to as well, Mr. Soames. It has been a pleasure. Thank you again for allowing me to search your beach and—and thank you for talking to me about Philip."

With a nod, Mr. Soames turned around and lumbered up the stone path.

Chapter Twenty-eight

Claire sat on one of Philip's Adirondack chairs and stared with blank eyes at the brilliant yellow and orange horizon. She mulled Mr. Soames' words and craved the change he saw in Philip. She yearned for the same peace Philip had.

She thought about her parents and concluded from her mother's words and actions and desires for the things of God she had most likely died a Christian. But, as wonderful a man as her father was, his life revealed no such evidence, and nothing could be done about it now. Overwhelmed by misery, she covered her face with her hands and sobbed.

Today's message had been about forgiveness—of God forgiving sins and of people forgiving others. Throughout the afternoon its weight on her heart and mind had become unbearable.

She could fight no longer and prayed aloud. "God, I've done a lot of stupid things…" She swallowed the lump in her throat. "…sinful things. Please forgive me and help me not to repeat them. I do believe Jesus died on the cross for my sins and rose again after three days. I accept Your gift of eternal life. Help me to be a person of moral strength and character like Philip, and please, please give me peace. Thank you, God. In Jesus' name, Amen."

She opened her wet eyes and drew in a long, halting breath of chilly air before releasing it in a long, slow stream. She rubbed her cheeks with her hands.

It felt as if a boulder had fallen from her chest as peace diffused through her heart and mind. After closing her eyes and leaning back, she heaved a loud sigh and flopped her arms over the sides of the chair.

The crunch of tires jolted her from her reverie. *Philip!* How could she escape without being detected? She sat up and pulled her arms in but not before headlight beams halted on the sand on either side of her. She sat there frozen, hoping she had not been detected. Then the lights swung away.

$$\mathcal{U}\mathcal{U}\mathcal{U}$$

Philip's eyes stung, and his shoulders ached from driving all day. He could hardly wait to climb between his own sheets and succumb to sleep.

As much as he liked being home, though, he dreaded facing everyone in town and wanted to see his tenant even less.

I can't stay away forever, God. You know I'm innocent. Please help me through this.

His headlight beamed onto the chairs and beach in front of him. Are those arms? He thought of the footprints and cigarette butts. *Oh, bother!* Maybe in his exhausted state his eyes were playing a trick on him. He swung up his driveway and brought the jeep to a halt.

He got out of his jeep, slammed the door, and trudged to the beach. What if it's Claire? He gritted his teeth when he saw her hair fluffing out one side of the chair. *Ugh! I don't want to deal with her right now.*

But now he had committed.

"Can't you manage to come here when I'm not home? You had a whole week."

She popped up from the chair. "I'm sorry. I shouldn't have stayed here, but—but..."

"No you shouldn't have!"

"I hoped you wouldn't see me."

With mounting agitation, Philip stepped closer to her and put his fists on his hips. She raised her face like a timid child. Only then, helped by the sun's last rays pointing above the horizon, did he see her blotched nose and swollen eyes.

She still looked as beautiful as ever.

He scowled, angry with himself for being attracted to her, and concentrated on the words he had rehearsed all week to say at this very moment.

But, she spoke first.

"Philip, you will never guess what I just did."

"I can only imagine."

"I became a Christian tonight…right here…just a few minutes before you pulled up."

His eyes bore through her. *No!* The embankment that had held so steadfastly broke, and the memories—oh, the memories—flooded his mind.

"See, you said you hoped I would become one, and I have. It just took a little time."

He groped for words, but none came.

Fidgeting with her fingers, she searched his face. "Do you not believe me? Aren't you glad? I thought you of all people would…"

"Yes, yes!" His words lashed like a blast of cold air. "Why wouldn't I be glad for you?" His coldness shamed him.

She blinked several times before continuing. "Also, I want to—wish to—ask for your forgiveness for speaking wrongly—for gossiping about you. I was envious of your sister thinking she was…" Claire licked her lips. "Well, I spoke when I shouldn't have about something I knew too little about."

Envious?

"Oh, Philip, if God can forgive me of wrongdoing, surely you can too!" Her lips trembled and tears trickled down her face. Her voice fell to just above a whisper. "I'm so sorry. I don't deserve it, but please forgive me."

Though still floundering in the flood of memories, her apology disarmed him, and his anger melted. God had kept him from uttering the bitter words he had planned to say, words he would have regretted. Humbled, he dropped his fists. "Yes. Yes, of course I forgive you."

Her shoulders fell. "Thank you."

"We'll consider the subject consigned to the past. Okay?"

"Can we start over?"

"Let's."

She wiped her cheek with the back of her hand.

"I need to go," he said. "Thanks for telling me about your decision, Claire. You won't regret it. Goodnight."

After she said goodbye, he turned and walked to his house, wondering if he dared believe her.

Chapter Twenty-nine

Sweat rolled down the only remaining gap between Claire's shirt and her skin. Wayward curls that had escaped her ponytail matted against her temples and neck. Sapped of energy, she leaned against the propped church door and sprawled on the top step, hoping for a breeze—any breeze—to offer respite.

Wiping her face on her sleeve, she grabbed her bottle of water and took a drink. *Yuck!* She emptied the bottle over the edge of the steps before thunking it beside her.

Lone Spruce Cove had come to life during the past week. Men made deliveries, fresh flowers filled window boxes, and windows sparkled from vinegar washes. The Saturday of Memorial Day weekend, the official start of "the season" had arrived.

From her vantage point Claire watched tourists bustle down the sidewalks and cars crawl along Main Street. Though she could not see it from where she sat, she pictured boats in all shapes and sizes glugging about the harbor. She looked forward to Monday and imagined herself on that amazing schooner. She closed her eyes at the thought of the cool ocean air blowing through her hair. Her body felt heavy as the sounds and movements on Main Street got farther and farther away.

What a busy morning! Pleased with the day's sales, Philip checked his watch. Was it two o'clock already?

Though the air conditioning had blown all day, he still felt hot and sticky. Leaving the shop in the capable hands of Emma and Marie, he stepped out into the muggy air. His glasses fogged, and he swiped the hazy patches with his finger. He licked his lips as only one thing occupied his mind—a bottle of Grace's icy French lemonade.

When he opened the door and stepped inside the tearoom, a welcome rush of cool air met him. Holly waited on a table at the back, and Grace sat on a stool behind the counter fanning her flushed cheeks with her apron.

"Well, good afternoon, Philip!"

"Hello, Grace! Did you have a good morning?"

"Very good! We've been out straight. This is the first time I've sat since 6:00!" She stopped flapping her apron and reached for a cup of ice water. "I really need to hire another person or two to help serve. Holly and I just can't do everything, and Tim has been here more than he should be." She took a long gulp. "How have things gone at the Compass Rose?"

"Great! It's been an awesome start to the weekend." He reached in his back pocket for his wallet. "I needed to get away for a minute though and thought I'd come in for—"

"Don't tell me!" Grace cut in, putting her hand up. "Let me guess. A piping hot cup of tea?" She sniggered as she rose and leaned over a galvanized tub filled with glass bottles of lemonade nestled in ice.

"Yes, that's exactly what I came in for. Hot tea! You know me so well."

Grace lifted two bottles, tiny bits of ice dripping down their sides, and clunked them onto the counter beside the cash register.

"Oh, one is enough," he said, thumbing through his bills.

"I'd like you to take one to Claire, if you don't mind."

His jovial spirit left him. "Grace…what are you trying to do?"

"What do you mean what am I trying to do? Claire came in here Monday morning over-the-top excited and told me all about the decision she made last Sunday night. She also said you were less than enthusiastic—like you didn't believe her. Apparently, your reaction confused her."

"Did you tell her anything?"

"No. You know I wouldn't do that."

"I'm sorry." He pulled a couple of bills out of his wallet. "I should trust you more than that."

"Come on. Give her some slack. She sure seemed different from when I talked with her last Friday." She hesitated. "I truly think it's real, Philip. Remember, not everyone is the same."

"I know."

"Besides," she said pushing the bottles closer to him, "she's been working long hard hours on that floor. The vestibule lights are already blazing every morning when I drive past—and you know what time I get here. I think she deserves a lemonade today, don't you? As warm as we feel, we've been in air conditioning all day."

"Wow! You sure know how to make a guy feel guilty." He reached back into his wallet, withdrew a few more bills, and tossed them onto the counter.

She punched numbers into the cash register and pushed half the bills back. "Her bottle is on me."

"Oh, no. If I've been given the task of delivering it, I'll pay for it."

"If you want to."

"I insist." He grabbed the bottles around the necks and headed for the door. "Thanks, Grace."

Cold penetrated his hands as he hustled the short distance. When he reached the church and saw Claire slouched motionless against the door, he flew up the stairs. After clunking the bottles on the top step, he bent over her.

Long, dark lashes rested on red, glistening cheeks. Rings of hair matted against her forehead and chin. "Claire?" She didn't stir. He got down on his knees and, laying his hand on her small shoulder, gently shook it. "Claire?"

Her body jerked, and her eyelids flew open. "Philip!"

"I didn't mean to scare you." He withdrew his hand. "Are you okay?"

She rubbed her eyes with her hands and blinked. "Yes, I'm a little tired, though, and awfully hot." She wiped her red cheeks with her shirt sleeve. "I leaned back and thought about being on the ocean and feeling the cool air blow through my hair, and I guess I fell asleep."

"You've been putting in long hours here, haven't you? What time do you get here each morning?" No way would he admit he noticed her car gone every morning when he got up.

"Oh, around 4:30 or 5:00, I suppose."

"And you leave around…?"

"Mmm, 6:30 to 7:00. Well, it was 8:15 last night."

"No wonder you're tired working hours like that. Here…" He picked up a bottle and handed it to her. "…this bottle of French lemonade will help." He picked up his own bottle and shifted back to lean against the door opposite her, stretching his long legs in front of him.

She took the bottle and again leaned against the door and closed her eyes. With face lifted skyward she rolled the icy bottle over her burning cheeks then up and down her slim neck.

"Ahh," she breathed. "This feels so good!"

Grace had been right.

Snapping the metal clip, he popped his seal, and a miniature swirl of mist curled from the opening. "Well, you can wear your bottle if you like, but I prefer to drink from mine," he said before taking a generous swallow.

Claire stopped rolling the bottle down her neck and giggled. "I suppose you're right." She broke the seal and took a long drink as well. "This is delicious! I've never had French lemonade before. Thank you."

"You're welcome." He exaggerated a glance to his right. "So, are you going to let me have a peek?'

"Oh, I see how it is. You give me this wonderful lemonade so I'll let my guard down and give you an exclusive look."

Feigning innocence, he shot an angled glance above him.

She giggled again. "You'll have your chance, Philip England, but in a few weeks along with everyone else."

He laughed. "Well, it was worth a try." He took another drink and set the jesting aside. "So when do you hope to be finished?"

"My goal is by the third week of June. I still need to get more red within the next two weeks for a tight ribbon design. What I've laid out will work, but I'm just not satisfied with how it looks. I *so* want to use the red sea glass!"

"How many more pieces do you need?"

"Ten to fourteen medium-sized pieces would be perfect." She told him about the church people who had given their prized pieces and the little boy who gave his precious treasure "for God."

An idea came to him. He looked at his watch. *I'll have to wait.* "Emma and Marie are going to wonder what happened to me." He drained the last drop then stood.

"I'm glad you came by. Even though people are all about, no one ever stops, and it gets a little lonely working here all day. Thank you again for the lemonade. I feel refreshed now."

Philip regretted it hadn't been his idea. At least he had paid for it. "Glad you liked it. It's my favorite drink. Grace has plenty of them if you ever need another one." With a wave he walked down the stairs and called back, "Goodbye, Claire. Have a good day."

"You too, Philip."

～～～

She watched him stride down the street. He greeted people and waved across the street at others before disappearing from view.

His attitude toward everyone—his attitude toward *her*—amazed her. He acted as if she had never spoken ill of him and as if he had truly forgiven her.

The healing balm of reassurance soothed her heart, and with renewed energy she jumped up to work again.

～～～

Positioned on her hands and knees, a clap of thunder yanked her attention from the floor to the angry clouds churning outside. She sat back on her legs and dusted her hands on her thighs.

Time to quit anyway.

Before covering the floor for church tomorrow, she picked up her level to check an area one more time. The glass and tile glimmered in the bright work lights as she placed it on top of them. She lay on her stomach and followed the ethanol-suspended bubble as it moved left then right then left again before stopping at the center of the vial.

Level. She thought of the riddle. "*Under pieces on a level plane*" Her eyes dropped from the level to the mosaic pieces then back to the level again.

"*Under...pieces...on...a...level...plane*" Though she had used her level several times this past week, the riddle had not come to mind before now. Could the "pieces" be referring to a mosaic? If that were the case, it would have to be *under* the pieces—under a mosaic.

What else could involve pieces of something being level or flat? An airplane leveling off? She snickered. No. A hand planer? That doesn't make sense either.

Another crack of thunder shook the church. Her weary mind whirled with thoughts of what the "pieces" could be referring to and what could possibly be under them.

I don't even know what I'm supposed to be looking for under those pieces!

Chapter Thirty

With a light heart, Claire held the Bible to her chest and remained sitting after the service ended. How different she felt compared to the past few weeks!

Pastor Tim must have gone over today, for Philip and Grace scooted down the far aisle and disappeared through the door below the exit sign. After chatting with a few people, Claire left, rubbing her fingers over the few pieces of red sea glass in her pocket, and moseyed down the path toward the docks.

The sun gleamed off Parker's silver sports car in the parking lot; however, the end of the dock gaped empty. She could not blame him for being out on the water today. The storms of last night had cleared leaving a cloudless blue sky surrounding the bright white sunshine.

She sat on a bench and enjoyed the harbor's activity for a while before getting up and retracing her steps. When she got to her car, she put the Bible on the front seat and grabbed her purse from under the seat. She didn't *need* to go to the Compass Rose, but those soaps and notepaper had caught her eye last time she visited.

She joined the busy crowd on the sidewalk and, along with two other women, entered the Compass Rose below the jingling bell. Marie greeted the others, then came over to Claire. "Good afternoon! So nice to see you again, Claire. Something in particular bring you in today?"

Claire glanced past Marie's ear toward the back room but said, "I came for some soap and notepaper."

"Well, you'll find the letterpress notepaper over there and the goats' milk soap right over here," she said, leading her to a display. Not missing a beat, Marie whispered, "Yes, Philip is in, but he's talking with Mr. Soames. I'm sure you have no idea who he is, but he's a very important person. He doesn't come in very often, so it's quite an honor when he makes an appearance. He owns most of the town, you know. No one ever says 'no' to him. He's just that sort of man."

"Oh! I—I didn't know that."

"I'll leave you to the soap," Marie said speaking a little louder. "My favorite is the Earl Grey." She picked up a sample and held it below Claire's nose.

"Hmm….this is going to be a hard choice, I can see."

When Marie went to assist other customers, Claire inspected the soaps. The round, light-colored soaps had varieties of tea as their predominant essence. She smelled each one and had just placed a chamomile tea soap beside ones made with raspberry green tea and peach tea in a wax bag when Philip and Mr. Soames emerged from the back room and headed down her aisle.

"Like I said, I should have more details by Tuesday morning. If you come over Tuesday evening, say around 8:00, we can discuss the festival in more detail. That should give you plenty of time to close up and get over to my place."

"I'll be there, Mr. Soames."

Mr. Soames' eyes lit up when he saw Claire. "Why, Miss Claire, my dear! What a delight to see you again." He picked up her hand in both of his and patted it.

"The delight is all mine, Mr. Soames."

Her eyes drifted over his shoulder to Philip who looked at her in shock.

Still holding her hand, Mr. Soames cranked his head over his shoulder. "And bring Miss Claire with you when you come."

Philip's eyebrows shot up. He opened his mouth as if he were going to protest but snapped it shut.

"You know you want to bring her along, so no objections from you now," he added, winking at Claire.

Philip's mouth opened again, but he pursed his lips and remained silent.

Claire could feel her cheeks flame. Mr. Soames gave her hand a gentle squeeze before letting go. "See you both on Tuesday evening then." Appearing content with the arrangements, he walked down the aisle and went out the door.

Philip didn't waste any time. "Where have you met Mr. Soames? How do you know him? *When* did you meet him?"

Claire savored her secret by studying the details of the tin ceiling in silence. She couldn't stop the smile from forming on her lips.

"Claire?" Philip crossed his arms and stepped closer. Having the advantage of height, she had no choice but to look him in the eye.

"I met him a week ago when I decided to check out his beach. He was sitting on his bench, so I sat and chitchatted with him for a while." She paused. "He certainly had a good deal to say about you."

"He probably told you all the naughty things I did as a little boy."

Her smile grew. "As a matter of fact, he did."

"Oh, great!" He rolled his eyes. "Seriously, though. I can't believe that in the short time you've been here, you've already managed to meet and find favor with one of the most influential men in the area. That's no small feat."

"He's a very kind gentleman, and I'm honored to know him."

"Well, if Mr. Soames wants you at our meeting, then you certainly must come. Why don't you meet me by my garage at 7:50? We can walk over together."

"Okay, I'll be there."

Philip turned around and went to the back room. Claire chose a ribbon-bound stack of paper with a raised compass rose design and headed to the cash register.

Marie spoke little as she rang up and bagged Claire's paper and soaps.

"That kayak is exquisite, Marie. I don't remember seeing it there before." Claire pointed to the two-tone wooden kayak hanging on the wall behind her. Its smooth, lacquered surface reflected the shop's golden light.

"Philip hung it last Friday. There are two others, but he hasn't had time to get them up yet."

"The detail and craftsmanship is amazing. I can't imagine actually using it in the water."

"Oh, people do, believe it or not, but if I had one I think I'd just hang it in my living room."

Claire agreed as she picked up the bag and took one last look at the kayak. It reminded her of a handsome Philip England in his kayak one foggy morning not long ago.

✒✒✒

That evening, Claire wrote on her new notepaper the following notes:

Under = underneath, at the very bottom

Pieces = tiles? mosaic?

Level plane = flat, level surface

She tacked the paper beside the riddle on the bulletin board and studied it for a moment. *How am I ever going to figure this out?*

✒✒✒

Philip tucked his shirt between his forefinger and thumb and wiped the smudges off his glasses. He turned to the window in his small office and held them up to the cool morning light. Satisfied, he put them back on and blinked to focus his eyes on the harbor below. People scurried about as they prepared to go out on the ocean for the day.

What a fabulous morning! I wish I could join them.

To his surprise, Claire caught his eye. She gathered a coat and a small box from her car, looked around, and headed for the docks. Parker then darted in her direction.

"Oh, no," Philip muttered. "Not the Hollenbecks!"

Parker drew her to him and kissed her cheek. *Ugh!* Her hand flew to her cheek, but she did not return the kiss. Parker then placed his hand on her back and led her to his schooner. They stopped and talked for a minute before he held her close and led her onto it.

Why don't you just scoop her into your arms and carry her on, Parker. Philip sighed. *Of all people, not him, Claire!*

Not far behind them, Parker's older sister in a profusion of head-to-toe color hastened from the parking lot to the schooner and climbed aboard.

119

Then from the far side of the parking lot walked a man who Philip did not recognize with his arm around the waist of someone he did recognize—Parker's beautiful younger sister. It had been a long time since he had seen her. Her straight black hair fell the entire length of her back and shimmered in the morning sun. White shorts accentuated her shapely bronze legs.

Philip closed his eyes and turned away from the window. Strong emotions flared and troublesome thoughts warred within him. He seized the broom and attacked the dirt and dust that dared land on the floor since last night.

I must talk to Claire about Parker. However, as soon as the thought arose, he remembered his own words about staying out of each other's personal lives.

Lord, he prayed, *please help me with these thoughts and emotions. Help me be strong and centered on You. And please, Lord, please protect Claire.*

Chapter Thirty-one

Claire took her coat and a box of chocolate-covered strawberries from her car. Seeing Parker nowhere, she walked toward the schooner.

Parker hurried up to her. "Claire, darling!"

"Good morning!"

In one motion Parker pulled her into his arms and kissed her cheek. Surprised, she jerked back and touched her hand to her face. "Parker, I barely know you!"

"That will change."

"But…"

"Oh, now, loosen up, Claire. There's nothing wrong with a little kiss from someone who adores you. Come, I've been looking forward to this." With his hand on her back he pushed her gently toward the dock. "We have a perfect morning, and this northeast breeze will keep us warm for a good part of the day. It's wise you brought that coat along, though."

The dock dipped and rose as they stepped onto it. Claire froze in front of the gap between the dock and the schooner and looked at the water. An unexpected wave of anxiety splashed over her.

"What's the matter?"

Feeling foolish, she didn't want to tell him. "I didn't think before now how deep the ocean is."

Parker laughed. "Of course it's deep!"

"It makes me nervous."

"*Pfft*. Don't be silly."

"Well, shouldn't we wear life vests?"

"It's not like you're on a little dinghy here. Think of this as a small house." He slid his arm around her and drew her close, saturating the precious air she sucked into her lungs with his sandalwood cologne. She sputtered to suppress a cough.

"You'll be safe with me." He pulled her up the small steps and onto the schooner. "Besides, I like having a beautiful woman close to me without a bulky life jacket between us." He winked. "Let's go below deck first."

The smell of coffee replaced the cologne and cleared her head as they walked down wide-planked, wooden stairs. Cool sunlight streamed from latticed windows overhead and from windows lining the tops of mahogany walls. Shiny brass fixtures and creamy leather couches exuded luxury.

"This is the galley; down there is the lavatory; and behind those doors are the bedrooms." When he moved within inches from her, she could feel his breath on her face. "Roam about. Get to know the place," he said in a low voice.

Unease prickled over her body.

"I want you to come back here alone sometime and—"

"Parker? Parker where are you?" Footsteps hastened above them and clomped down the wooden steps. "Are you down here?"

"Yeah, I'm down here," he called. Claire stepped back and thrust the box of strawberries toward him. "These need to be refrigerated."

Grumbling something under his breath, he took the box. A woman in pink shoes below white pants covered in splashes of pink, green, and orange walked down the steps balancing overstuffed bags on each arm.

Immediately Claire recognized her.

"Parker, help me with these will you? They're heavy." Parker grabbed a bag from her as she reached the bottom step. She narrowed her dark-brown eyes at Claire. "So, you must be Claire. I'm Barbara, Parker's older sister." She then turned her petite frame and placed the other bag on the small counter in the galley. Her twirling orange earrings, the color of her glasses, were the same ones Claire saw at the Compass Rose.

More commotion ensued overhead before a pair of long deeply-tanned legs sashayed down the stairs followed by ones in pressed, cuffed pants. The woman halted and from behind dense lashes scrutinized Claire from head to toe with blue eyes so pale they looked transparent.

"I assume you're Claire."

"Yes, I am. Nice to meet you…"

Silence overstretched the moment before Parker spoke, irritation chafing his voice. "Vanessa. This is my younger sister, Vanessa. And this is Stewart, her friend."

Stewart shook Claire's clammy hand and gave her a single nod.

Claire smoothed the coat draped over her arm in order to dry her sweaty hands. *I'm on this luxurious schooner on the gorgeous coast of Maine. I'm not going to be afraid of the water. I'm not going to be anxious.*

Parker cupped his hands together. "Ok, now that introductions are over, let's get underway." He grabbed Claire's hand and hauled her up the stairs.

Vanessa rolled her eyes. "Settle down, Parker," she whined. "Do you always have to be so adrenalized?"

Chapter Thirty-two

As the *Lady Katherine* glided from the mouth of the harbor, Claire sat motionless by Parker as he guided the spoked wooden wheel. He gave her a short sailing lesson and pointed out different parts of the ship. She hoped the knowledge would ease her anxiety.

"There's our estate and the spruce tree I told you about," Parker said as they slid past a turreted mansion sprawling along the rocky point. A large, lone spruce tree stood in repose between it and the ocean.

"Here, take the wheel," he said sliding off the seat behind it.

"Me?" Panic seized her. "I don't know how to do that!"

"There's nothing to it." He extended two fingers toward a rocky island far ahead of them. "Focus your eyes on that island and move the wheel to aim the bow at the center of it."

She slid from her seat to his and gripped the wheel with all her strength. He switched the engine off then covered her white knuckles with his hands and pried the tips of her fingers from the wheel. "It's going to be okay, darling. Loosen up. You're doing just fine."

Stewart, Barbara, Vanessa, and Parker flew into action, positioning themselves by the tall, wooden masts. Like a synchronized team, they untied ropes and assisted each other in raising the sails. The impressive, red sails rippled then snapped violently in the wind until they swelled taut.

Dad would have loved this!

Parker returned with a wide grin and took over the wheel. "So, what do you think?"

"Oh, it's grand!" she said, thankful to return to her seat.

While Parker followed the coastline south, she marveled at how different things appeared from her ocean perspective. Then, with a start, she straightened and looked behind them as the corner of Philip's house disappeared. She had been too intent on steering and watching the sails to notice the cottage and house as they sailed past.

I wonder what Philip is doing right now.

Her mind drifted to his kind green eyes and to how people described his character. Once again, his attitude toward her on Saturday then on Sunday at his shop warmed her—and calmed her. She felt so undeserving of his forgiveness. She wished he—

Parker cleared his throat jerking her from her contemplation. Surely he hadn't read her thoughts! Parker's profile, perfect like the carving of a Roman emperor, remained fixed, though, and dark sunglasses covered his eyes. Silent, he sat at the helm—silent? A rare occasion indeed!

Barbara, crocheting a hat in fluffy fluorescent-pink yarn, sat diagonally from her and made no effort at conversation. At the bow, Vanessa struggled in the wind to braid her hair as Stewart worshipped her every move.

Claire pulled back the sleeve on her long-sleeved shirt and twirled her gold bracelet around her wrist. *I can't believe I'm doing this. I hardly know these people... and I'm entrusting them with my life!*

Without warning, the wind raked her hair from her face and pulled it toward the ocean. Her eyes grew wide as the schooner leaned deeply on its side—the side Claire sat on. She cast a wary glance over her shoulder as her body slanted closer and closer to the water. How cold and deep the water must be! Her chest heaved, and grasping the seat with both hands, she dug her fingers into the cushion.

"Hey, you're going to put holes in my cushion," Parker chided.

"Are we supposed to be leaning this much? Will we tip over?"

Parker laughed. "It would be very difficult to tip over. Claire, this is what happens when we sail." He spoke as if she were a child. "The wind fills the sails, and the ship heels to one side."

"Are you *sure* we don't need to wear life vests?"

"Of course I'm sure." He made no attempt to hide the irritation in his voice. "I suppose if you really want to you can. They're over there." He wiggled his finger in the general direction of the cabin. "But if you put one on don't complain to me that you're uncomfortable."

"Or to me either," Barbara added while looping yarn around her crochet hook.

"It's unlikely you'll fall over those roped railings…and we won't push you off the ship either, will we, Barbara?"

Without missing a stitch, she smirked. "Well—no, we probably won't jettison anyone today."

Claire didn't care for their amusement at her expense. "I guess this Midwestern gal just isn't used to being on the ocean."

"You'd better get used to it if you're going to live on the coast of Maine," Parker said.

She closed her eyes as the wind combed her hair, the moment she had wished for a few days earlier. Unfortunately, she did not feel as blissful as she had imagined she would.

The moment passed quickly, however, as Parker pointed out a place that had been marked on the navigational chart in the Chart and Sextant. He identified landmarks and engrossed her in local folklore and tales of ships that once sailed along the coast. *These stories—these places—sound familiar.* She calmed as she drank in Parker's intriguing narrative.

Before long they sailed into an area densely scattered with islands. On the small bare ones, seals sunned themselves on wet rocks. Thick forests dominated some islands, while houses crowded along the shores of others.

Ahead on their right, white sails dotted the entrance to Hydeport's busy harbor. The car ferry slid across the bay in the distance.

"This is the Spice Chest," Parker said. "Here is Sage Island. That is Ginger Rock. The one with all the houses on it over there is Basil Isle."

"Do people actually *own* these islands?"

"Some are viable, year-round communities like the island that ferry goes to. Some are owned or held in trust by the State of Maine or by the federal government. Of the rest, some are still bought and sold, but most have been owned by the same families for generations."

"Does your family own an island?"

"Unfortunately no."

"I can't imagine owning an island."

Parker opened his mouth as if he were going reply but shut it again as Stewart, Vanessa, and Barbara appeared from the cabin. They carried individual trays of lobster rolls, coleslaw, pickles, and Claire's chocolate-covered strawberries. Stewart handed Claire a tray.

The sun smiled upon them one last time before thick clouds rolled over its countenance. Parker pushed his sunglasses to the top of his head and glanced skyward.

Barbara swallowed a bite of strawberry. "So, Claire, are you feeling more comfortable now that you've been out here for a while?"

"A little. Parker has kept my thoughts occupied with his stories."

"You've been nervous about being out here?" Vanessa asked.

"I didn't expect to feel uncomfortable, but having never learned to swim, I'm a little afraid of the water."

"*Tsk!* You've never learned how to swim?"

Vanessa's condescension filled Claire with shame, and her cheeks flared. "I suppose my parents never expected I'd ever have the need to learn."

Barbara spoke again. "So, tell me about your family. Are they all still back in—where is it exactly?—the Midwest somewhere?"

I will not cry. "I'm from the Chicago area. My parents passed away in an accident last December. I have no siblings and no other relatives—at least that I'm sure about." She bit into her lobster roll and hoped no one would notice her shaking hand.

"That's so sad, Claire," Stewart said. "How did it happen?"

Claire swallowed. She tried again to get the lobster roll past the lump in her throat.

Vanessa admonished him. "Oh, Stewart, obviously it's something Claire doesn't want to talk about." She turned back to Claire. "I find it hard to believe you don't have any relatives."

"Well, then how did you end up here at the Cove if you're from the Chicago area?" Barbara asked.

With one last effort, Claire downed the bite of lobster roll. "Well—I—I'm here doing some research—about a—a private matter."

Vanessa stopped chewing her pickle and studied her for a moment. "That sounds cryptic."

Barbara scowled before sitting up straight. "Hey, look, Parker, there's the *Dry Bones!*" A schooner with multiple white, puffy sails painted a striking picture on the horizon.

"Ah, yes. So it is. She must be on her way to Nova Scotia."

"*Dry Bones?* It sounds like a pirate ship," said Claire thankful for the change in subject matter. "How did it get its name?"

"Yeah, it does, doesn't it?" Parker snorted while everyone watched the schooner speed north. Parker sighed. "I have no idea why Ezekiel Goldblum named her the *Dry Bones.* I just know that he has one of the nicest schooners on the eastern seaboard."

"And *you* can't beat it!" A wicked laugh erupted from Vanessa. "The *Dry Bones* is the one ship Parker has never been able to beat in all of the tall-ships races over the years." She turned to Stewart and Claire and needled further. "Can't you just see the envy in his eyes?"

Parker flashed his eyes at her before looking back at the *Dry Bones.* "You wait. This is going to be the year I beat old Zeke. I have plans up my sleeve. Besides, no one makes a fool of a Hollenbeck."

"Yeah, yeah—you're not a failure. We've heard it a million times."

Parker bristled. "Hey! If I want something I take it no matter what. The means is not relevant."

"Oh, stop being so sore about Zeke and the *Dry Bones,*" Barbara said. "He's not making a fool of you. He's an expert seaman as well as a super nice guy, and you know it. You're just pricked because his ship is more impressive than ours."

"People will see the *Lady Katherine's* red sails, and I guarantee Zeke won't get all the admiration this year."

"Will you be in all the races this season?" Stewart asked.

"You bet! The one-day races are the fourth weekends in June and July. The Maine Coastal Regatta, a four-day race this year, is over the Fourth of

July weekend. There are a few others in August and September, but I'd have to check my calendar for the exact dates."

"So, a tall-ships race is…what exactly?" Claire asked.

Barbara answered. "Tall ships are simply tall-masted sailing vessels with any number of sails…like the *Lady Katherine*. In the local races, the ships gather at certain harbors along the coast then race to a specified location. Seeing them together in full sail is quite impressive, and the races attract huge crowds."

Claire's eyes widened. "It sounds fabulous."

Barbara frowned at Parker. "The races are meant as friendly competitions to encourage camaraderie and fun, but *some* people—whom I won't mention—turn them into events of intense rivalry."

"I don't like how the sky looks," Parker announced.

The wind had changed and bit through Claire's clothing. She rubbed her hands up and down the sleeves of her shirt.

Parker put on his jacket and zipped it. "Barbara, you and Claire gather those trays and fix some coffee." As Vanessa slipped jeans over her shorts, Parker motioned for her to take the wheel. "Let's go, Stewart."

When Claire and Barbara returned with covered cups of steaming cappuccino, Stewart and Parker had loosened the ropes and moved the boom, filling the sails on the opposite side of the ship. Stewart now sat at the helm.

After a wide, u-shaped turn, their journey back to the Cove had begun.

Barbara and Vanessa sat on one side of the ship while Parker and Claire huddled opposite them. Claire wrapped her cold fingers around her cup of cappuccino as untamed wisps of creamy vanilla brushed her nose before whisking away.

Looking bored, Vanessa asked, "So, where do you live, Claire?"

Parker perked up. "Yes, were *do* you live? You've never told me that."

Glad for an easy question, Claire brightened. "If you know where the English Rose estate is, I rent the cottage there—Julie's cottage, people call it."

The wind flapping the rigging and the waves sloshing against the hull amplified the long silence that ensued.

Barbara pivoted her eyes between her siblings. Parker raised his brows before becoming preoccupied with a spot on the floor. Stewart stared at the water in front of them.

Vanessa jutted her lower jaw to one side and glared at Claire. "Well, now. Isn't *that* cozy."

Chapter Thirty-three

Uh-oh. What did I say? "It is a cozy cottage," Claire stammered.

Vanessa rolled her eyes. "That's not what I meant."

"That's were I've seen you before," Barbara said. "You were in the Compass Rose a few weeks back when Philip and I had our heated discussion about one of my favorite paintings. I knew I recognized you from somewhere."

"Yes, that was me."

Parker swallowed a final gulp of cappuccino and nestled it between the cushions beside him. "I've told Claire you two are artists." He put his arm around her. "She's an artist too, you know."

"I'm...sure...she...is," Vanessa said. Her eyes steadied on Claire.

Barbara asked, "What's your specialty?"

Claire told them about tiling floors then about branching into mosaic work. She described the church project and her plans after its completion.

Vanessa asked, "So, you're self-taught, huh?"

"For the most part, yes."

"Vanessa and I have attended some of the best art schools both in the States and abroad. Vanessa specializes in abstracts and modern art while I'm an impressionist painter. In fact I've painted that cottage you live in."

Parker spoke up. "You must send Claire an invitation to your gallery night on the 10th, Barbara. That way she can see Vanessa's and your work." He turned to Claire. "Then you can meet Margot. She owns the gallery and is very influential in the art community. Wonderful woman!"

"I would love to meet her."

Barbara frowned. "I doubt Margo will be able to help her much, Parker."

"Nonsense! Send her an invitation."

Barbara sighed. "Fine. Claire, I'll send you one this week." She mumbled under her breath. "Even though I'm sure you won't be able to afford much."

Claire's jaw dropped. "How do you—"

"Splendid!" Parker said clapping his hands together. "Come, darling. Let's go sit toward the bow."

Vanessa stood, grabbed some empty cups, and stormed below deck. Barbara took Claire's cup and followed her.

Claire held onto Parker's arm as they walked toward the front. Leaving the security of her seat unnerved her. When they settled on top of the cabin, she thrust her hands under her thighs and wrapped her fingers around the thin wooden railing that edged the top. She leaned close to Parker for warmth but could not stop shivering.

"Stay here. I'll go below and get a blanket for you. Be right back." He got up and walked to the helm and stopped to talk to Stewart.

Claire stared at the rushing water and tightened her grip on the railing of the tilting schooner. *No one would even know if I fell overboard!* Her chest tightened, and through chattering teeth, she forced her breaths into a regular pattern. Voices drifted up from the propped-open hatches on either side of her. The voices grew louder.

"It's *mine*!" Vanessa said. Claire jumped when a drawer slammed directly under her.

Claire heard Barbara's voice but could not distinguish her words.

"I'm going to do whatever it takes. No one—*no one*—will stop me!"

Claire bent to hear Barbara's reply. "I know I can't stop you, so I won't even try. Just don't get hurt—again."

"I'm too smart to get hurt this time. I know what I want, and I'm going to get it."

"Don't get so worked up about her. She's only marginally attractive and could never, ever be a threat. She is unrefined and naïve and—"

"—and a so-called artist who tiles bathroom floors!" A shrill laugh pierced Claire's ears.

Barbara laughed too. "Did you see her nails? Clearly she hasn't had a manicure in months—if she's *ever* had one."

Claire pulled a shaking hand from under her thigh. Dry, rough skin surrounded uneven and unpolished fingernails. Working on the mosaic had taken its toll. She stuffed her hand back under her leg.

Barbara then said, "I just don't see what Parker sees in her."

"He's just pathetic."

"I think she's after his money."

"Oh, without a doubt! I mean that sob story about her parents and not having family is pretty farfetched. I'm so embarrassed Stewart got caught up in it. What an idiot!"

"Well, little does she know…" The exchange halted when Claire heard Parker's voice, and Barbara and Vanessa moved away from the hatch.

She turned her face into the wind to dry the tears that dribbled across her temples into her hair. Her heart ached for comfort. Oh, to be enveloped in the arms of someone who loved her and wanted to take care of her!

Parker arrived carrying a wool blanket. He wrapped it around her shoulders and crossed it across her knees before gently tucking the edges around her ankles. "There. How's that?" He ran his hands up and down her upper arms, then sat and enfolded her in his arm.

Craving his attentiveness, she released her grasp on the railing, rested her head against his shoulder, and sunk into his embrace. "Thank you, Parker."

Silence hung between them for several moments before he spoke. "So, have you liked being out here today?"

"I don't think your sisters care much for me."

"*Pfft!* Don't worry about them. They just need to get to know you better, that's all. They're probably jealous of you." He pushed a wayward curl off her brow. "I'm sure there are many women who are jealous of you." He gave her a light squeeze. "Now, back to my question, huh? How have you liked it?"

She struggled to be truthful. "It's been quite a day. I've learned so much from you and feel privileged to have sailed on the *Lady Katherine*."

❀❀❀

The corner of Parker's lip turned upward. *Mission accomplished!*

"Do you think we'll get to the harbor before that gets here?" Claire asked nodding toward a curtain of rain on the horizon.

"I do," he lied.

As if a board had been thrust down her back, Claire sat up. She pulled her arm out from under the blanket and pointed to a small island. Parker dropped his arm. "Look!" The gold bracelet swung on her wrist. Pleased she wore it, his mind raced to the next gift he would lavish on her.

"Those houses there!" Though the island had several houses on it, three perched in a row—a purple house, a turquoise house, and a pink house—dominated the view.

"Yeah?"

"I didn't notice them before."

"That's because when we sailed south earlier we passed by the other side of the island."

"Oh."

"Why? They're quaint, but—"

"I recognize those houses."

"From a postcard or calendar?"

"No, no. From my dad. When I was a little girl, he would tell me stories about a little old sailor named Briny Bry and his adventures on a small wooden boat with a large white sail. On each adventure Briny Bry would sail past an island on which a purple house, a turquoise house, and a pink house sat all in a row."

Briny Bry. Parker raised one eyebrow. "Interesting."

"Oh, his stories were so engaging. I loved them and always begged him for more. He'd tell me about stormy seas and pirates and buried treasure on rocky islands."

"Treasure? There is nothing more captivating than buried treasure. Was any treasure buried on the island with the three houses?"

"I don't remember." She snuggled back under the blanket again. "I never imagined any of his stories had any truth to them or were about real people or places." Her voice softened. "But they must have been."

Hmm. "You'll have to tell me more about your father's stories."

Chapter Thirty-four

Claire brushed through her hair one final time smoothing the soft curls that framed her face and cascaded down her back. While skimming on a thin coat of lip balm, someone knocked on her door. She checked the clock by the bathroom mirror—7:40.

She went to the door and opened it. Philip stood holding a box of red roses beneath a transparent lid. Her heart leapt.

✿✿✿

"Sorry to impose," he said. "I know it is earlier than we agreed, but these have been sitting on my side doorstep all day. Apparently the deliveryman didn't receive clear instructions from whoever sent them to you." He couldn't help his business-like tone, but he felt ridiculous giving her a dozen roses from another man. He handed her the box. "I figured you'd want to get them in water as soon as possible."

Her shoulders sank. "Oh."

Was that disappointment in her voice?

"Yes. Yes, thank you. I'll be right back." She took the box and disappeared into the cottage.

He tossed his flashlight into the air and caught it. Of course he had read the note attached to the lid. Only the address had been written on the front of the unsealed envelope, and, after all, he had to see who they were for.

He flung the flashlight higher and with more intensity as he ruminated on the words he read. *Dearest Claire, Every time I am with you, I grow fonder of you and long for the next time we will be together. With Warm Affection, Parker*

How dashing! Such gallantry! "Whatever," he mumbled under his breath. Claire was his tenant, and that was it. Who she saw and what she did in her personal life did not concern him. Besides, he hardly knew her. *I will not be interested in her other than as a friend.*

However, as soon as she stepped out of the cottage his stoic determination fluctuated.

"Thanks for waiting."

"Not a problem." Her smile further melted his resolve, and he forced himself to be formal. "Shall we?" He led her toward his garage.

"Aren't we going to go along the beach?"

"No. We'll take the path I always use. It runs through the woods between my house and the Soames'. I have this," he said, rattling the batteries inside the flashlight, "since I suspect we'll be there well past nightfall."

"What is this meeting about, anyway? I can't imagine why Mr. Soames would want me to come."

"One never knows the reasons behind the requests of Harvard Soames. However, I know we will be talking about the Small Ships Festival coming up the third weekend of June."

"Small ships? I thought it was tall ships."

"Ah, so you've heard all about the tall ships." Of course she had! The Hollenbecks would have told her about them.

He led her to the back of his house and across a carpet of grass to a well-worn path that cut through the woods. They fanned the air around their faces in an attempt to stave off the thick clouds of blackflies and mosquitoes.

"Our little town doesn't have a big enough harbor to host a tall ships event, so we developed the Small Ships Festival as a spoof, I guess you could say. All the ships at *this* festival are little. We have toy ship races, model shipbuilding competitions, games, food, music, crafts…Well, you get the idea."

He whacked at a prick on his forehead and rubbed his fingers over the spot. "It's held every Father's Day weekend and offers something for every member of the family."

"It sounds like fun!"

At the edge of the path, they passed through a break in a rock wall then walked across the vast manicured lawn to the stone path that linked the beach to a sprawling two-story house. They stepped up a wide staircase leading to a well-lit veranda that wrapped around the home's back and side. A fan in the ceiling rotated above them.

Philip rapped on the storm door before turning to Claire. "I've come to this back door since I was a kid."

"Wait!" In a flash she pulled a tissue from her jacket pocket, stepped close to him, and bounced up onto her toes. Staring at his forehead, she slipped her fingers through his hair and cradled his head close. With quick circular motions she wiped his forehead with the tissue.

She smelled of soap—peaches with a hint of tea. Long lashes separated over her aqua eyes. Through her parted mouth, rapid breaths warmed his skin and fogged a corner of his glasses. Only inches separated her lips from his.

He swallowed. *It would be so easy to—*

As if she heard his thoughts, she stopped wiping and met his stare. Her breaths quickened on his skin while she spread her fingertips through his hair. Her gaze fell to his lips then back to his eyes again before her cheeks reddened.

"I—I—you were bleeding. A mosquito…"

At that moment the inner door rattled and sucked the storm door inward.

"Thank you," Philip whispered.

Claire whipped her hand down and lowered her heels. They both turned toward the door just in time.

By some miracle, Philip kept his composure. "Good evening, Mrs. Soames. It's so nice to see you again. This is my…" He paused and swallowed again. "…tenant, Claire."

Chapter Thirty-five

Nested in a large brown chair, Claire listened to Philip and Mr. Soames as they discussed the schedule, the sponsors' contributions, and other details of the festival. Mrs. Soames, quiet and unassertive, sat to her left, Mr. Soames across the coffee table from her, and Philip at her right.

As the men talked and still at a loss as to why her presence was requested, Claire's mind wandered while sipping the last of her chamomile tea. Holding the delicate teacup and saucer with their gold-highlighted pinecone and tassel design, she contemplated how lovely it would be to smash them into shards and piece them onto a mosaicked mailbox.

Mr. Soames tamped some papers on the coffee table, awaking her from her muse. "And that brings me to you, Claire."

She straightened. "Yes?"

"Last year our festival coordinator decided not to help anymore." He glanced at Philip who did not look up from reading the paper he held. "So, last year I was the coordinator, and it took a lot out of me…"

"I didn't know that." Philip's head shot up from the paper. "I wish you had told me."

"Well, Philip, no one else could on such short notice. You had your hands full, so I wasn't about to complain." He directed his attention back to Claire. "It's too much for me, and if you will, Claire, I'd like to personally ask if you will be the coordinator this year?"

Philip set the paper on the table. "Why, yes, of course. Perfect!"

Claire looked from Mr. Soames to Philip then back to Mr. Soames who winked at her. She hid a smile behind a brief sip of tea. "What would I be doing as the coordinator?" She intended to accept but didn't want to sound too eager.

"Philip?" Mr. Soames motioned.

"You would help direct the crafters to their booths—it would be a great way for you to meet these people—and be in charge of the musicians making sure they know where to go and tending to their needs." Enthusiasm bubbled in his voice. "You would also help me keep the events on schedule. Oh, there are many duties. We can go over them all sometime so you'll know what you're doing and when."

"In a way you would be Philip's right hand lady for the day," Mr. Soames said with another wink.

His efforts at flaming the friendship between her and Philip humored her. "I would be honored to be a help—to you both," she said.

"There! That was easy!" Mr. Soames said slapping his hands on his knees. "Now for the final piece of business." He turned toward Philip. "I've saved this for last because I know you'll be disappointed, but the High Seas Quintet won't be able to perform this year."

"What? Oh no! What did you find out?"

"I checked this morning like I said, and even though we've had them booked since last year, they cancelled due to a 'once-in-a-lifetime opportunity to perform in Europe,'" he said, fingering quotation marks in the air, "and their schedule cannot be rearranged."

Philip sighed. "I'm so disappointed."

"I called around, and the only one available that weekend is…" He raised his eyebrows at Philip.

"…the Maritime Consort."

"Yup…but only because they had a cancellation that weekend."

"They are good—the best—but they're *so* expensive. Our sponsors have given their budgets already, and I can't imagine anyone will give more."

"We could always go without music."

"We could, but the atmosphere just won't be the same."

"Atmosphere?" Claire dared ask.

Philip answered. "We always have an instrumental group play seafaring-style music—you know, like sea shanties, maritime folk, and fiddling tunes—on the evening before and during the day of the festival. It gives the grounds an atmosphere of being on a 1800s ship or in an old shipping port."

"Oh, I see."

He turned back to Mr. Soames. "Okay, how much?"

Mr. Soames pushed a small piece of paper toward Philip who picked it up and cringed. "Let me make some phone calls. I'll get back to you by Thursday evening if I think we can gather enough money to have them come, but we shouldn't count on it."

"Very well." Philip stood and tossed the paper on the table. "Thanks for all your work, Mr. Soames."

With the discussion over, Philip and Mr. Soames walked toward the back door. Mrs. Soames gathered her and her husband's dishes and followed them. Still holding her cup and saucer, Claire stood and glanced at the price while collecting Philip's dishes. This Maritime Consort *was* expensive!

After saying their goodbyes, Philip and Claire stepped outside into a dense fog. It didn't take long for the lights of the Soames' house to disappear, and Philip clicked on the flashlight.

"I'm awful glad you brought that. Even with the flashlight, I don't know how you know where to go."

"I've traveled between their back door and my home so many times I could do it blindfolded." Batting at mosquitoes, they hurried in silence across the lawn.

After they started on the path through the woods, Philip cleared his throat. "Thank you for being willing to be the coordinator. I should have realized it was too much for Mr. Soames to do at his age. You must have made quite an impression, Claire, for him to personally ask you to take his place."

Their feet trod on thick wet grass. "I'm delighted he asked me. He is a kind and thoughtful man."

"He is. He comes across as a gruff man to be feared, but he truly has a generous and tender heart."

Philip pointed the beam at the garage as they reached the corner. "Do you mind stepping into the garage for a just few minutes? I know it's late, and you must be tired. But I'd really like to show you something before walking you home."

She tried not to sound too eager. "Sure!"

"Here. Please hold this for a second." Philip handed her the flashlight and opened the garage's double doors. The pungent smell of wood stain and polyurethane greeted her before he flicked on the blaring overhead lights. An unfinished wooden kayak perched on a table at the center of the floor.

"You?" Claire walked to the kayak and ran her hand down the length of the smooth, dusty surface. "*You* make these?"

"You sound so shocked." Philip laughed. "I can make things too, you know."

"I'm sorry! I didn't mean it that way. I guess I never expected—well, you know, you're just so busy with your store—and…"

"Yeah, yeah, admit it. You didn't think I had it in me." He slapped a mosquito on his arm.

"No. That's not it. It's just that—it's just that you never cease to amaze me. That's all."

"Oh, I'm just teasing you." Philip flipped a switch sending a large fan whirring to life. "I make these in my spare time, yes, of which I have very little. Most get made during the winter. I come out here, stoke up that little woodstove over there, and work on these on snowy winter days when there's no place to go—even if I were able to get out of the driveway."

"Then the ones hanging in your shop…?"

"Yes, I made them. I could probably make these full-time and earn a decent living but would rather keep this solely as a hobby right now."

"Did you make the one you take out on the ocean?"

"You've seen me out there?"

Claire nodded. "A few weeks ago. I was on my beach and greeted you." The image of him in his damp red shirt flew to the forefront of her mind, and she looked back at the kayak.

"I didn't see or hear you. If I had, I definitely would have said something.

Sometimes I get preoccupied with thinking or praying and don't pay enough attention to my surroundings. Yes, I designed and made that one as well."

Feeling foolish for having jumped so quickly to conclusions that weekend, she touched the smooth seams of the kayak one more time. Admiration for not just the craftsmanship but for the one who made it swelled within her.

"These are not why I asked you here though. I need to show you the things in my printer's drawers."

"Printer's drawers?"

He took the flashlight from her hand, flicked off the light, and stuck it in his pocket. He led her to a worktable beside the fan. "They're long wooden, sectioned drawers. Letterpress printers stored their pieces of movable type in them, but I have other things stored in mine that may be of interest to you." He clicked the switch of a fluorescent light dangling above the worktable.

Claire gasped.

"These two don't include my pieces of pottery or metal or other miscellaneous things, but they *do* contain my collection of favorite glass finds."

"Oh, Philip!" Claire gaped at the sections filled with frosted marbles— "This green one looks like a piece of lime candy."—and glass pieces embossed with words and pictures and intricate designs. She circled her finger around the rim of a cobalt-colored bottle top.

Her hand hovered over a purple, fleur-de-lis-shaped perfume bottle stopper. She followed it's perfect, sea-smoothed lines with her finger. "How beautiful! You must have been thrilled when you found this."

"I was."

Philip lifted the drawer and placed it to one side revealing the drawer beneath it. Jeweled pieces in orange, yellow, and pink nestled beside glass in unusual shapes. She fixated on the sections of red ones—sugared, embossed, and shaped.

"These red pieces are why I'm really showing you these tonight." He reached for an empty glass jar on the shelf above them and unscrewed the lid. "When you spoke of the people at church giving up their red pieces for the mosaic, I felt ashamed knowing that I had held my special pieces back."

"But you gave all your other red ones," she contested. "Other than the tiniest pieces, I used all the ones in your collection."

He picked up some red pieces and placed them into the jar. "I know, but I gave what was unimportant to me. If a little boy can give his one and only favorite piece 'for God' as you told me, I too can give up my special pieces."

He dropped the last red piece in the jar. "There aren't many, but there should be enough here for you to complete the project. Take them all and use what you think you'll need. You can always return those you don't use."

He picked up the cobalt bottle top and the green marble she had admired. "Can you use these too?"

"I could, but…"

He held up his hand to quiet her before tossing them in, screwing the lid on the jar, and handing it to her.

Her mind raced to where she would place the pieces as she took the jar from him. "Thank you, Philip. You're right. These are exactly what I need."

"I figured as much. Come. I'll walk you back to the cottage."

The fog had thickened, blanketing the lights of the garage within a few steps. Philip turned on the flashlight, yet the fog claimed most of its beam.

"I'm sorry about the problems with the musicians and hope something works out."

"I'm going to pray about it and then be content with whatever the outcome is."

"Pray? You would pray about something like this?"

Philip pointed the beam in front of her feet. "Absolutely! I talk to God all the time and about everything—from little things like not being able to find my car keys to big things like wisdom regarding an important decision. I talk to Him just like you and I are talking now, either thanking Him for things or asking Him to help with something."

"I haven't thought much about praying since I prayed to become a Christian. I guess I need to work on that."

"You could always start out by praying about a few things at a set time of day then build from there."

"I'll do that."

As they reached the cottage, she stretched her hand and felt for the latch.

"Wait! Before you go in…"

She pulled her hand away.

Philip stuffed the flashlight under his arm, its beam pointing behind him. In the darkness, she felt his hand slide down her arm until he reached her empty hand and turned her palm up. "Here, this is for you," he said. He pressed something small and hard into it before covering her hand with his and closing her fingers around the object. He kept his firm, gentle hand wrapped around hers for several seconds.

"What is it?"

"Look when you go inside. It's something I'd like you to have." He released her hand and reached back for the flashlight to point it back at the latch.

It did not take long to figure out what it was, and she clenched her fist as her fingers grasped the latch. "Thank you, Philip. Good night."

"Good night, Claire."

∿∿∿

When the lock on the cottage door snicked behind him, Philip switched off his flashlight and allowed the smothering fog to envelope him. He rubbed the itchy bump on his forehead then ran his fingers through his thick hair, wet from the fog.

He tried to deny it. He tried to convince himself he shouldn't.

But he found it impossible to stop the love for her that grew within him at a most alarming rate.

There. He'd admitted it.

Something deeper than Claire's compelling beauty struck him that night when he saw her standing there in the shop. No one would ever believe him if he told them he had prayed for months his future wife would simply walk through the door of his shop one day and he would just *know* she was the one.

No one would ever believe him if he told them he had given up on marrying and during the long drive to Chicago had told God he would be content being single for the rest of his life if that was His will.

How disappointed he had been when she said she wasn't a Christian—then she became one. Did she really? She had never been less then truthful with him, but could he trust her?

He must watch her and get to know her. That would take time. No one could know about his feelings for her, and he must not let his guard down—not even for even a moment. He almost did on the Soames' porch tonight.

Her living only several hundred feet away made things more complicated. What will the townspeople say? He didn't want to do anything to compromise her character or reputation, and he had his own to uphold.

Then he remembered the bouquet of roses.

Chapter Thirty-six

Claire picked up the paper with the names and dates her mother had written and tapped her finger under the freshly inked date beside her name. The date of her birth. The date of her salvation. Now only one date remained unwritten.

After sticking the paper between two, onion-thin pages, she closed the Bible, snapped the clasp, and slid it beside the peanut butter jar brimming with the stunning red roses that had no scent.

Taking Pastor Tim's advice, she had read a portion of the book of John every day. How things had changed since, with little desire let alone comprehension, she had attempted to read the Bible as a teenager! Though tired this morning, she hungered for its words until she had finished the entire book along with a few chapters of Acts.

She picked up the fleur-de-lis bottle stopper and admired it for the umpteenth time. She closed her hand and imagined Philip's long warm fingers over hers.

Last night's limited access to his private life further heightened her interest in him. Although he kept a door shut between them, he had allowed her a keyhole peek at the depth of his integrity, unwittingly endearing himself to her.

Like a pinwheel in a stiff wind, her mind spun all night, and she had awoken late after a short, restless sleep. At least she had solved one issue. *I'll take care of that on my way to town.*

Her eyes flew from the bottle stopper to Parker's note propped against the peanut butter jar. Grace's warning regarding him confused her. He did not seem like the man she described.

Sure he had his faults, but he spoiled her and had been tender at the exact moment she needed it most. His connections impressed her, and she esteemed his intelligence and self-assurance—qualities she wished she possessed. She wondered if he were a Christian as well.

She recalled her mother recommending she find a man of character and principles who would respect and care for her. She also had emphasized the importance of choosing a man who not only had strong Bible beliefs but who also lived them—whatever that meant.

Still holding the bottle stopper, she stood and walked into her bedroom. She placed the delicate piece inside the gold bangle bracelet lying on top of the dresser—two very different gifts from two very different men.

"But I'm drawn to them both," she admitted to her reflection. *Lord, help me know which one to give my heart to.*

～

"So nice to see you, Miss Wycoff. What can I do for you this morning?" Mr. Gibbons closed the door to his office and sat behind his desk. His moustache twitched above his pasted smile.

Claire handed him a piece of paper with a name and a monetary amount on it. "I'd like a cashier's check in this amount made out to Harvard Soames. Please put this name on the memorandum line," she said pointing to the paper. Mr. Gibbons' face exuded curiosity. "I do not want my name associated with this check and will count on you not to disclose it."

"Yes, of course, this will be done in the strictest confidence."

"Also, I would like the check hand-delivered to Mr. Soames today shortly after 4:00. I'm willing to pay for the delivery if necessary."

"I will deliver it myself at no extra charge."

"Again, timing and anonymity is vital."

"Whatever you wish, Miss Wycoff. You have my word."

～

The little boutique had a better selection of dresses and footwear than Claire had expected. Though not overly friendly, the efficient clerk helped Claire select a gauzy aqua dress.

"It matches your eyes beautifully," the clerk had said, "and these strappy shoes are chic."

With bag in tow, Claire left the shop and hasted to the tearoom for a pot of tea.

"Well, hello!" Grace said while bending to slide a tray of molasses cookies into one of the glass cases. "What an unexpected surprise!" She straightened and glanced at the clock. "You're out of routine this morning."

"I had some business to attend to and decided to come by before working the rest of the day."

"Ah, I see. So glad you did. It's a little slow right now. Help yourself to wherever you'd like to sit. Scone of the day and black tea?"

"Perfect!"

The rich scents of cinnamon and ground coffee swirled in the air as she wound her way through the tables to the coveted window seat. After sitting, she set her bag on the floor then watched the beehive of activity below her. The *Lady Katherine* rolled back and forth, straining her ropes.

"How's the mosaic coming?" Grace asked as she put Claire's cup, saucer, and milk on the table and poured the steaming liquid.

"It's coming along quite well. It should be done by Father's Day."

"How exciting!" Grace sat beside Claire. "Have you gotten enough red pieces yet?"

"Yes, I have plenty now."

"Wonderful!"

"Have things been going well for you here?"

"Yes, it's been quite busy. I advertised more this year, and it's paying off. I've sold quite a few of those teakettles. All the pink ones are gone already. I should have ordered more of them."

"They're so pretty. I just love mine." Claire glanced back at the docks again and thought she saw someone's head disappear below deck on the *Lady Katherine*.

⁓⁓⁓

Grace followed Claire's attention out the window and scowled at the imposing schooner.

"May I ask you a question, Grace?"

"Sure!"

"Do you think Parker Hollenbeck is a Christian?"

Grace sat motionless, but inside she wanted to scream. Hadn't this girl listened to a word she'd said? Ten minutes in Parker's presence should have answered her question clearly. *Lord, help me be patient and answer wisely.*

"Usually if someone's a Christian they have a desire to do what's right and to do things that please God like reading their Bible, praying, telling others about Him, going to church…that sort of thing. You could come right out and ask him, but if he were to tell you he is yet shows no obvious, consistent desire for the things of God, I would doubt his honesty."

"These things you said—that's what living your Bible beliefs is?"

"Yes, I guess you could say it that way."

"Okay." Pensive, Claire picked up her teacup and swished the tea around at the bottom of it.

Grace continued. "You could invite him to church to see if he goes. Be careful, though. Just because someone goes to church or says they're a Christian doesn't necessarily mean they are."

Claire rested her teacup on its saucer. "Thank you, Grace. I'll invite him to church the next chance I get."

Grace looked behind her and rose. "I see customers and had better get going." She gave Claire's arm a gentle pat as she left. "Feel free to ask any questions anytime."

⁓⁓⁓

Memories of her father passed through her mind. Claire sat and stared out the window and considered Grace's words.

Two men jumping off the *Lady Katherine* onto the dock grabbed her attention. She recognized the one in the flannel shirt and scruffy beard— Hugh Wycoff. The other man, younger and looking equally as rough, though clean shaven, must be Jake Wycoff.

Claire grimaced as they flicked lighters and lit cigarettes while walking away from the docks. A chill ran through her. Why on earth would they be on Parker's schooner?

Chapter Thirty-seven

Claire's shoes clicked on the brick sidewalk as she passed the converted gaslights and red, brick buildings of Hydeport's artsy Old Port District.

She compared her invitation to the sign centered below a black lantern. The two-story building blazed with warm light from its large, arched windows. She had expected a small gallery but found quite the opposite.

She walked up the steps of the Sea Spray Gallery and Arts building and handed the girl at the door her invitation. A woman in a tailored lavender dress complimenting her straight silver hair offered Claire a genuine smile and an extended hand. "I'm Margot, the owner of this gallery. I don't believe I've met you before."

Claire shook her hand. "Nice to meet you. I'm Cl—"

"Claire! This is Claire Wycoff, Margot." Parker hustled to them. "Hello, darling," he said before turning to Margot. "This is the girl I told you about."

"The mosaic artist?" Margot asked, directing her attention back at Claire.

"Yes, I'm almost done a project in the vestibule of the church in Lone Spruce Cove."

"So I've heard."

"It will be revealed on Father's Day."

"She has other mosaics planned, though," Parker added.

"I'll have to make a point of seeing the vestibule whenever I get over to the Cove. However, you'll have to bring in some of your other work sometime, Claire. Call me when you have something ready, and we'll set up an appointment." Checking over Claire's shoulder she said, "I should be going. Nice to meet you, Claire. Enjoy the evening."

"Thank you, Margot," Claire said.

With a nod, Margot moved on.

Parker swept his arms wide and lifted his palms upward. "What can I say? You're now in the loop. Am I good or what?"

"I certainly appreciate it."

"Anything for you, darling." Parker wrapped his arm around her waist. "Let's go see my sisters and get that out of the way." Parker introduced her to few people, but when he did he presented her simply as "Claire, an artist new to town."

Standing alone in a yellow pantsuit with matching flower earrings, Barbara regarded their approach with little interest. "I see you've met Margot. At least I don't have to introduce you now."

Parker's attention flitted about them. "Oh, Barbara, of course I'd be the one to introduce her."

"I recognize your style, Barbara," Claire said, eyeing a coastal scene beside them. "Your work is splendid."

Without acknowledging her compliment, Barbara said, "Three of us are represented tonight, and our work is intermingled on both floors." She pointed above them. "Mine are mostly the same style as you see here. You won't have any problem identifying Vanessa's modernist and abstract pieces even without looking at the cards, and Terri Blankenship's are the fabric and handmade paper pieces."

Laughter erupted, and the three of them turned to see Vanessa in the midst of a large group of people—mostly men. Wearing a red, clingy dress and high-heeled shoes, she looked as if she had just stepped off the cover of a magazine.

Parker dropped his arm from around Claire's waist. "Looks like we're missing out on something."

Barbara rolled her eyes before moving in the opposite direction. "I'm going this way."

"Come, Claire. Let's see why they are having such a good time."

Nothing about the scene interested her. "Actually, I'd like to look around a bit if you don't mind."

"Oh, come on. Come with me."

More laughter rang in the air.

"I'd like to have the time to look at your sisters' artwork, Parker."

"Very well," he clipped. "I'll come find you in a little while."

The rich vibrato of a cello echoed throughout the glossy-floored gallery, and Claire lingered at each spotlighted piece and pondered their names. She studied one of Vanessa's works with its brooding colors, heavy ambiguous brushstrokes, and dark name. All her pieces had similar, oppressive themes that both surprised and disturbed Claire.

She poked her head into a side room where Barbara's infamous nude painting hung alongside others that did not interest her. Claire instantly liked two of Terri's works made of handmade paper imbedded with dried rose petals and embellished with tiny pieces of purple sea glass. She selected the price cards beneath them claiming them as hers.

During the hour she had been on the first floor, she had not seen Parker once. She retraced her steps hoping to find him before heading upstairs. She craned her neck while passing a previously unnoticed and secluded alcove between a column and one of the large arched windows at the far end of the gallery.

Vanessa's red dress swooshed in the small space as Claire approached it. Philip, in jeans and a tweed sports coat, faced Vanessa with his hands on his hips. Claire could only see part of the side of his face and the back of his head as he and Vanessa exchanged hushed words. What a striking couple they made! With unmistakable longing, Vanessa reached up and curled her elegant fingers around his arm and leaned into him.

She certainly wasn't his sister! Unable to bear seeing what would obviously happen next—Philip wrapping his arms around Vanessa—Claire snapped her head to the side. The thought of him kissing her clenched her heart.

Claire turned and hurried to the wide staircase, grasping the railing for support as she climbed to the second story. She tried to calm herself with each step. *I will not be irrational. I will not be envious. I will not get involved in his personal life. I will not be attracted to him.*

Now distracted, she did not pause as long at each piece on the quieter second floor—at least until she came to one painting.

She stopped and drew her breath in.

Larger than most and enhanced in an ornate, gold-gilt frame, Barbara's painting of the cottage mesmerized her. With the cottage slightly left of center, sailboats dotted the ocean beyond it, and pink roses splashed both the cottage and the hill above the beach with color. Crossing the threshold, a woman with long dark hair carried a bouquet of pink roses on her arm.

This is my cottage! That's me! Claire grabbed the card below it and laid it on top of the other two in her palm. *I love this!* Desperate to get her mind off Philip and Vanessa, she closely examined the details of the painting.

"Claire?"

She closed her eyes. *How can I face him?*

Chapter Thirty-eight

His pulse drummed upon seeing her. The long dark curls cascading down her back rivaled any of the surrounding artwork.

"Hello, Philip," she said without turning around.

He stepped beside her and clasped his hands behind his back. Despite his movement, her gaze remained fixed on the painting with eyes mirroring the deep aqua of her dress—his favorite color. "What are you doing here? How did you know about this?"

"You sound surprised."

"I admit I didn't expect to have the pleasure of seeing you here tonight."

"I received an invitation to come."

The Hollenbecks—of course.

"This painting of my cottage—well, your cottage—captivates me."

Philip frowned

"What are *you* doing here?"

"I've come to Margot's gallery nights for years. This is where I find fresh talent for the Compass Rose and festivals."

"I see. That makes sense."

"Hey, speaking of festivals, you will never guess what happened. I haven't seen you to tell you."

Claire turned toward him.

"An anonymous donor paid for the Maritime Consort to play at the Small Ships Festival. Mr. Soames had made calls to all the sponsors for donations, and everyone said 'no.' But, apparently someone had a change of heart because a check was delivered to him to cover the entire cost."

A faint smile crossed her face.

"It's an answer to prayer. I just know you'll like their music, Claire."

"That's great. I'm glad you're pleased."

"Oh, I am!"

"I'll look forward to hearing them then."

Awkward silence followed, and they both turned back toward the painting.

Philip spotted the empty card holder. *Yes! Someone finally bought this.*

"I would think you would want to buy this painting, Philip, since it's your cottage. Barbara did an incredible job on it. I see she painted it a few years ago." Claire pressed him. "Why wouldn't you want it?"

"Why *would* I want it when I can look down and see the cottage, its little beach, and the ocean from my bedroom window any time I wish?"

Claire opened her mouth to speak, but a cold voice behind them commented first.

"Yes, Philip, but you won't always be able to view the scene with a beautiful woman at its door."

Philip and Claire spun around and saw Parker standing with his arms crossed. Philip glared at him.

Parker addressed Claire. "I've been looking all over for you, darling. I last saw you while I was talking with Margot and observed you witnessing Philip and Vanessa's intimate conversation in the alcove. You certainly disappeared fast."

Oh, no! Philip concentrated on remaining expressionless.

Claire dropped her head and fiddled with the cards in her hand.

Parker raised an eyebrow at Philip and drew a smug smile across his face.

Philip clenched his jaw and balled his hand into a fist.

He watched as Parker cupped Claire's elbow. "Come. Let's look at the rest of the artwork together. After all, it's because of me you're here."

Behind wayward curls, questioning eyes peeked up at Philip as Parker led her away. Philip released his fist only to ball it again. Though he had kept his anger in check, his conscience throbbed with regret.

After walking past several pieces of artwork, Parker dropped his hand from Claire's elbow and spun her around.

"I want you staying away from Philip."

"But he's my landlord. We live on the same property."

"You can always move." Parker jutted his chin out. "You're a talented and beautiful young woman who needs to be protected from the advances of inferior men."

"Inferior? Philip isn't inferior. Everyone speaks well of him."

"Hey, I've known Philip a lot longer than you have and know things about him you don't."

"Parker, I have no intention of moving out of that cottage anytime soon."

"We'll see about that."

"But, Philip and I—we're—we're—friends." She swallowed hard and rubbed her upper arms so that her hands wouldn't shake. "That's all..." she whispered as the disappointing truth of her words sank in. "Just friends." She heaved a sigh. "Besides, for being so inferior, Philip is apparently good enough for your sister."

"Bah! There is no comparison between Vanessa and you. She's going to do what she wants to do, and I can't control *her* foolish actions."

A dark memory buried deep within her lifted its head and roared a warning. Refusing to acknowledge its presence, she forced it back and shushed it with her trustful reasoning. *No, Parker is different.*

Distracted by a curvy young woman standing in front of one of Vanessa's paintings, Parker quickly changed the subject. "The gallery will close soon. Go on ahead and finish looking at the artwork without me but make sure I see you again before you leave."

"I will."

Parker walked over to the woman and started a conversation.

Claire ran her fingers up and down her arms once more to calm her trembling. She had one last wall of artwork to look at before heading downstairs to purchase her selections.

~~~

Outside the Sea Spray, Claire waited for Parker and almost gave up when he came bursting through the door.

"You've been hard to keep up with tonight!"

Unimpressed with his efforts and wanting to go home, she got straight to the point. "I'd like to ask a favor of you."

"Whatever your heart desires."

"Will you go to church with me this Sunday?"

The smile fell from his face.

"You *are* a Christian, aren't you?"

"Sure—sure—of course, I am." He rubbed his hand over the back of his neck. "Yes, I'll go with you to church."

"Good! I'll look forward to seeing you at 10:30 then."

He opened his palms toward her. "Your wish is my command."

"Good night. Thank you for encouraging Barbara to invite me and for introducing me to Margot."

~~~

"It's been a productive evening!" Barbara said while driving up the dark highway between Hydeport and the Cove.

Vanessa wiggled her shoulders. "Oh, yes. It definitely has been—in many ways."

"I'm thrilled the cottage painting sold."

"At least you made some good money off that."

"Margot refused to tell me who bought it. She said the customer requested that under no circumstances was she to reveal the name. But…" Barbara's lips curled into a sly smile. "…when Margot wasn't looking I just happened to find the list under the counter."

"You are *so* sneaky. Who bought it?"

"She didn't write the name down, but she did write where it's to be delivered."

"And?"

"Oh, I'm relishing this moment."

Vanessa shoved her arm. "Barbara! Get on with it!"

"The delivery address is Philip's house."

"No way!"

"Yes!"

"Oh, how terribly interesting!"

"Girl, your charms must have worked tonight."

"Of course they worked. They always work."

Chapter Thirty-nine

As usual, Philip sat where he could keep an eye on Claire. Each Sunday morning she relaxed more and more and talked and laughed and made new friends. A change? Maybe.

He always found some excuse to talk to her but not this week. What must she think of him?

Today, serious and unsettled, she lingered by the door, looked around outside, then wandered about only to repeat her motions. Finally she sat down, but her head kept turning toward the door long after the service started. He wondered who she expected to see.

～✑✑✑

Perhaps Parker languished in bed from a fever. Maybe he injured himself in a car accident. Possibly his law office called him back to Boston because something terrible happened in one of his cases. No doubt at that very moment he felt badly about not being at church.

She flipped the crinkly pages of her Bible to the next reference.

No, he stood me up.

～✑✑✑

"Grace, I'm here to buy a celebratory lemonade," Claire announced. She plucked an icy bottle from the galvanized tub and clinked a fistful of change onto the counter.

"You're done?"

"I'm done—and two days ahead of schedule!" Triumphant, she raised her bottle into the air, sending a piece of ice streaming down her arm.

"Hooray! I can hardly wait until Sunday morning."

"It feels so good to be done. I'm going to go home and rest before the festival this weekend. I've been at the church so much these past several weeks it will seem strange to be home this time of day."

"Well, you deserve it. Enjoy your day!"

Claire left the tearoom buoyant and satisfied and couldn't help greeting everyone she met on the way to her car.

Covered with a sheet, the mosaic would be dry and ready for the dedication Sunday morning. She only regretted not finding a piece of red sea glass herself to include in the ribbon.

When she drove down the driveway, seeing Philip surprised her. He waved and after pointing to a large package on his doorstep, strode in her direction. She rolled down the passenger-side window.

"You're home! That can only mean one thing."

Claire beamed. "It does! I'm done!"

"Wonderful! I'm looking forward to seeing it Sunday. I suppose I still can't get a sneak preview?"

Claire grinned. "No!"

He pointed his thumb over his shoulder. "That package has your name on it. It's pretty heavy, so I'll bring it over to you. I also have the list of things you'll be doing tomorrow afternoon and Saturday. Is this a good time to go over it?"

"Sure. If you haven't had lunch, I'll make us some sandwiches. We can have a picnic on the beach and go over the list."

His hands clutched his stomach. "That sounds great. I'm starving."

She picked up the bottle and swung it from side to side. "I suppose I could even share this with you."

Philip's eyebrows shot up. "Ohh! I'll be right over."

Claire hurried home, rubbed a wet washcloth over her face, and ran a brush through her hair. Over the past few days she had worked very hard at convincing herself that she and Philip could only ever be friends.

Now if her heart would just comply.

∿∿∿

Philip arrived at the French doors cradling the large cardboard package in his arms. Claire zipped over and flung open the doors. "I figured you'd be back here," he said while setting the package down and supporting it as it tottered on the threshold. "Bought some artwork last week, I see."

"How do you know?"

"The return address gave it away."

She chuckled. "Oh, I suppose it would. Yes, a few pieces spoke to me, and I had to have them. Will you please slide it over there against my worktable?"

Without setting foot in the cottage, he pushed the package over and rested it against her worktable. He then remained in the doorway leaning one arm up against the doorjamb and holding a clipboard under his other arm.

"Just a second. I'm almost done," she said, returning to the kitchenette.

Philip took advantage of the opportunity to look around. The pink teakettle in the tidy kitchen reminded him of the roses around the property, a little bouquet of which drank from a glass tumbler on the table. The antique Bible she carried to church lay beside them. Tiles, sea glass, and sketched designs graced her worktable.

He squinted at a white bulletin board pinned with a partial map and an odd assortment of little pieces of paper.

Claire handed him a box lid containing the sandwiches, grapes, and a bag of potato chips. She grabbed the French lemonade and two glasses from the counter. "Perhaps someday we can talk about that map." She nodded toward the bulletin board. "It's a project I need help with—help from someone I can trust. Today's not the day, though, with the festival coming up."

"Sounds intriguing. I'll look forward to the conversation, but…" He eyed her hands. "…until then, I'm looking forward to some of that lemonade. I got you hooked, didn't I?"

She thunked him in the arm with the bottom of the bottle. "Yeah, so you could weasel some out of me when given the opportunity."

"I'm innocent. You offered, remember?" He laughed as they walked across her small lawn. "Here, let's eat on these rocks. They're easier to sit on than the sand."

After sitting down, Philip said, "I pray before meals to thank God for the food. Would you like to join me?"

"I haven't prayed before a meal for years—well, other than at Thanksgiving. I sure have a lot to learn." She frowned as she bowed her head and closed her eyes.

Philip smothered a smile before bowing his head and praying a simple prayer.

"That was nice." She opened the bottle and poured the lemonade evenly into the glasses. "I'm going to do that before meals now," she said, handing him a glass.

His fingers brushed hers as he took the glass. He could hold back no longer. "Claire, regarding last Friday night…"

She did not look at him as she handed him a sandwich. She picked hers up and squished the edges.

"I want to set something straight with you regarding Vanessa. I want to tell you about her."

Chapter Forty

Claire shook her head.

He swallowed hard. "I want to tell you that she and I—"

"No—no—whatever you want to say, I don't want to hear it. You don't need to set anything straight with me."

The events of last Friday night had weighed on his mind all week. He *had* to tell her but never expected she wouldn't want to listen. "I wish you would let me. It would be good for both of us to be open—to be honest."

"We agreed not to get involved with each other's personal lives, and I'm determined to respect that as I know you will."

"We did agree to that, didn't we?"

She squashed the soft center of her sandwich. "We certainly did, and I've learned my lesson well, Philip. I don't want to ruin our—our rapport by talking about our relationships."

He bit into his peanut butter sandwich and munched it with slow, laborious chews, finally choking it down with the help of the lemonade.

She rolled her now-flat sandwich into a tight tube. "I just hope that no matter what we can at least be friends—good friends." She quietly breathed her words. "It would mean the world to me."

"It would to me as well."

He crunched into a potato chip. *But I don't want to be* just *friends.*

The paper on the clipboard flittered in the breeze. Perhaps after working together this weekend she would be willing to listen. With that ray of hope, he perked up. "Well, shall we go over the plans for the festival then?"

⁂

After arriving on the grounds under a high, warm sun, Claire and Philip worked down the checklist throughout the afternoon, directing food and game vendors, setting up the judging tables, and making sure the vendor booths had been placed correctly. When they discovered six booths had been erected in the wrong area, they laughed so hard while struggling to move them that Claire's sides hurt.

Philip introduced her to countless people—to some as the coordinator and to others as his friend. It had been a long time since Claire had been to or involved in something lively and exciting. She relished having a day full of life and happiness void of loneliness and anxiety.

As evening fell, people lined up at the food vendors tempted by the scents of baked beans and popcorn. Giggles and laughter rang from children bouncing on an inflatable pirate ship.

At the center of the grounds, strands of lights twinkled on the gingerbread-trimmed gazebo with its opposite staircases. The members of the Maritime Consort rotated both instruments and musicians, filling the air with tunes played on period instruments made of strings and bellows and other materials.

With less than an hour remaining before the musicians and vendors were to close down, Philip bid Claire goodnight and headed to the Compass Rose. Claire bought a blueberry ice cream cone and joined the others who sat on the grass around the gazebo.

"Somehow I knew you'd be here tonight." Parker sat beside her and rested his arms on his knees. "I could pick you out of any crowd."

After being with Philip all day, she could arouse no enthusiasm to be with Parker. As she nibbled on the bits of blueberry in her ice cream, Parker jabbered about the festival, the vendors, the competitions, and even the Maritime Consort as if she knew nothing about anything.

"I think this festival is childish in light of the other festivals up and down the coast that celebrate real ships—tall ships like the *Lady Katherine*."

"This festival sounds like fun to me," she replied licking her sticky fingers. "I'm looking forward to being here tomorrow."

"You don't want to waste your time here. Come sail with me. I'll leave first thing in the morning, and we can be together all day."

"Thank you for the invitation, but I won't be able to go with you."

"Why not?"

"I've been asked to be the festival coordinator."

Parker jerked his head back. "Ah, England doesn't need you. He can handle this trifling festival himself. Besides, I thought I told you to stay away from him."

"Philip didn't ask me. Harvard Soames did, and I agreed to do it for him."

He tented his hands and drummed the pads of his fingers together. "Oh, I guess it's pretty hard to say 'no' to Harvard."

She bristled. "Besides, I *want* to be here."

Parker shrugged. "Fine. When can we get together then? Let's have dinner tomorrow night. There's a great little place in Hydeport. I'll pick you up around 7:30."

"That won't work out. Why don't we go to church on Sunday instead?"

"Church? That's not going out."

"Sure it is. By the way, what happened last Sunday? I waited for you."

"Let's see—last Sunday…" He brought his hand up to his chin and tapped his finger against his lips. "That's right, something came up."

"That's all? Something came up? You could have at least let me know you weren't going to be there."

"You don't have a phone, so I can't call you and tell you these things."

"There are other ways."

"Okay, okay—I'll come to church."

"This Sunday would be perfect. I finished the mosaic in the vestibule, and at 10:30 it will be revealed and dedicated."

"I'll come—well, I'll *try* to come. I have several big cases open right now, you know, and may have to head to Boston if something unexpected comes up." He stood and brushed his hands across his pants. "I need to go do some things. Maybe I'll see you tomorrow when I'm back from sailing. Goodnight, darling." With a high head and a quick stride he disappeared into the thinning crowd.

Claire sighed and rose to leave as the musicians began their final song. Entranced by its slow, haunting tune, Claire stopped and leaned against a tree to listen. She imagined it to be a love song and daydreamed about Philip until the last chord faded into the night air.

"Its words are about a fair young maiden who pines for her love, a handsome ship's captain, who is out to sea."

She stood straight and turned around. "Mr. Soames, I didn't know you were there."

"I know you didn't. You looked like you were doing your own pining, so I waited until the song finished."

She lifted the back of her hand to a burning cheek.

"Thank you, by the way," he said.

"For what?"

"For this," he said nodding toward the musicians as they bustled about, packing up their instruments and equipment. "I'm not so old that I can't figure some things out, you know."

Claire dropped her hand. Her eyes shifted from the musicians back to Mr. Soames. "Does Philip know?"

"From what I can tell, he has no idea."

"Please don't tell him."

"Your secret is safe with me." A tender smile crinkled his cheeks. "Why did you do it?"

She fidgeted with the gooey napkin in her hand. "To please Philip."

"I figured as much." His eyes twinkled. "Your parents left you a wealthy young woman, didn't they, my dear?"

She widened her eyes. "How do you know? Mr. Gibbons didn't..."

"No, no, believe it or not he is too professional for that. Let's just say I had my suspicions and the check for the Maritime Consort confirmed them."

"I can't get away with anything around you, can I?" Pain stabbed her heart, and her voice quieted. "I had no idea my parents had so much life insurance on them, but I'd give every penny and more to have them back."

"I believe you would, Miss Claire. They must have also taught you to be generous."

"They did. Many times they told me that if I ever became wealthy I should never flaunt it. They said I needed to be wise and prudent but generous, and my mother, by example mostly, showed me that an anonymous giver is the happiest."

"Sound advice—sound advice indeed."

She wound the napkin around her fingers. "It's so strange, Mr. Soames. They always spoke as if—as if they knew I would be wealthy someday. It pains me to think that perhaps they had premonitions of their deaths."

He rested his crooked fingers on her arm and patted it gently. "I'm sure they didn't, my dear. No doubt they simply saw how bright and talented you are and realized the potential you had to be successful in all your endeavors."

She placed her hand over his and forced a smile. "Thank you, Mr. Soames. What would I do without you?"

He squeezed her arm and dropped his hand. "Goodnight, Claire."

"Goodnight."

On the way to his car, Mr. Soames saw Philip coming from his closed shop. "Good evening, Philip! Going to make your final check of the grounds?"

"Why, Mr. Soames, you're here late tonight!"

"You know I can't resist the atmosphere of the evening before the festival. Besides, I hear it's supposed to be pretty hot, and I don't know if I'll be able to come tomorrow."

"It *is* supposed to get hot with the potential for storms at the end of the day. Hopefully we'll have good weather until 7:00."

"I was just talking with Claire a few minutes ago." Mr. Soames enjoyed watching Philip's eyes light up and dart past him in search of her. "How did it go with her today?"

"Splendidly!"

Mr. Soames chuckled at his enthusiasm.

"She's smart and funny, and we had so much fun despite all the work we had to do. You know, I feel as if I've known her all my life. I can't tell you how much I'm looking forward to working with her tomorrow."

"I bet you are." Pleased he hadn't lost his matchmaking skills, Mr. Soames bid Philip goodnight.

Philip knew Claire would be gone, but he looked for her anyway as he made one last check of the festival grounds. He could barely contain his excitement knowing she would be with him from sun up to sun down tomorrow. How he loved being with her. How he loved her!

No way could tomorrow be anything but a great day.

Chapter Forty-one

Like an organza bridal veil, haze draped over the blushing sun as it peeked above the horizon. Claire stepped from her car in white sandals that synchronized with the tiny daisies that danced across her blue cotton skirt and blouse—the coolest outfit she owned. Her thick braid, tied on the end with a blue ribbon, draped over her left shoulder and rested against the crisscrossed strap of her small purse.

As planned, Claire met Philip by the gazebo at 6:30, and with heads bent close, they pored over the schedule. She would direct vendors to their booths between 7:00 and 9:00, making sure everyone opened by 9:00 when the musicians played their first song. Starting at 9:30 and on each hour after that, the shipbuilding competitions would take place. After lunch, the small ships races would start at the docks at 1:30. When not assisting the musicians and vendors, she would organize the competitors before each event and make sure Philip had the awards.

"Well, I'm here!"

Philip stiffened. He and Claire looked at each other before turning around. Vanessa, wearing an aqua shirt and khaki shorts, stood smiling smugly.

Philip glowered. "What do you mean you're here?"

"To fill in for Abel Longpre." Her hand flew to her mouth. "You mean he didn't tell you?"

"Didn't tell me what?"

"That he couldn't be here today."

"No he didn't tell me. I saw him Wednesday, and he never said a word."

"Well, apparently he can't make it. He and Parker talked late last night, and Parker volunteered me to fill in for him." Her voice dripped with syrupy sweetness. "I know how important Abel's role is, so how could I not agree to help?"

Claire scowled. *And just* what *would we do without you, Vanessa?*

"I can't believe Abel didn't tell me. Judging the competitions is a big deal to him."

Claire scrawled dark pen lines through the tasks she had already completed then scratched over them again with harder, darker impressions.

"Well, whatever the case, I thought since I had to be here, I might as well come early to help."

Philip crossed his arms. "Claire is the coordinator, Vanessa, and has things under control."

Claire stood taller and wrote her name twice in an effort to look important.

"Nonsense! You can never have enough help, and there's nothing I'd rather do than be here with you, Philip. Besides, unlike Claire, I know all the vendors, and they know me."

Claire pressed on the pen so hard she scratched a hole in the paper.

"Vanessa, I think it would be best for you to leave."

"You and I both know you need me. There," she pointed. "The Jeffers are here and have booth 39." Philip watched her as she took off toward the couple and directed them to a tented booth along the path.

Claire checked her clipboard. Sure enough the Jeffers had been assigned booth 39. She jammed the clipboard under her arm and twiddled the pen between her fingers as she waited for him to turn his attention back to her.

Philip finally turned around. "I'm sorry. Once Vanessa's mind is set on something, she'll muscle her way in whether she's wanted or not."

Of course he would defend her. She had not forgotten the scene in the alcove. "I'm quite acquainted with Vanessa's ways, Philip. You don't have to make excuses for her on my account."

"Excuses? I wasn't making an excuse. I didn't ask her to be here..." He paused. "I don't want her here either, but my hands are tied now."

Yeah, right! He would have been more insistent on sending her home if that had been the case. Claire pulled out the clipboard and shook it in front of him. "So, do you want me to do this or Vanessa?"

"You, of course!"

"I suppose I am doing this for Mr. Soames, aren't I? At least he must think I'm competent enough."

"Claire, you *are* competent. There is no one—"

"Philip! Someone needs you!" Vanessa said, running up to him. "Over here. Come with me."

Claire pursed her lips as Philip sighed and followed Vanessa. *This is going to be a long, lonely day.*

Chapter Forty-two

Vanessa's intervention confused the vendors over who was in charge. Once Vanessa finally headed off toward the docks, no doubt in search of Philip, Claire visited each vendor, introducing herself and offering assistance, to reestablish her role.

"I don't know who you are," one old man griped. "You're not from around here, are you?"

"No, I'm not. I moved to the Cove only last month."

"What's your name again?"

"Claire, Claire Wycoff."

"You related to Hugh and Jake? Those boys are trouble."

"I'm not sure."

"What do you mean you're not sure?" He glared at her. "Look, I don't want you around my booth unless you're going to buy something. If I need help, I'll ask Vanessa."

"Now, now, Mr. Howard." Philip spoke from behind her. "I can vouch for Claire. Harvard Soames asked her to help this year, and she is quite trustworthy. Guess we had better let you finish setting up. It's almost 9:00. Have a successful day, Mr. Howard."

"Come," he whispered in Claire's ear as they left the booth. "He's always a grump. He doesn't like people, especially from out of state. If it weren't for his unique items and quality workmanship, he would probably do very poorly at these festivals. Don't let him get to you."

"Oh—whew! I thought it was me."

"It could never be—"

"Philip, Philip!" Marie yelled running up to them. Her cheeks flushed crimson, and she panted close to the point of hyperventilation. *What now?*

"Okay, just catch your breath."

Marie sucked in a breath. "Oh, Philip, it's *terrible!*"

Philip looked at her bug-eyed. "What?"

"You *must* come to the store."

Seemingly from nowhere, Vanessa appeared beside Philip much to Claire's annoyance.

"I stepped out of the store to get a cup of coffee. Emma had just put the till in the cash register drawer when two women came into the store. One woman asked her about the soaps."

"Slow down, Marie."

Marie wiped sweat from her forehead with the back of her hand. "Emma thought she shut the drawer, but when she went back to the register after showing the woman the soaps, the other woman was gone and the drawer gaped wide open—empty!" She dragged in a deep breath, "Oh, Philip, all the money is gone, and Emma is in tears."

Claire's heart burst with empathy.

"Oh, no!" Philip groaned. "Okay," he said clasping his hands, "let's just try to remain calm. Have you called the police yet?"

"No. I ran here first."

"Come on then. Let's go." He and Marie dashed toward the store.

Vanessa followed at their heels—of course. Claire gripped the clipboard wishing she could go too but knew she had to remain and oversee her responsibilities. After all, she was the coordinator. Poor Emma! Poor Philip! Claire prayed a silent prayer for them both.

While checking on the final few booths, she saw Sasha Harriman draping silver jewelry over fresh green apples. A hand-wrought sign made of silver wire forming the name "Sasha's Silver" sat propped on the table.

"I didn't know you were here," Claire said. "I must have missed you when you arrived. Though I'm the coordinator this year, Vanessa must have beaten me to you."

"Ah, so you're the one to blame for having to endure a few moments in Vanessa's presence."

Claire snickered. "Sorry!"

"I'll forgive you this time."

"I love your display! The silver really pops against those apples. I didn't know you made jewelry."

"Oh, this is my fun outlet. I'm an emergency room nurse at St. Joe's in Hydeport, but after a day in the ER I go home, focus my attention on making something pretty, and destress until I'm calm enough to sleep."

"Good for you! Your jewelry is fabulous." A siren screamed louder and louder. Claire's mind sped to Philip and Emma. "My mom was a nurse too. She worked in ICU for years."

"I'd take the ER over ICU any day. You said 'was.' Is she retired now?"

"No, she and my father died last year in an accident."

"Oh." Her voice softened. "I'm so sorry." The siren stopped, and Sasha poked her head out the booth. "I wonder what's going on."

"I know what it is." Claire told her about the theft at the Compass Rose.

"Poor Philip—and on today of all days!"

When a customer entered the booth, Claire said goodbye and left. The time for the first competition had come, and Claire carried the first box of awards to the judging tables set up in the parking lot by the docks.

While the other two judges, Ron and Andrew, sat ready for the competition, Claire organized the children into lines. At 9:50, with Philip and Vanessa nowhere in sight and with Ron and Andrew's agreement, Claire appointed herself a judge.

With moms and dads in tow, children presented their handmade ships. Though Claire loved all of them, the ship made entirely of noodles won first place, and just as she finished presenting the awards, Philip and Vanessa arrived.

"You started without us?" Vanessa chided. "You don't *ever* start a competition without Philip."

"But—"

"I wish you hadn't, Claire," Philip said, tension evident in his face.

"But, I thought we needed to stay on schedule." She looked from Vanessa to Philip. "Ron and Andrew thought we should start too."

Vanessa lifted her chin in the air. "Obviously you don't know how things work around here."

Philip held up a hand. "What's been done has been done. Let's just get going with the next event."

Baffled, Claire quickly organized the second group as Vanessa planted herself by Philip's elbow at the judges' table. Eager to get away, Claire gave Philip the next set of awards and excused herself to check on the vendors and musicians.

When she returned for the final competition, Vanessa had already organized the lines. "I have this." She flicked her long fingers. "You can go."

Claire plunked the awards on the end of the table and waited for Philip to finish talking with Ron.

The sun baked Claire's cheeks and exacerbated the humidity that clung to the air. She swiped a drop of sweat that ran down the side of her face before leaning heavily on her knuckles on the end of the table. She half-heartedly surveyed the closest line of impatient competitors.

Protecting his ship in the crook of an arm, a man with dark hair like her father and about his age pulled a cigarette out of its package with his lips. *Dad used to do it like that too.* The man swayed from side to side then ran his hand over his abdomen. He withdrew a lighter from his pocket.

Claire stared at him. *No! Don't do it!*

She watched as he scowled at his shaking hand, then forced the flame. As the flame leapt into the air, he looked over it and locked eyes with Claire. An expression of horror crossed his bright-red face, and he opened his mouth as if to say something. The cigarette dropped from his lips, and the lighter bounced on the ground.

"No!" Claire cried as the man collapsed. The ship splintered on the pavement. A woman screamed.

Philip spun around and ran behind Claire. "Someone, call 9-1-1!"

Fast, shallow breaths heaved Claire's chest.

Bending over the man, Philip called to her. "Claire, quickly, go get Sasha!"

She froze.

"Claire!" he yelled.

People crowded around. Everyone talked at once. Vanessa pushed her way through the crowd. "Go get Sasha!" Philip told her. She obeyed in a flash.

"Everyone, please, move back," Philip said.

Sweat coursed down Claire's face. Her lungs tightened with each rapid breath. She folded an arm across her abdomen as nausea waved through her stomach. Dizzy and weak, she reached for the closest chair and plopped down on it, thumping the side of her head on the table. Her arms dangled at her sides. The voices and noises around her got farther and farther away as first tiny sparks of light then blackness encroached on her vision.

Chapter Forty-three

Scooched beside her, Philip moved aside the thick braid that lay across Claire's mouth. Sweat glistened around her closed eyes. The color of her face matched the white table. "Claire?"

She didn't move.

He stroked her cheek and pushed aside some wayward curls. "Claire?"

Still no response.

An ambulance wailed in the distance. He spoke louder. "Claire, are you okay?"

She scrunched her eyebrows. Her eyes fluttered open, and she blinked over a blank stare.

"Are you okay?" he repeated. The ambulance drew closer.

He dropped his hand as she slowly lifted her head and leaned against the back of the chair.

Philip grabbed his water bottle from the table and unscrewed the cap. "Here, drink some of this." He cradled her head and touched the bottle to her lips. She reached for it, but her hands trembled too much to take it. Water dribbled down her chin.

The blaring siren silenced as, directed by a sheriff's deputy, it pulled slowly through the crowd. Sasha, Vanessa, and another deputy knelt beside the fallen man.

Philip withdrew the bottle from her lips, returned the cap, and searched Claire's face. "Do you need a doctor?"

She slowly shook her head.

"Can you walk?"

She nodded.

"Let's get away from here then." Holding the bottle in one hand he wrapped his other arm around her shoulders and lifted her to a standing position. "Let's go to Sasha's booth." He held her close as they walked away from the crowd. Though quite aware he held the woman he loved, his concern clouded any delight in the situation.

She stopped and put her hand on his chest. Her breathing quickened. "Philip, it was the lighter wasn't it? That's what killed him." Her bottom lip quivered.

"No, no," he replied. He tenderly rubbed his hand up and down her arm before leading her on again. "Don't cry. He's not dead, Claire. He's going to be okay. The lighter had nothing to do with his collapsing."

She stopped again. "He's not dead?"

"No, he's alive. Sasha took good care of him." He urged her on.

"It wasn't because of the lighter?"

"No."

Thankfully void of customers, they arrived at Sasha's booth, and he eased her into the lone chair.

"How about another sip of water," he said unscrewing the cap and handing her the bottle.

Shaking only slightly now, she raised the bottle to her parted lips and drank.

He knelt on one knee and studied her. Though the heat may have contributed to her fainting, he suspected from her reaction to the man and his lighter that she suffered from the memory of a painful experience. He longed to comfort her, to hold her in his arms until her distress eased, but knew he couldn't.

"Sasha said the man passed out from sunstroke—no surprise in this heat. He's in good hands now and will soon be on his way to St. Josephs."

Color returned to her cheeks. "I'm so relieved he's alive." She took another sip. "He was just—he looked like my father. He shook and—and lit that flame.

He looked at me so strangely like he *knew* he was about to—like he—"

"Philip, here you are! I've been looking all over for you." Vanessa cut in from the opening of the tent. "You're needed *right now* down at the parking lot."

Philip looked from Vanessa back to Claire. He didn't want to leave her but knew he had to and slowly rose to his feet.

"Go ahead. I'll be right there," he called over his shoulder.

"I'll wait for you."

"I said 'go,' Vanessa."

Claire gave him a weak smile. "Go ahead. I'm okay now. I'll stay here until Sasha gets back."

Leaning his hands on the ends of the armrests he bent close and whispered, "It's important to me that you're okay. Come to me if you need anything, all right? Meanwhile I'll pray you find peace from whatever has caused you this upset."

Her eyes widened then pooled with tears.

He stood and spoke louder. "And remember, the man will be all right. Okay?"

⌇⌇⌇

A while later Sasha returned to the booth. "And here I thought I wouldn't have to work today," she whined.

Still sitting in the chair with thoughts of Philip's tenderness and care, Claire fanned her face with a paper bag.

"I certainly appreciate you sitting here for me. I wouldn't want someone taking off with my apples. I worked too hard to find just the right ones."

Claire giggled. "You had a few sales, so I guess it was good I was here."

As she stood, she recognized the scrutiny a nurse's eyes can give and wondered if Philip had requested it. She took money from her purse to purchase a pair of earrings she had set aside and placed the cash on the table before tucking the earrings into her purse. "The man—Philip said he'll be okay."

"That's true. He passed out from dehydration and sun exposure. He'll be at the hospital for a little while, but he should be just fine." She paused. "How about yourself?"

"I feel much stronger now. Thank you."

"And you're keeping hydrated?"

Claire held up Philip's empty water bottle as she left. "I guess I owe Philip a drink, don't I?"

During the lunch break, Claire wandered the grounds to help where needed.

Powerful fans blew across the musicians' flying fingers as a spirited jig leapt from the gazebo. Claire tapped her finger to the rhythm on a plastic bowl while standing outside a sweltering booth. She scooped the last spoonful of corn chowder into her mouth then tossed the bowl into a garbage can close by. Though it made no sense to eat hot chowder on such a steamy day, the peppery milk filled with onions and corn revived her.

Other things energized her as well.

"I will forever be grateful, Claire!" a vendor exclaimed as she walked toward her. "In all the years I've participated in festivals, no one has ever volunteered to watch my booth and give me a break."

"I'm delighted to help. You'll be happy to know you had three sales."

"Wonderful!"

Claire picked up a button card and flitted it between two fingers. Though the vendor had many cards filled with buttons made from locally sourced rocks, Claire craved to know more about this one. "Did you find this locally?"

"Yes, isn't that a beauty? It's the only blue granite I've ever found, and believe me I've seen a lot of rocks over the years."

"Where did you find it?" Claire tried to sound casual, but inside she could barely contain herself.

"I found it several years ago on Dovetail Beach."

"Where's that?"

"In Hydeport. Because it's so pretty, I haven't wanted to give it up, but," she chuckled, "I can only keep so many rocks. It was time to turn it into a button. Most people don't want just one button, though."

"I certainly do," Claire said pulling money from her purse.

"Mom's in the kitchen. Do you want me to get her for you?"

"No, that's fine," Claire said. "I know she's busy. I'll catch her later. I've just come for two bottles of French lemonade."

"We've sold an awful lot of these today," Holly said, as she pulled the bottles from the ice-filled tub.

"I can see why. It's blistering out there."

After paying for the lemonade and leaving the tearoom, Claire, with a bottle in each hand, swung her arms as she searched for Philip. Not finding him among the vendors, she descended the path toward the docks. The bony masts of the *Lady Katherine* skewered the air above the harbor. Such a short sail for Parker today?

About to give up, she saw Philip and Vanessa talking and laughing with two other couples. Within a few yards of approaching them, Philip and Vanessa turned to face each other, and took long simultaneous drinks from bottles of French lemonade.

Claire's carefree arm-swinging stopped. Her feet couldn't move another step.

Vanessa lowered her bottle. With provocative eyes, she captured Philip's attention and pressed a slow, enticing kiss into the air.

Philip sputtered on his lemonade. With eyes fixed on her, he pulled the bottle from his lips and wiped his mouth on his wrist.

Claire's shoulders sank.

Vanessa curled up the corners of her mouth, slinked close to Philip, and put her hand through the crook of his arm. She turned toward the two couples…

Claire pivoted her head then wheeled around. *What was I thinking?*

Just because Philip had helped her and comforted her, he did nothing more than what a friend would have done. During the past hour or so she had foolishly built his attentiveness and tender words into meaning something deeper than friendship.

Why would Philip ever want her over the beautiful and tempting Vanessa Hollenbeck anyway? She hung her head and looked from one bottle to the other. *I hope Sasha likes French lemonade.*

Chapter Forty-four

After tipping the bottle of lemonade Vanessa bought him and experiencing her brazen attempt at seduction, realization slapped Philip across the face, sending lemonade spurting back up his throat.

Grr! I've been so blind!

During his brief moment of recuperation, Vanessa snuggled close and addressed the two couples. "Yes, it'll take a lot of late nights, but Philip and I will work on it together—just like old times."

Philip flared his nostrils and jerked his arm away from her. "I'll do nothing of the sort, Vanessa." He turned to the others. "I'm sorry. You'll have to find someone else for the project. Excuse me, please." Clenching the bottle, he spun around and stormed away.

A short distance ahead, Claire, holding a bottle of lemonade in each hand, trundled in front of him. Having escaped her braid, strands of hair swirled wildly in the blasting, hot wind that had picked up.

Oh, no! She must have seen what just happened.

He wondered if…

He heaved a loud sigh. *I bet she came to give me one of those lemonades.* He gritted his teeth. *Why am I so brainless?*

He massaged his forehead, hoping to dissolve the invisible band compressing it like a vise, then hurled his bottle into a recycling bin, shattering it to pieces.

Claire avoided Philip and Vanessa and busied herself lining up the competitors gripping their little ships along the dock for the first small-ships race. Despite being in a shallow, protected area of the harbor, water sloshed high above the sides of the docks while billowing gray clouds churned overhead.

At the sound of a whistle, the children put their ships in the water and guided them with long sticks hoping their ship would not only stay afloat but also be able to cross the finish line marked by a flag along the shore. The ever-increasing wind, however, made both accomplishments difficult.

As the last race concluded, Claire glanced skyward where gray clouds had turned to black. She placed the box of awards on the judges' table and hastened toward the joggling white-tented booths on the festival grounds.

She approached a sheriff's deputy standing by the gazebo. "Sir, are any storms heading this way?"

"Yes! Severe storm warnings are out for the entire area. I don't see this festival going on much longer."

She thanked the officer and suppressed the anxiety that rose within her by focusing on finding Philip. Vanessa walked toward her as a deep rumble rolled in the distance. She did not want to speak to her but knew she had no choice. "Have you seen Philip?"

"Why?"

"I need to talk with him. It's important."

"What about?"

"Come on. Where is he?"

Vanessa sneered. "I know where he is, but I won't tell you where unless you tell me why you need him."

"I'm not going to play your game, Vanessa," Claire shot back.

Vanessa shrugged then proceeded toward Main Street.

Ohh! If Philip wants that kind of woman, he can have her!

More thunder roared, this time closer. The muggy air stilled, suffocating her. Looking skyward she decided what to do—Philip or no Philip. Claire raced to each booth and instructed the vendors to pack up.

"But it's not five o'clock!" one person complained.

"A severe storm is coming, and no one will be here anyway," she answered.

"But, Philip is adamant if we close up early we won't be able to participate next year."

"As the coordinator, I'm taking full responsibility and will ensure you're not penalized."

Mr. Howard crossed his arms. "I refuse to leave."

"Suit yourself," she answered. *What an impossible man!*

Saddened, Claire watched the members of the Maritime Consort fold their music stands and pack their instruments.

Tentacles of lightning stabbed the air and growling thunder shook the ground. People ran to their cars. Vendors scrambled to box their wares. A vehement wind whipped through the grounds, toppling garbage cans and breaking branches.

While Claire struggled to carry a tote to a vendor's car, Philip rushed up to her.

His hands flew into the air. "Claire, what have you done?"

Panting and drenched in sweat, she dropped the tote at her feet and stared at him as if he had struck her. Her untamed mass of curls, free from the ribbon that had instead entwined itself around her purse strap, danced in the wind. "What do you mean, what have I done? I couldn't find you. *Someone* had to make a decision. People's safety is at risk!"

"But you didn't ask me. You just up and dismissed everyone—the vendors—the musicians—everyone is gone!"

Large drops splatted on the tote. "Philip, I took the responsibility into my own hands because—because *your* Vanessa would not condescend to grant me access to you." Overwhelmed, she picked up the tote and hustled toward the vendor's car.

～✇✇～

Rain battered in through the openings opposite him. Philip slid down a support beam until he landed on the floor of the gazebo. Water dripped then splattered in all directions as he combed his fingers through his hair, adding more water spots to his glasses.

Beside him a pair of sandals lay strewn on the floor. He rolled his eyes. *How can someone possibly forget her own shoes?*

He jumped as a flash of lightning synchronized with a crack of thunder above him. At least the heavy rain held off until most of the vendors had left. He assured those he could that they would not be penalized next year for leaving early.

He looked out the opening to his left at the havoc the storm had wreaked on the festival grounds. He needed to get to the Compass Rose, but thankfully the storm prevented him and offered him this short respite.

He pulled the shirt that had suctioned to his chest then took off his glasses and rubbed them against it, smearing the water spots into wet streaks. *Tsk!* He straddled the glasses on his elevated knee and rubbed his burning eyes.

Why did Vanessa have to come? If the gallery night hadn't proven how stupid he was, allowing her to stay today cinched it. He clenched his fists. "I do not *think*!" he yelled aloud rapping his knuckles on the floor.

He replaced his glasses at the sound of empty tin cans striking the roof above him. White hailstones shooting in myriad directions bounced down the steps and on the ground.

"Ow! Ow!"

Footsteps pounded on the opposite staircase.

"Ouch!"

Philip sat up straight. Claire crumpled on the top step under the security of the roof and massaged her bare red feet.

The sandals! He picked them up, went to her, and dropped them in front of her.

She jumped, then puckered her eyebrows. "What are you doing here?" she shouted over the clatter of the hail.

He sat beside her and crossed his legs. Neither spoke while the hail pelted above them. Claire stopped rubbing her feet and buckled on her sandals. The hail melted back to rain.

"I thought you'd be long gone by now," Philip said breaking the silence. Thunder boomed overhead.

Claire sighed. "Oh, Mr. Howard decided he would leave after all but only once everyone else had gone and, of course, only once the rain started in earnest."

She tugged at the hair and ribbon wound around her purse strap. Philip leaned his elbows on his knees, engrossed in her futile efforts.

"Some people are so stubborn. I helped him despite his unpleasantness, and he decided that maybe, just maybe, this once, he could use a little of my help. He kept a good eye on me, though, to make sure I didn't steal anything."

Her fingers followed a section of hair to a small key on a gold chain that lay against her shoulder. She wrapped her fingers around it before tearing it free from her hair and tucking it beneath her blouse.

"I kept slipping in my sandals and didn't want to break my neck, so I took them off and left them here thinking I'd pick them up on the way to my car." She yanked at the ribbon succeeding only in tightening it further. "Have you ever run through hail before in your bare feet? It hurts! It's cold too." She pushed her bottom lip out like a child.

Philip snorted as he tried to stifle a laugh. "I can't say I've tried that." He tilted his head back unable to hold it in any longer and laughed.

"What's so funny?"

"You are. Oh, it feels so good to laugh. After a day like today I'm not sure whether to laugh or cry—but I'd much rather laugh."

She frowned. "I don't feel very funny." His laughter infected her though, and soon she turned up the corners of her mouth and giggled. She dropped her hands from working the tangle and stood up. Philip stood as well.

She pulled her skirt and blouse away from her body and twisted streams of water from their edges leaving them scrunched and uneven. She tugged at the tangle of hair, ribbon, and purse again. "I'm such a mess! Just look at me!"

Philip crossed his arms. The rain had spiked her long lashes. Around her pink cheeks, droplets dangled like diamonds from the tips of each curl. *Look at you? I can barely keep my eyes off you.* "I don't think you look so bad."

She rubbed her scalp and pulled the snarly knot away from her body. "I don't know what to do about this. It pulls and hurts."

Philip dug his jackknife from his pocket. "May I help?"

"Please do."

He took the clump from her hand and after drawing his knife through the ribbon several times gently pulled the pieces from her hair and put them into his shirt pocket.

∿∿∿

Claire's pulse quickened as Philip's hands, strong and nimble, worked at freeing lengths from the matted tangle. She dared not look up and willed the strength not to fall in love with him.

After releasing the last few strands, she tried in vain to tame her breathing as he lingered and caressed a handful of hair between his hands rubbing the wet curls between his long fingers.

As if he had grabbed a hot ember, he dropped her hair and stepped back, snapping his jackknife closed. "I need to get to the store." He turned around and walked a few steps.

She lifted her hands to her cheeks to cool them.

"Claire, one thing," he said turning back to face her.

She dropped her hands.

"I owe you an apology."

"An apology? For what?"

"You made the right decisions today—to start the first competition without me and to send everyone home early. My pride got in the way, and I had no right getting angry at you. I'm sorry."

Why did he always have to do or say something to magnetize her heart when she knew he belonged to someone else?

She acknowledged his coveted validation with a nod before spinning around and fleeing down the steps into the rain. If she had stayed she would have tried to convince him to choose her instead of Vanessa, and hearing his rejection would have been unbearable.

Chapter Forty-five

"So, Lord," Pastor Tim concluded, "we dedicate this mosaic to You. May all who enter through these doors know and remember that You are the only way to heaven. In Jesus' name we pray, amen."

Mumbles of "amen" reverberated around the vestibule and from the overflow in the sanctuary and out the double doors down the steps.

"Do you have anything you'd like to say, Claire, before we take the sheet off?"

She stepped toward the center of the room. *I'm not going to cry.* In the ensuing hush, the envelope in her cold wet hands crinkled as she twisted it into a tight coil.

"Thank you for the privilege of working on this mosaic and for the pieces of sea glass many of you gave to complete it. It's fitting that this mosaic is being dedicated on..." She swallowed hard. "...Father's Day since my father was the one who encouraged me to learn to lay tile and design mosaics." Her voice quavered, and she wrung the mangled envelope until her hands hurt. "And I'm grateful for the impact this project and its verse had on me so that now I'm a Christian."

After breathing a quick breath to relieve her anxiety, she nodded to Pastor Tim, and together they pulled aside the sheet.

People craned their necks. A few women gasped. Claire's eyes flew to Philip who stood opposite her, but he did not lift his attention from the mosaic. Applause rang throughout the crowd; then everyone talked at once.

189

People patted her on the shoulder. Others shook her hand.

The little boy tugged on her skirt and pointed to the red piece he gave. She grasped his hand and allowed him to lead her to it. He bent and picked at the hardened grout.

"It's in there to stay now," she said, "but it's a very special piece and one of the prettiest in the entire mosaic." After a few more tries at dislodging it, he gave up and scampered off.

"I'm speechless," Philip said as he stepped toward her and took her hand to shake it. "The design, the mastery is phenomenal…." He covered her hand with his but didn't let go. "…it's exquisite, Claire. Well done!"

His approval meant the world to her. Powerless, her cheeks warmed. Oh, she hated it when she blushed!

✍✍✍

Her suspicion confirmed, Grace jabbed an elbow into Philip. He dropped Claire's hand.

"All right, you've hogged the artist too long," she interrupted, cutting in front of him. "I'm the one who discovered her, remember, so I have priority."

She had been watching them for weeks now but had seen them interact on only a few occasions. Did they realize how obvious their attraction to each other was? A knowing smile crossed her lips. She sensed hesitations on both sides, though. She understood Philip's but hoped Claire's wasn't because of Parker Hollenbeck. She would keep a close eye on these two to see what she could do to help.

✍✍✍

Claire held up the chunk of granite beside the button card she had pinned to the bulletin board. The azure-blue button with its bits of black mica, sparkling quartz, and feldspar matched her rock exactly.

"*Blue surrounds yet blue releases…*" Blue *granite?* Did granite surround something? If it was granite, then what was it releasing? She scribbled her thoughts beneath her other notes, then placed the rock on the table beside the scrunched envelope. The envelope had been affixed to the front door of the church and given to her by Pastor Tim. She picked up the note and reread it.

Dearest Claire,

I apologize for not being able to attend the dedication of your work, but I had matters to attend to. I'm sure you did an amazing job. I have a race this Saturday, so let's meet before it for coffee. Meet me in Hydeport at the dock by the Lady Katherine *at 4:30 a.m. I'll bring cappuccino and pastries.*

We'll watch the sun rise on Dovetail Beach.

Fondly, Parker

She tossed the note onto the table. *I see how it is. He doesn't come for me but expects me to go running to him.* She crumpled her nose. But—he wanted to go to Dovetail Beach, and she wanted to search for blue granite there. She would meet him, but only this once, since she wanted to search that beach and see those tall ships.

Feeling restless, she opened the French doors. The scent of wild roses coaxed her into the backyard, and the resonance of the waves once again lured her down the sandy path. Movement at the end of the beach surprised her.

～✲✲✲

Grinning, Philip walked up to her. "Ah, you caught me! I didn't expect you to be down here this evening for some reason. Guess I should have known."

She looked past his shoulder toward the end of the beach.

"I was just checking for evidence of trespassers."

Her eyes widened. "Did you see anything?"

"No, nothing fresh." He didn't tell her he had checked other times during the past month and had seen large shoeprints and more cigarette butts. "I'll be gone for a few weeks but will be back by July Fourth. Do you mind keeping an eye around the place?"

"Not at all. Anything to help."

"Great! I figured you'd be willing." They ambled along the beach. *Should I ask her?* Her words at the dedication today had given him hope.

"Any progress on the theft from your shop?"

"The deputy interviewed Emma, the other customer, and the shopkeepers on either side of me. He concluded an opportunist saw the open drawer and decided to steal the cash tray. I suspect she won't ever be caught. I knew the drawer wasn't working properly and could kick myself for not fixing it right away."

"I'm sorry."

"It's a hard lesson learned, but I'm eager to move on." He cleared his throat. "Speaking of moving on, now that the vestibule is done and you have a little more time on your hands, will you be able to finish any projects to sell in the arts and crafts fair in August? I'm sure Sasha would be willing to share her booth space with you. The fair is much smaller than the Small Ships Festival—just arts and crafts vendors."

"I would love that! It will be fun to work toward something this summer."

"Good! I hoped you'd want to participate."

They walked in an awkward silence to the rocky barrier. "I need to get packed for an early start tomorrow."

"You're a busy man, Philip."

"Too busy sometimes."

"Have a safe journey. Perhaps I'll see you on July Fourth." She turned to scramble up the path.

. He flicked the jackknife in his pocket. *Ask her!* "Claire?"

She turned around.

"My two sisters, their families, and my parents, if they're up to it, will be here for Fourth of July weekend. We always have a big celebration on the beach after closing the shop on the Fourth. We build a driftwood fire and cook hotdogs and watch the fireworks shoot over the harbor."

"Sounds wonderful."

He swallowed. *I can't believe I'm nervous!* "Would you like to celebrate the evening with my family and me? Well, unless you have plans already?"

She cocked her head. "Just your family will be there?"

"This year it's just us."

"I have no other plans. It sounds like fun. Okay, I'll be there."

"Great!" He knew he'd look forward to it more than he wanted to admit.

Chapter Forty-six

The sky had brightened from black to pale blue, and despite the early hour, a few people moved about Hydeport's dimly-illuminated docks. Several large ships with their masts lancing the dissipating morning mist rocked in sync with the water. Claire settled upon a bench above the *Lady Katherine* and waited for Parker.

Emerging from his ship, he beamed his perfect smile as he approached her. "I just knew you'd come," he said, carrying a basket. "You really should get a telephone, you know. Calling would be much simpler than leaving you notes—as charming as it is."

"I don't want a telephone," she answered. "And, I've never stood you up yet, now, have I?"

Seemingly oblivious to her jab, Parker said, "You might as well come with me in my car. Dovetail Beach isn't very far away."

After getting into Parker's car, they zoomed out of the parking lot and turned down a narrow road hugging the bay. On one side mansions faced the ocean. On the other side, bordered by large slabs of granite, a rocky beach stretched from the road and disappeared into the water.

Along the way, Parker blathered about a case he had worked on all week for a statesman she didn't know. Without warning he swung into a tight U-turn and stopped in the center of a space marked for two cars.

They got out of the car, and Parker, with basket in tow, grabbed Claire's hand and led her to the end of a section of rock that jutted into the ocean.

Parker retrieved a cloth from the basket, snapped it in the air, and smoothed it on the rocky surface before motioning for her to sit. "The rocky protrusions on this beach dovetail into the ocean—thus, the name," he explained while placing a plate of swirled cinnamon twists between them. He offered her a porcelain mug and poured steaming hazelnut cappuccino from a thermos. He then set a nosegay of red roses beside her.

She held the roses to her nose. They had no scent.

"Am I impressing you?"

"Everything is lovely."

"This is a famous spot to view the sunrise. You'll see pictures from here on postcards and in calendars. It will rise over there between those two islands."

Steel gray water lapped against the rocks as lingering wisps of mist vanished. A long thin coral line stretched across the clear, ever-lightening sky. Islands and a steady progression of boats dotted the water.

Claire nibbled on her delicious cinnamon pastry while Parker fidgeted and talked nonstop about the upcoming race. Though charming as always, he acted unusually intense today, and Claire wished he would relax and enjoy the sunrise.

"Ten ships will be in the race today. You really must come back to this spot and watch them sail south. The first ship will leave the harbor at 9:00."

"I'll do that." *Then look for blue granite.*

His eyes glinted in the progressing light. "I'm going to beat the *Dry Bones* today."

"How can you be so sure?"

"If I set my mind on something, I'm always confident of its outcome."

She sipped the last of her cappuccino. "I wish I were always so sure of things."

"You don't need to be. Let me handle things for you. I'll always know what's best for you."

His words troubled her as the golden orb lifted its warm head above the ever-moving ocean. Orange gave way to pink, surrendering finally to a wide brushstroke of yellow. When a long reflective arm reached out to her from between the two islands, she wrapped her arms around her knees, hoping to draw from its warmth.

She thought of Philip. Emptiness had filled her since he left, and Parker did not fill the void.

"Come, darling, let's walk along the beach," he said, cutting into her thoughts. He bounced to his feet and extended his hand.

As much as she loved walking beaches, she had wanted to bask in the glow of the sunrise a bit longer but rose and grasped his hand. *Perhaps the exercise will help him relax.*

Thankful for an excuse to let go, she withdrew her hand and seized a tiny piece of brown sea glass by Parker's foot. "I'm surprised you want to do this now. You seem too restless to stroll the beach." Not that their brisk walk could be considered a stroll.

"Do you like beaches?" he asked.

"I love them. There is no place I think I'd rather be."

"You like beaches then," he repeated as if making a mental note. "I like them okay, but I'd rather be on the ocean. Speaking of which, we should probably head back. I need to get ready for the race."

After turning around, Parker bent by an area peppered with large rocks. "Hey, look at this!"

Claire stopped in her tracks. The piece of brown sea glass dropped from her hand. "Where did you find that?"

"Right here," he said, pointing beside him.

"I can't believe it." She took the rock from his hand and examined it. It matched her piece of blue granite in color, texture, and approximate size.

"Nice piece of granite. Interesting color, too. I don't know if I've ever seen a piece quite like this before." Parker paused. "Have you?"

Transfixed, words tumbled from her lips. "Yes. Yes, I have two pieces of granite just like it."

Parker raised his eyebrows. "Two?" Pressing his hand on her back, he nudged her to walk again. "Where did you get them?"

"One is a button I bought at the festival last weekend. The lady made it from a little piece she found on this very beach. I confess to wanting to come here to see if I could find more. The other one..." She bit her lip regretting she had impulsively spoken.

"Yes? And the other one?"

"The other one," she started again, "was my father's. I discovered it in his safe deposit box after his death."

"Really? You discovered a chunk of blue granite like this just sitting in his safe deposit box...with nothing to explain it?"

"Well, there was a paper with it."

"Did he tell you or did the paper say where the rock came from?"

Feeling as if she were being cross-examined and unable to think straight, she lifted a hand to her forehead. *Why so insistent? Why the pointed questions?* "Well, not exactly. I have a few ideas where it may be from, but—but I don't want to talk about it right now, Parker."

He reached over and grabbed the rock from her hand. "Here, I'll take this and hold it for a while. I can see it's bringing back painful memories of your parents."

Upset that she had spoken about her father's granite and the riddle, she fell silent.

Once they reached their breakfast area, Parker stuffed everything into the basket and handed her the nosegay. He lifted her chin and ran his thumb across it and over her bottom lip.

When she looked into his eyes, she expected to feel at least some of the same adoration for him as she did for Philip. Instead, the two men contrasted more than ever.

"I have something for you, darling." Parker reached into his pants pocket and withdrew a small shiny object. He loosened a clasp, pinched her shirt, and affixed a gold brooch. "I had this made especially for you. It's a replica of the *Lady Katherine*—red sails and all."

"Oh, Parker!" She lifted it with her finger. "It's beautiful, but..." The still-rising sun glinted off the faceted rubies and polished gold. "...you shouldn't have. I really can't accept..."

"Nonsense! Anything for my girl."

"*Your* girl? But—"

"You're not anyone else's are you? You haven't been sneaking around dating anyone when we've been apart have you?"

The times she had been with Philip could hardly be considered dates. Besides, she knew Vanessa held his affection. "No."

"Good."

"Parker, I don't want you to get the wrong impression that—"

"Shh!" He covered her mouth with his fingers. "I'm claiming you. You're mine, and that's all there is to it."

"But I—"

"No buts!"

～✺✺～

Claire waved back as Parker disappeared below the *Lady Katherine's* scrubbed deck. She weaved through the thickening crowd and lingered to watch the tall ships come to life with activity in preparation for the race.

The gathering throngs, however, hampered her exit from the parking lot, and the snarled traffic prolonged her return to Dovetail Beach. She arrived at the crowded beach just in time to see the *Dry Bones* parade past. In its wake, the wind billowed the red sails of the *Lady Katherine*, and as it skimmed past Claire rested her hand on its resplendent duplicate resting on her chest.

After the last ship sailed past and the spectators thinned out, Claire wandered the beach but ended up with nothing more than a pocket full of sea glass and a kink in her neck from looking down too intently.

She rested on a flat rock and rubbed her neck. Parker's words—*I'm claiming you. You're mine.*—replayed in her mind. The familiar words sent a prickling sensation careening to her extremities. *Not again, Lord. What have I done? I can't go through it again. What do I do?*

Chapter Forty-seven

With four days to spare, Claire popped her rent payment through Philip's mail slot, then returned to her car and drove to the Cove.

After parking and entering the far side of the post office, her footsteps echoed off the empty, box-lined room, and her keys jangled as she pushed her key into the brass lock.

Tap tap tap! Bending over the customer service counter, Lorna gestured through the glass door separating them and mouthed "Come." Claire stuffed her mail, including a small box, into the top of her purse, whapped closed the little door, and pulled her key before heading to the service area and opening the glass door. All eyes in the small grouping of people focused on her.

"Maybe you can tell us, Claire." A sly grin graced one corner of Lorna's mouth. "You've been seen with Parker Hollenbeck, so you probably know. Did he or didn't he cheat at the tall ships race on Saturday?"

"Cheat? I have no idea what you're talking about."

Lorna shoved a pencil behind her ear, forcing a tuft of red hair into a horizontal position. "Come on, Claire."

Everyone stared at her.

"I know he was in the race, but other than that, I know nothing. I didn't even know he won."

"Uh-huh," a man said.

"Right," someone else drawled.

Lorna continued. "Well, it's all around town that he won by cheating.

Someone said he used a motor hidden under his schooner, but no one can prove it. The race officials checked but found nothing." Adding drama to the juicy news, she sucked in a breath and held it a few seconds. "Cheating is instant disqualification, you know."

"I would expect it to be so, but..." She wanted to say that Parker would never do such a thing, but he did say he would beat the *Dry Bones*. Perhaps he had cheated. The thought sickened her.

"But what?" Lorna insisted arousing a pitiful moan from her chair as she shifted her bulk.

"I'm sure he has more character than to cheat at something so important."
People snickered and mumbled around her.
Lorna chuffed. "Ha!"

"Wouldn't surprise *me* if he cheated," one man said, his elbow resting on the counter. His eyes narrowed at Claire. "I don't know why anyone would want to keep company with Hollenbeck." More whispers and head nodding followed.

"We'll all know in due time. A person can't get away with much around here—not even rich folk like Parker Hollenbeck," Lorna said.

"He's gotten away with things before," another lady said, casting a glance at Claire, "but I guess people who aren't from around here wouldn't know that."

"Maybe when you see Parker again you can find out all the details of what really happened out there in the bay and come back and let us know," Lorna said, looking collectively at the others who muttered their agreement.

Claire could hardly get out of there quick enough.

⟋ɛɛɛ

The strawberry scone sat cool and untouched on its plate.

Too many things disturbed her about Parker. How could she possibly defend so many concurrent opinions about his character and reputation? How could she believe his claim of being a Christian? How could she be with him when every time she thought about Philip? And after his words to her last Saturday, how could she not be afraid of him? She knew what she had to do, but it wasn't going to be easy. And it had to be done soon.

"I see Holly has taken good care of you," Grace said as she approached her.

"She has, as always."

Grace pulled out a chair and sat. "I've been eager to ask you. Have you discovered any evidence indicating Parker is a Christian?"

Can this woman read my mind? "None, and quite the opposite!" Claire sipped some lukewarm tea. "I've decided not to see him anymore."

"Have you heard what's going around town—about how he won last Saturday's race?"

"Lorna couldn't wait to ask me about it today."

"Do you know anything about it?"

"Other than he determined to win it, no."

"I see."

"I know you tried to warn me about him, Grace, and I should have listened to you. Of course, I had to go do my own thing." Claire set the teacup on its saucer. "But, the next time I see him will be my last. It's time to be done with him and move on."

"Good! I'm glad you've been able to see through his persuasive charisma."

Grace smoothed her hands over her apron. "So…" She lifted the edge of it and smoothed it again. "Could there be anyone else you're interested in?"

Claire averted Grace's eyes.

"Philip England is the most honorable, eligible man around, you know. I wish he were the right age for my Holly, but he is much too old for her."

Claire said nothing.

"I know you care for him, Claire. It's obvious when you're around him."

Care for him? Claire shifted in her chair. *Oh, Grace, if I could only tell you how much I do!*

"Well, will you answer me this? What's wrong with him?"

Claire's voice dropped to just above a whisper. "There is nothing, absolutely nothing wrong with him. It's just that—it's just that his affection is obviously directed toward someone else."

Grace snapped her head back. "It is?"

Claire nodded.

"Are you sure?"

Claire nodded again.

"Who?"

"I can't say."

"Why?"

"I just can't say, that's all."

Claire felt Grace's eyes study her for a minute before she frowned and rose. "I don't know about that. I wouldn't give up on him just yet." She looked around her. "I need to get back to the kitchen."

Claire sighed before reaching into her open purse. She rifled through the mail and lifted out the small box. A postmark from Atlanta, Georgia marked one corner, and a box number with Lone Spruce Cove's name and zip code marked the opposite side.

She tore the brown paper and held a box heavily inked in a blue, green, and purple paisley design. She lifted the lid. Tucked in purple tissue coiled a length of blue ribbon—similar in color and width to the one Philip had cut from her hair.

Grace, that's the problem. There's nothing, absolutely nothing wrong with him. I'm in love with him, and he can never be mine.

Chapter Forty-eight

Claire slid a spatula under a hot cookie and lifted it to test its firmness. *Perfect!* She licked sugar crystals off her finger. While reaching for a dish rag, a soft knock sounded at the front door. Rag in hand, she hurried to open it. A woman stood there holding a silver, trophy-shaped vase of dead roses.

"You must be Claire. I'm Julie."

A needle of guilt pricked Claire's conscience. Up close she looked much like Philip.

Julie held out the urn. A sealed envelope with Claire's name penned on it dangled from one of the handles. "This was sitting on the steps at the house when I arrived. I'm sorry you didn't get it earlier. It must have been beautiful."

Claire warmed to her and took the vase. "Thank you for bringing it."

"We are all arriving later than we thought this weekend. My sister and parents won't be here until tomorrow morning. Philip ran into heavy traffic around Boston but should hopefully make it home before dark."

Claire opened the door wider. "Won't you come in?"

"Oh, I'd love to! I confess I've been eager to see how you've fixed it up. Do you like living here?"

"It's perfect in every way."

Julie peeked into the bedroom as they passed it. "I see you've added some..." Julie stopped and stared at the painting above the bed. "Was that painting there when you moved in?"

"No, I bought it at a gallery last month."

"May I ask why you bought it?"

"Well, first of all I couldn't believe it was a painting of this very cottage. Then I imagined the girl in the picture, even though her hair is darker than mine, to be me. If I—when I—leave here someday, I wanted to be able to look at the picture and remember living here."

Julie smiled at Claire. "That makes sense. I can see why you were drawn to it then."

Claire showed her the rest of the cottage and offered her a sugar-coated, peanut butter cookie from the cookie sheet. "I thought I'd make both chocolate chip and peanut butter cookies for tomorrow night."

"I could smell these all the way up the drive." Julie took a bite. "Mmm! These are delicious! She pointed to the plate of chocolate chip cookies. "Chocolate chip is Philip's favorite kind. He hates peanut butter and wouldn't eat anything made with it if his life depended on it."

Claire snickered at the memory of him eating every bite of the sandwich she had made for their impromptu picnic.

Before leaving, Julie stopped just outside the cottage door. "Even though Philip will be at the shop all day, please come over to the beach earlier and visit with us. He's told us a great deal about you, and we're all looking forward to getting to know you better."

"I will. Bye." As she closed the door behind Julie, she smiled at the thought that Philip had spoken well of her to his family.

~~~

Its flourish forming the "i" in her name, Claire readjusted the fleur-de-lis bottle stopper on the square sign one more time before setting it aside. She leaned her elbows on her worktable and rested her chin in her cupped hands. Her mind drifted to a week and a half ago—the night of July Fourth.

Though she thought of her parents often that day, she had little time to feel sad. Spending the day on the beach, Philip's sisters, brothers-in-law, nephews, and parents included her in everything and made her feel as if she were a part of their family.

Philip's arrival in the evening had completed the gathering. Claire had laughed as he fell exhausted on the sand after giving his young nephews endless piggyback rides and teased him mercilessly about not eating her peanut butter cookies.

His presence had calmed her when the bonfire roared to life. Then, when her anxiety soared as high as the fireworks and she jumped at each explosion, he had plunked one of his nephews onto her lap who succeeded in allaying her fears with his countless hugs and cuddles.

Philip had kept his distance, however, and knowing her place, she honored his loyalty to Vanessa.

But.

As the fire's warm glow had flickered on their faces, she found him watching her, and as discrete as she tried to be, he caught her looking at him as well. When their silent exchanges lingered, her heart would jolt before he looked away.

A cool, off-shore breeze blew through the window and swept across her face, bringing her back from her reverie. She ached for him, yet nothing could be done about it. *I have to put him out of my mind.*

She rose from her stool and closed the window. Grabbing her scissors she stepped though the French doors to snip some roses when she heard a car. *He's home already? Must be later than I thought.*

A knock hammered on her front door. She tossed the scissors and roses on the step before rounding the cottage.

A chill sprinted up her spine. "Parker? What are you doing here?"

"I've come to see you, of course. Let's go down to the beach."

She looked beyond him at Philip's empty driveway.

"Oh, come now, darling." He turned her about and, with his arm around her shoulders, propelled her around the cottage and down the path to the beach.

"It's only Thursday. I never expect to see you during the week like this."

"Ah, I've surprised you! Perfect! I'm glad to see you're alone."

"Parker, of course I'm alone!"

As they walked along the beach, his arm slipped to her waist, and he pulled her closer. "I drove from Boston just to be with you tonight."

"Whatever for?"

Parker stopped, dropped his arm, and spun her around to face him.

God, give me strength to tell him I don't want to see him anymore.

"I can wait no longer. It's time—and the sooner the better." He reached into his pocket, took her left hand, and slipped a large, pear-shaped diamond ring on her finger. "I want you to be my wife."

Claire's mouth dropped open. The diamond glistened like an oversized teardrop on her finger. "*Marry* you?"

Parker wrapped one arm around her shoulder and, threading the fingers of his other hand through her hair, pulled her toward him. With unyielding strength, he crushed her against him and covered her lips with his.

Chapter Forty-nine

I'm going to do it. Philip whistled as he locked the store and headed for his jeep. *Besides, how can I be sure unless I get to know her better? Maybe tonight she'll want to come back into town for an ice cream.*

His whistling stopped when he rounded the back of the buildings.

In the shadows of the parking area, Vanessa leaned against his jeep. One high-heeled shoe touched the ground while the other hung by its heel from the footboard. Her aqua dress, one he remembered well, fluttered up in the breeze, revealing her legs.

Lord, please give me wisdom, he prayed as he walked toward her. *And strength!*

"I've been waiting for you."

"What do you want, Vanessa?"

"Oh, come, love. So cold?" she pouted. Swinging her foot down, she placed her hands on his upper arms and stepped close to him. "We both know we're meant for each other. I know deep in your heart you still love me. Of course, I've never stopped loving you. Let's put the past behind us and start over."

As if her hands were coated with mud, he reached up, grabbed her wrists, and pulled them off. "You know we can't, and you know why we can't." He crossed his arms. "So why exactly is it that after—how long has it been now? over two years?—you've suddenly decided to pursue me?"

"You've been encouraging me. You eagerly engaged in our little intimate discussion at the gallery…"

"Be sensible, Vanessa. I thought you actually had something important to ask me. That's *it*."

"*You* pulled me into the alcove for privacy and did more than just answer my questions—you lingered."

"Lingered? Yeah, for maybe ten seconds. I should have known you were setting a trap."

"A trap? You can't deny you enjoyed being close to me again both at the gallery and at the festival."

"I do deny it."

Her honeyed voice slowed to a drip. "I know you came to the gallery just to see me that night; besides, you bought the cottage painting. You can't deny that, 'Anonymous' purchaser or not…" She carved quotes in the air with her slender fingers.

"First of all, you know I go to all of Margot's gallery nights. I dreaded seeing you and Barbara that night but was there only to support Margot. I approached you and suggested we speak in the alcove only because Barbara said you had something crucial to ask me. Secondly…" He felt his face grow hot. "I did not buy that painting." He struggled to control his anger. "I *wouldn't* buy it."

"But I know for a fact it was delivered to your house. That alone proved to me you wanted me back."

Ahh! That's what that was. "Claire must have bought it." He ran his fingers through his hair. "That must have been what I carried to the cottage for her."

Vanessa's countenance changed at the mention of Claire's name. She narrowed her eyes into slits. "Oh, yes, your little tenant."

Philip stood akimbo. "So, I've found your sore spot. I think you're only pursuing me because Claire is living at the cottage." He bounced his head up and down. "Yes—yes, this all started after she arrived in town. You don't like her living so close to me, do you? You're worried we'll fall in love. You're envious of her."

"Envious of Claire?" A high-pitched laugh twittered from her throat. "I could never be envious of her. She's plain and is nothing more than a common laborer. She's not from around here. She's *nothing*." Vanessa jutted her chin out. "I can have anything and anyone I want which is something she could never say."

How dare she talk about Claire like that! Seething, Philip glared at her. "You may think you can have anyone you want, but I assure you, you can never have me."

Her eyes flamed.

"The relationship we had at one time is over, Vanessa, *over*! I am not the same man from the past, and you just need to accept that."

She crossed her arms and turned her head away from him.

"Unfortunately, you have never changed. Thanks to you and your half-truths, I struggle trusting others, but with God's help I'll overcome it despite you."

She chuffed and pulled her hair over her shoulder.

"You only do or say things to benefit yourself. You never think of others and how your actions may affect them."

"That's not true!"

"Oh, and who paid off Abel Longpre so that you could take his place at the festival? Did you really think I wouldn't find out?"

"I didn't pay him, Parker did."

Philip gritted his teeth. "Vanessa, you may be beautiful on the outside, but you're deceptive and ugly on the inside. No matter what I may have said in the past, you are not the one I love and never will be."

Vanessa placed one hand on her hip and pointed her red fingernail inches from his face. "Well, if you think you love your little tenant and are planning to run to her you won't succeed."

"And what is that supposed to mean?"

A churlish smile spread across her face. "My brother is proposing to her as we speak and is going to whisk her away as soon as he can get his hands on her."

What? Surely not. "You're lying."

"I'm not!"

"She actually wants him?"

"She's been quite clear that she loves him, so, of course, she'll marry him."

The possibility of her words being truthful, even in part, dealt him a sickening blow. "I don't believe you."

"She needs him, and he needs her." Vanessa lifted an eyebrow. "At least he needs her long enough to get what he wants from her."

Philip clenched his jaw as concern for her safety now closed in on his mind.

"Just think about it, Philip." She dipped her words in wickedness. "They're probably kissing passionately on your beach at this very moment."

Chapter Fifty

Claire squirmed under Parker's suffocating grip and moved her head away from his unwelcome lips. "What are you doing?"

"What I've wanted to do for a long time."

She pulled her arms out of his embrace and pushed against his chest. "Stop! Let me go!"

Parker grinned and, with both arms now around her back, strengthened his hold. "I'm not letting you go, my darling."

"Why do you think I would marry you?"

"Don't you find me attractive?"

"Well, yes—"

"Doesn't my wealth and status impress you?"

"Yes, but—"

"There then."

"But there's more to marrying someone than that."

"You've gone out with me several times now, haven't you?"

"Of course."

"You've accepted my gifts and advances. I've had nothing but encouragement from you. You had no problem with my claiming you as mine."

"You wouldn't let me say otherwise!"

A laugh erupted from Parker and echoed off the cliff.

"I've gone out with you, yes, but it was to get to know you or—or to do something new or interesting." She again wiggled in his arms. "But, *marriage?* We hardly see each other. We barely know each other."

Finding her struggling futile against his strong arms, she eased her resistance.

His laugh calmed. "Ah, but I know you better than you think, and that's what's important," he boasted. "I know about your life and work back in the Chicago area. I know about your parents. I know you are a very wealthy young woman. I know that your former boyfriend's name is Daniel Smith, though I haven't located him yet. There are a lot of Daniel Smiths in Chicago."

Claire stiffened and stared at him.

"I'm an attorney, don't forget—and a good one. It's my business to know things about people." The look in his eyes sent a shiver up her back. "You're a beautiful woman, Claire, so youthful and full of unaffected spirit. You're perfect for me." He pulled her against him and kissed her again.

Squirming and pushing, she contorted her body to look back toward Philip's house. *Where are you?*

Parker gave her a sharp twist, forcing her to face him. "England's not home, Claire. You want me, not a simple shopkeeper full of dull religious talk and stuffy morals. Besides, he's already taken."

"He and Vanessa…" She couldn't finish.

"Yes, for some unknown reason he's the only man Vanessa has ever loved and wanted. I'm not about to let you force your way between them now that they've rekindled the past."

Weakness overcame her.

"When the date of their marriage approaches, you'll need to consider your living arrangements. I assure you once Vanessa is the mistress of this estate, you will not be welcome here."

She slumped in his arms and dropped her head against his shoulder. His sandalwood cologne nauseated her.

"That's a girl. Don't fight me." His grip on her loosened, and he rubbed his hand through her hair and kissed her forehead. "See what I'm trying to tell you? I want you, and you need me. Soon you'll have nowhere to live and nowhere to go. Be my wife."

She raised her head.

"Come with me tonight. We'll elope." His cold hungering eyes looked black in the fading sunlight. "Then you'll be all mine."

She shivered again before rearing back. This time he let her put some space between them. "But...but..." *What do I do, Lord?*

"Ah, but you need assurance. As I was saying, I know how your parents died—terrible way to die—though clearly it was your father's fault."

His words stabbed her heart. "How could you say such a thing?"

"It's the truth, darling. The truth hurts sometimes."

"It's not true!"

"Hugh and Jake, yes, are your cousins. I've known that for quite a while now. You have no other living relatives. I know why you moved to Maine." He leaned and whispered in her ear. "I know your secret." He kissed her ear and the side of her face.

She bent her head away from his lips.

"Your cousins are also searching for the granite deposit."

The purpose of the riddle!

"But we can find it before they do if you and I combine our knowledge and resources to solve the riddle. Once that beautiful granite is extracted, we'll be wealthy beyond our dreams, and our circles will not be confined to Boston and this pathetic little community. I'll finally be able to run for the Senate. Just think, darling, you'll be a senator's wife."

"You're using me!" Her chest burned, and tears welled in her eyes. "You don't want to marry me because you love me. You just—"

"Don't be silly. Of course I love you. Do you really think I would lie to you? Why else would I want you to marry me?"

"For the money!"

"No, it's not just because of that. I have money without you—though more is always better. It's because I want you, Claire, and I want what we can accomplish together." His grip around her arms tightened.

She wiggled and strained to get away. "You want that granite deposit."

He squinched his eyes. "Don't resist me, Claire." Vines of agitation coiled around his charisma, and he talked through his teeth. "I'm used to getting what I want, and I want you all to myself. I know someone in Hydeport who could marry us tonight."

His composure rattled her. "Tonight? No, I will *not*! I do not love you, and—and—"

"Your love for me will come in time."

"But, I *can't* marry you."

"You can't? And why exactly is that?"

"B—because you…" *Lord, I'm afraid!*

"Yes?"

"Because I—I don't think you're really a Christian. I will only marry a Christian." *There. Something he couldn't deny.*

Parker jutted his chin as if his collar had suddenly tightened. His nostrils widened as he drew in a long, slow breath. His smile belied his piercing eyes. "Ah, but you underestimate me, Claire," he whispered. "I will be whatever you want me to be and will persuade you otherwise when I can't." He thrust his hand through her hair again and forced his lips onto hers.

She writhed then jerked her head aside and, with a mighty shove against his embrace, freed her arms from his imprisonment. In an instant, she drew her right hand up and raked her fingernails cross his left cheek before pulling the diamond ring off her finger.

"Ow!" he yelled. He released her and lifted his hands to the deep gouge she inflicted.

She stepped back.

Blood oozed from his cheek and dripped onto his hands and shirt. "What have you done?" he snarled. "No one ever makes a fool of me and gets away with it."

She hurled the ring as hard as she could over his shoulder. He twisted his body and reached a bloodied hand to catch it, but it sailed over him.

"Why, you—" He sped after the expensive ring before the surf dragged it into the ocean.

She turned, fled across the beach, scrambled up the bank, and raced to the cottage. Grabbing the scissors from the back step, she flew through the open French doors and locked them.

Through the window she saw Parker running up the pathway. Her chest heaving, she sprinted to the front door to lock it before dashing into the closet in the darkened hallway and closing the pocket door. *Lord, please help! Don't let him get in.*

Mimicking Claire's heart, Parker pounded his fist on the back doors. The lock rattled. "Let me in!" he barked. He slammed his body against the door and banged on the windows. He growled her name before all fell silent.

She waited. Nothing.

Wham! Wham! Wham! She jumped as Parker pummeled the front door. His voice boomed while he tried the latch. "You just wait until I get my hands on you, Claire!"

Cowering in the back corner, she pointed the scissors toward the pocket door. She tugged at a flannel shirt hanging overhead until it fell and wadded it against her knotted stomach, willing her shaking to stop.

The hammering stopped. She heard a car door slam and the sound of an engine fading into the night.

Eerie silence crept through the dark shadows of the cottage.

She sat erect and strained to hear the slightest noise. The faint sound of a car reached her ears. *He's back!* She sat shaking but silent as every part of her focused on listening. After waiting an eternity, she could bear it no longer. She dropped the scissors and sobbed into the flannel shirt until the beating in her head became intolerable and choking breaths spurted from her lungs.

She could flee to Philip's house. Would he be home now? He would be kind and understanding and perhaps even protective. *No, I can't do it.* The confirmation—the finality—of his impending marriage to Vanessa filled her with despair. A fresh round of sobbing ensued.

She chided herself for not listening to Grace—for becoming entangled in Parker's web. She wiped the lingering smell of Parker's cologne off her face and neck. Desperate to erase his kisses, she rubbed her lips against the flannel shirt. Over and over she abraded them until she tasted blood.

The taste of blood.

Her mind sped to the night at the coffee shop with Daniel. As the memories returned, her body tingled as if she had been an onlooker instead of a participant.

Chapter Fifty-one

"Claire? What are you doing here? I thought I told you not to come here unless I'm with you. Who else has been here?"

"I've only seen Zach."

"Zach, huh?"

"Oh, Daniel. He and I have barely spoken. I've been too busy working on this floor. So what do you think?" The project had been behind schedule, and she had wanted to get the tiling done to please him.

"Not bad. It'll pass for a coffee shop bathroom. Are you done then?"

"Yup! I just need to clean these tools then I'm going to head back to my place."

"Now? But I just got here. Wait for me. I should only be another hour—hour and a half at most.

"But I'm exhausted and really want to get home before dark."

"You're not stopping anywhere on the way home are you?"

"Looking like this? No."

"Anything from your attorney yet?"

"Not as of this morning."

"Ugh! What's taking so long?" He had booted a block of wood out the open back door.

"We'll know the total in time. I never expected anything from my parents, so whatever the amount I'll be content."

"It's us, not just you, remember, and every dollar matters. Speaking of us, you've had plenty of time to think it over. When are you going to marry me?"

215

"Oh...Daniel, I'm just not ready yet."

"How much more time do you need? Don't I mean anything to you?"

"Of course you do."

"You don't show it. I've held your hand ever since your parents died and helped you with your finances, gotten rid of your annoying friends, and even gave you this job. And what have I gotten in return? A girlfriend who could care less about me and my feelings."

"That's not true. I do care for you, and you've done more than I could ever repay."

"Then marry me. I've already claimed you as mine, so marrying me will be your repayment."

"But it's been so hard to move on from my parents' deaths let alone think about getting married right now. There are too many things to sort out in my mind."

"Don't you see? That's what I've been trying to tell you. You can't function without me. With all the crying and moping around you do all the time, who else would put up with you?"

"But I'm still grieving." She had barely started to heal from the rawness of her parents' deaths.

"What does grieving have to do with getting married? Besides, you should be over their deaths by now. After all, it's been three whole months!"

"But—"

"Snap out of it, Claire. I'm tired of waiting around for you to make up your mind."

She had inched closer to the back door as his agitation mounted.

"Look, this job should finally be wrapped up by the middle of next week. Let's get married next weekend. We'll fly to Vegas. I'll plan everything."

"But I—I'm not sure I..."

"What? What could you possibly not be sure about?"

"I'm just not sure I love you enough to marry you."

"Love? Who said anything about love?"

"You mean—you want to marry me but you don't love me?"

"Don't you get it, baby? Your parents' deaths have made you unstable and incapable of giving or receiving love. No one will want you, but I'm willing to *take care of you despite that. Come on. What's your answer—yes or no?"*

His degradation had sent her self-confidence spiraling. *"I can't."*

"Can't or won't?"

"Won't."

"Don't reject me, Claire. I may not give you another chance."

"But…"

"Something's going on between you and Zach isn't there?" Never before had she seen such fury in his eyes.

"Of course not!"

"Zach? Get over here!"

His hands had felt like sandpaper as they clenched her wrists.

"Daniel, that hurts!"

"Zach? Where are you?

"Maybe we shouldn't see each other anymore."

"Don't even think of leaving me or you'll regret it. You're mine."

"No, Daniel! You're hurting me! I want to leave."

"If you try anything, don't ever forget there's nowhere in this city you can hide where I can't find you and bring you back."

"Let go of me!"

"Yeah, I'll let go of you all right!"

The memory of Daniel hurting her, something he had not done before that night, sent her huddling further into the corner of the closet. She squeezed her burning eyes as hot tears flooded down her cheeks.

As the clunking of Zach's tool belt had gotten louder, Daniel had shoved her out the back door of the coffee shop. She had tumbled to the bottom of the steps bruising her arms and legs and biting a hole in her tongue. He had lobbed a hammer at her that had breezed by her hair as it whizzed past. Who knows what else Daniel would have done had Zach not intervened and told her to run.

Just as she had done then, she hid.

In the darkness, fear tormented her and loneliness scorned her once again. Too spent to pray, she clutched the flannel shirt and curled her body into a tight ball, weeping until she fell into an exhausted sleep.

v v v

I can't believe she's going to marry Parker—of all people! I can't believe she loves him.

Philip's mind overflowed with consternation. Should he have been bolder? Should he have asked her out earlier? How could he have misjudged the attraction between them?

As he sped along the highway home, he hoped for the first time ever that Vanessa had lied to him.

At least if she had told him the truth, she saved him the pain of making an idiot of himself. Perhaps the reluctance that had kept him from declaring his affection had been a blessing in disguise.

While lifting his finger to push down on the turn signal, Parker's sporty car careened out of his driveway and zipped away from him toward Hydeport.

No!

Philip gripped the steering wheel and gave it a quick twist. After his jeep lurched down the driveway, the sight of Claire's car and the dark cottage melted away any concern for her wellbeing and rendered him numb.

She left with him. She really left with him. He halted in front of his garage, got out, and trudged into his house.

As the night progressed, he struggled to rein in his thoughts as he worked on paperwork. His mind wandered as he read his Bible and prayed. He doubted sleep would come, but had to give it a chance, since only a few hours now remained before dawn.

Sticking to his nightly ritual of the past month and a half, he clicked off the lamp on his bedside table and looked down through the window before removing his glasses. The moon, like a pearl nestled on a silk pillow, cast its luster across the rippling ocean and shrouded the beach and cottage in shadows. No golden glow emanated from the cottage and warmed his heart tonight.

He wrestled with the thought of the woman he loved being in Parker's arms—perhaps at this very moment.

He yanked his glasses off and threw them on the table. *Oh, Claire, how could you!*

Chapter Fifty-two

The bell jingled, and Philip looked up from scribbling on a piece of paper. "Grace? What are you doing here?"

She could tell in an instant something was amiss. "I couldn't catch you in time after the service. I've left the tearoom in Holly's hands, so I'm only here for a second. Have you seen Claire? It was unlike her not to come to the tearoom yesterday, and she hasn't missed a church service since she's lived here."

He answered in a monotone. "I have no idea where she is."

"I'm worried she's ill."

"I'm sure she's fine." He darted the pencil into a cup beside the cash register. "I'm going to make a phone call." He turned his back and strode to his office.

Grace scowled as she watched him go and put her fists on her hips. Marie walked up to her. "What's eating him, Marie?"

"I don't know. He's been awfully quiet since Friday morning, and when he does talk, he's short-tempered. Emma and I wish he'd just go home."

"Mmm. You haven't seen Claire have you?"

Marie shook her head.

Grace sighed. *I'm going to get to the bottom of this.*

～ɛɛ～

Early Monday afternoon, Grace rapped on the cottage door.

Nothing.

She knocked harder. "Claire? Claire? are you home?"

Silence.

Splatters of rust-colored paint had dried on the latch. She bent for a closer look and flicked at the paint with her fingernail. *Looks like blood.* Her heart quickened. She pounded her fist on the door. "Claire? It's Grace. I'll break in if I have to!"

The lock ticked, and four fingers curled around the edge of the door as it cracked open.

Grace leaned toward the narrow opening. "Claire?"

An aqua eye, rimmed by puffy-red crinkles and underscored by a line of purple, blinked at her before the four fingers opened the door wider. "Oh, Grace, you came!"

～～～

A cascading pile of wet tissues and five cups of tea later, Claire swiped at yet another tear with her knuckle and folded her hands in her lap.

Empathetic, Grace had kept silent as Claire spoke. After draining the last swig of now-cold tea from a green tumbler, she clunked it on the table. "You haven't really grieved since your parents' deaths, have you?"

Claire shook her head.

Sympathy swelled in Grace's heart. "Have you not talked to anyone about it?"

Claire picked up a wet tissue and wiped a drip from her nose. "The loneliness since their deaths has been almost unbearable at times. Daniel drove away the few friends I had, and you've been the only person patient enough to sit and listen. It feels so relieving to talk about it though. Somehow telling you about the guilt I've felt—saying it out loud—helps me realize how unrealistic I've been."

"You haven't been unrealistic, Claire. Your feelings have been normal, but I'm glad you realize you have nothing to feel guilty about. It simply wasn't your time to die."

"I see that now, but it's going to take a while to accept it."

"Of course it will." Grace traced the tumbler's classic motif with her fingertip. "Do you see any similarities between Daniel and Parker? A pattern perhaps?"

Claire hung her head then nodded.

"And what type of men are they?"

"But they both did so much for me, and I..."

"Claire, what type of men are they?"

Claire gulped. "Selfish?"

"And?"

"Controlling?"

"Uh-huh." She leaned closer to Claire. "While not all are violent, controllers can make a person's life miserable no matter how charming they are or what they do for you."

"I've been so gullible—so stupid."

"Oh, now. The main thing is you got away from these guys before it was too late. Learn from your experiences by recognizing and avoiding this type of man *before* you get involved with him."

"I should have listened to my parents. I should have listened to you."

"It's all in the past now. It's time to move on."

Claire drew in a stuttering breath and released it slowly. "You're right."

"Just remember, though, not all men are the same."

"I never really loved either of them, you know, and Daniel was wrong. I am capable of loving." She tapped her fingertips against her chest. "So capable it hurts." Her voice softened to a whisper. "But the one I truly love I can't have."

Claire's anguish crushed Grace's heart. "You haven't said one word about him during the last hour and a half. You're still not going to tell me what you know are you?"

She shook her head. More tears rolled down her cheeks.

"And it has something to do with why you haven't gone to him since last Thursday?"

Claire nodded.

They sat in silence for a moment. *I'm going help resolve this if it's the last thing I do!* A plan formed in Grace's mind.

"Well, Philip or no Philip, don't ever forget you have friends—true friends—who care about you and will help you if you ever need it. None of us is ever too busy. You don't have to run. You don't have to hide."

"But what if Parker finds Daniel and tells him where I am?"

"Daniel wouldn't be in the Cove long before the whole town would know, and you'd have half the church at your side supporting you in an instant."

Tears raced down each cheek.

"It would help if you had a phone. There *are* ways to keep Daniel from calling you, you know."

"I know."

"Listen, you don't have to suffer in fear and loneliness again. In fact, it's impossible for you to ever be truly alone again, since God is always with you no matter what."

A weary smile crossed Claire's face. The sores on her lips crackled and started to bleed. "Thanks, Grace. I needed this, and I so needed you to come."

Grace patted her hand then pushed the tumbler toward Claire as she rose. "I should get going. You know, sipping hot tea out of a tumbler is not working for this girl," she said pointing to herself.

"I'm sorry!"

"No apologies necessary. We'll have to see what we can do about it, that's all."

Claire rose as well.

"You need to get out of this cottage. You've been cooped up for too long. Come, let's go outside. It's a lovely day." Grace led Claire into the sunshine and onto the stones that led to the beach's zigzag path. She motioned to the hesitant Claire. "Come on!"

Claire bit her lip.

"You did the right thing in resisting Parker and fleeing, but you can't live every day as if he were going to return to harm you. I can't say this with certainty, but he probably would've come back already if he intended to hurt you. No doubt his anger has passed, though I'd stay clear of him from now on if I were you."

"Believe me, I plan on it."

"Do you realize if you had married him you would have been his fifth wife and the stepmother to, let me see, at least seven children that I know of?"

Claire sucked in a quick breath.

"By remaining miserable and fearful, you are allowing Parker Hollenbeck to control you whether he's around or not. I know with God's help the fear and heaviness of heart will dissipate, and you'll start living again."

Claire looked back toward Philip's house. "I don't know if some of the ache will ever go away, though."

"You can't avoid Philip forever, Claire. It's best to get things out in the open. Be frank and truthful with him. Then you must simply accept whatever happens and move on."

Chapter Fifty-three

Grace leaned out the car window. "Remember our agreement. I won't tell anyone about anything you told me including the blue granite—unless for some reason I *absolutely* must—and you won't go into that cottage for at least an hour. Also, you'll turn your lights on tonight and won't tell a soul I was here today."

"Agreed!" Claire lips bled again as she gave her a half-cocked smile.

"Promise?"

"Promise!"

Grace headed back to town, parked behind the row of buildings, and hurried to the tearoom. "Do you mind staying for just a little bit longer, honey?" she asked Tim. "This is important. I'll explain later." He nodded as she picked out one of the pretty teacups from the morning's shipment and wrapped it in tissue. After placing it into a small box, she hastened to the Compass Rose.

"Is Philip here?" she asked Emma, glancing around the shop. Emma frowned and jutted her thumb over her shoulder in the direction of the back office.

When Grace popped her head in, she found Philip standing, staring out the window with his arms crossed. "Afternoon, Philip. Will you do me a favor?" Without waiting for an answer, she held out the box. "This came in a shipment this morning and is for Claire. Will you please take it to her?"

He continued staring out the window. "Sure. Throw it on the desk, and I'll leave it on the doorstep tonight."

"I'd really like it if you took it to her now."

He turned toward her. "Now? I have a shop to take care of."

"I know, but it's slow right now. Emma is here and is very capable. Besides, you want to get out for a few moments, and you know it." She nodded in the direction of the window.

He huffed.

"I can't tell you what to do, but I think you should check up on her. If she—"

"She won't be there, Grace. She left with someone Thursday night. The cottage has been dark and quiet ever since, and her car hasn't moved. She's *not there*."

Grace kept her voice quiet and steady. "But if she happened to be there and needed your help in some way you'd feel bad when you learned about it knowing you could have helped her sooner."

He stared at her for a moment before expelling an irritated sigh. "Oh, all right. I'll go."

~⁓⁓~

Philip stepped from his SUV and slammed the door. "I know she's not here," he muttered aloud. With the box under one arm, he knocked on the cottage door, then bent over the latch. *What's with the red paint?*

He knocked again. No answer. The closed Roman shade prevented him from looking in the window. Perhaps he could see through the windows at the back. He turned left and rounded the cottage.

He stopped.

With head craned looking behind her, Claire ran full speed toward him. A pair of scissors in her right hand pointed directly at him.

Philip pitched the box into the grass and in an instant grabbed her wrist with his left hand. As she whammed into him at full momentum, he engulfed her body with his right arm and held her against him.

She screamed. "No, no, don't hurt me. Let me go!" Shaking, she pushed against his chest and cried hysterically. "Don't hurt me!"

"Whoa! Whoa!" He released his arm from around her but still held her wrist at arm's length. "I'm not going to hurt you, Claire."

She choked on her breath. "It's you!"

"Of course it's me! If you promise not to impale me with those," he said, eyeing the scissors, "I'll let you go."

She sniffled and wiped her nose on her free arm. "I promise."

Philip gradually loosened his grasp, and her wrist and the scissors fell to her side.

"I wouldn't hurt you!"

She forced breaths from her chest and lifted a shaking hand to rub her eye with a knuckle.

"Who did you think I was?"

"What are you doing here? You're hardly ever here during the day like this."

"Claire, I live here. What are *you* doing here?"

She opened and closed the points of the scissors a few times. "I'm cutting roses. I heard a car and—and a voice and a knock, and thought I heard someone coming around the cottage that way," she said, pointing to the corner behind her.

He looked over her shoulder and scanned the premises. Thankfully, he didn't see Parker. He bent and picked up the box in the grass. "Grace wanted me to bring this and check up on you."

Claire accepted the box. "Dear Grace," she whispered.

Philip searched her face. Her swollen, blood-shot eyes had sunk into a pallid face. Dried blood caked on strange sores on her lips. "What happened? Have you been ill?"

"No." She turned and walked toward the French doors then picked up a cut rose lying in the grass. She set the box and scissors on the step and placed the rose on top of others that had been gathered into a pile on the stoop. She then occupied herself rearranging the pile of roses for a few moments before straightening. "I'm enjoying the roses while I can."

Seeing her again, especially when he hadn't expected to, disconcerted him. He thrust his hands into his pockets and strode past her to stand behind the rosebushes on the edge of the cliff. Not even their sweet smell offered any solace.

He felt Claire's presence beside him but couldn't look at her. He kicked at a rock sticking above the ground until it loosened. A seagull called above their heads before it swooped down and skimmed the surface of the water beside the weir poles.

She spoke first. "I suppose I'll be leaving here soon. When do you think I should move?"

He flicked the jackknife in his pocket back and forth. "I suppose for the sake of everyone as soon as possible."

⁓⁓⁓

His words sunk Claire's heart further. "I shall truly miss being here," she said. "I'll miss everything about it." *Especially you.*

Philip bristled. "Well, you'll have your own estate to enjoy—one much grander than this."

How did he find out I have money? Does he know about the riddle too? "I suppose the whole town knows everything."

"It's hard to keep big news quiet in a small town like this, Claire. You know that. Rest assured though. No one learned anything from me." He kicked the rock, sending it flying through the bushes. It bounced on the beach below them. "Your marrying Hollenbeck will undoubtedly give people plenty to talk about for the rest of the month."

"Marrying *Parker*? I'm not marrying Parker!"

Philip's head whipped toward her. "You're not? You haven't?"

"No!"

"But, aren't you engaged? You didn't elope? I was told…" He swallowed. "…that you were going to marry him—if you haven't already."

"No! No, he tried very hard to convince me to marry him, but I refused."

"But I thought you had—" He could hardly say the words. "—had left with him Thursday night. I saw him hightailing from my driveway as I came home. The cottage—it's been dark ever since."

Claire's voice quieted. "I've been hiding inside the whole time."

"Hiding?"

"I've been afraid."

"Afraid? Of what?"

She moistened the dried blood on her tender bottom lip with her tongue.

Philip's eyes flared. "Did Hollenbeck...? Did he hurt you?"

"No, not exactly."

"What does that mean?"

"Well, I made him very angry with me. He almost tried to force me to marry him—as if someone can actually force someone to marry—by telling me all these things and holding me tightly and kissing me."

Philip closed his eyes and clamped his teeth. His neck turned red as he ran his fingers through his hair.

"I scratched his face and threw his engagement ring on the beach behind him and escaped by bolting to the cottage when he went after the ring. I locked myself in and grabbed my scissors to defend myself in case he could get in. I think if he had been able to get in he—he might have hurt me."

"And you were afraid that—ahh, you thought I was Parker and had returned for you."

She nodded.

"Oh, Claire, I'm sorry. I'm so sorry. Here all of this happened on my own property, and I didn't protect you."

His tenderness worsened the ache in her heart.

"You should have come to me right away. Why didn't you? Why have you stayed away from me the past four days?"

"I—I couldn't go to you."

"Why?"

Tears spilled from her eyes. Grace's words burned in her mind. *Be frank and truthful... accept whatever happens and move on.* "Because Parker confirmed that you will be marrying Vanessa, and the finality of it—of knowing that you would be forever hers—left me..." She rubbed a rose petal between her fingers and whispered, "...heartbroken."

Heartbroken? Is it possible? As hope surged within him, Philip fought to stay composed.

He lifted her chin with his forefinger and slid his thumb across it and up her soft cheek to whisk away a falling tear. "I assure you, Claire, I'm not marrying Vanessa."

Her eyes grew round, and her chin pushed atop his finger.

"She's not a Christian, and it would never work. Besides, I don't love her." He yearned to hold her in his arms and comfort her and tell her about his relief and about his love for her. But not now. She needed time.

And he needed time. He needed to use his head and not his heart. He wouldn't be able to bear another crushing mistake.

Chapter Fifty-four

As Claire stood in the empty post office, Lorna shuffled from one side of the back room to the other, carrying an armload of envelopes. "I'll be right there," she called through the doorway. "I need to have these ready for pickup at noon."

"No problem," Claire shouted back before dropping the small box she held on the counter. She reread the address she had penned—"O.U.C.H., Attn. Hollenbeck". *I wonder if the other attorneys at his law firm cause as much pain as he does.* Mailing the brooch and bracelet back would not make him happy, but it would give her closure.

"Sorry about that, Claire," Lorna said as she heaved herself onto her chair. "Now, let's see. What do we have here?"

Claire pushed the box toward her.

"Did you ever find out if Parker cheated in that race?"

"I never asked him."

"Too bad! We'd all really like to know."

Well, you won't find out from me!

"You know, Marcy Hill said her husband was talking with Ron and Donna Stuben who were in Hydeport—it must have been two weeks ago now—for one of their district meetings. After their meeting they went to the Harborside Café for a cup of coffee before heading home."

Lorna swatted a shock of fuzzy-red hair that limped over one of her eyebrows.

"You know who they saw there? Parker—sitting by himself in a corner. He looked really upset and kept trying to pull his jacket up over this horrible scratch on his cheek. Ron said he had blood all over his shirt too. Of course, Ron had to ask him how he got the scratch, and Parker said it was from a cat."

Lorna held out her hand. "That will be $3.15."

Slashing Parker replayed in Claire's mind. She avoided Lorna's eyes as she handed her a ten dollar bill.

"Now, Donna said it didn't look like a scratch from a cat. The scratch was bigger and deeper than a cat scratch, but Parker insisted it was and even said he was determined to put the cat down for good someday soon. Imagine that? Put a cat to sleep just because it scratches you? Some people are just plain mean. Poor cat. Don't you think it's mean?"

Claire steadied her breathing to stay calm. "I couldn't say. I've never owned a cat."

Lorna suspended the change in the air above Claire's hand. Her tone changed. "I suppose you don't know anything about that scratch."

"Neither Parker nor his sisters have ever mentioned to me that they had a cat."

Lorna dropped the coins in Claire's hand.

Claire placed them in her purse as she turned to leave. "Thank you, Lorna. Have a pleasant day."

She breathed a sigh of relief as she hurried to her car.

✀✀✀

Grace wiped her hands on her apron and scanned the tearoom. Claire sat by the window smoothing clotted cream over a gingerbread scone. She walked up to her. "I didn't know you were here."

"Holly has taken good care of me." She set the knife on the plate. "This scone is delicious."

"Glad you like it. It's a new recipe." She sat next to her. "So, what are you up to today?"

"I'm spoiling myself. I had an early breakfast on the beach, snipped a huge

231

bouquet of roses, took a long bubble bath, and read several chapters of a novel I found last week at a book sale. I stopped at the post office—but only because I had to—and now I'm having my favorite light lunch before shopping the rest of the afternoon."

The many talks and prayers were paying off, and Grace delighted in Claire's steady improvement since two weeks ago. "What a wonderful day! It almost sounds like you're celebrating something."

"I am. It's my birthday."

"I didn't know that! Why didn't you tell me?"

Claire scrunched her nose. "I'm not going to go around and tell people it's my birthday."

An idea popped into Grace's head. "Well, happy, happy birthday! Your tea and scone are definitely on me today."

"No, no. I never would have told you if I knew you were going to do that."

"I know, but I insist. It's the sort of thing friends do for one another."

Claire beamed.

"Now if you'll excuse me, I have something I must do."

Grace walked to the far side of the cash register, scratched a note on a piece of paper, and shooed Holly out the door with it.

↬↬↬

"Thank you for the tea and scone."

"I wish I could make your day more special or have you over for dinner, but since Tim is up in Augusta today, it's only Holly and me until closing," Grace said as she walked Claire to the door.

"I feel safe and loved today, and I've had good wishes from you, one of my dearest friends. Nothing could be more special than that."

Grace gave her a light hug. "Going to the Compass Rose today?"

"Yes! I'm going to buy a pair of sterling, chair-shaped earrings I noticed in the window display the other day."

Claire left the tearoom and walked to the Compass Rose. The earrings still sat in their sandy display.

As she entered the shop, Philip fanned a stack of paper bags in the air above the counter. "Good afternoon, ma'am!" A boyish grin spread across his face. "So nice of you to visit my shop today. Is there anything I can assist you with?" He placed the bags under the cash register and reached for the remaining stack.

"Well, sir, I'm interested in a pair of the silver Adirondack chair earrings in your window."

"I'm sorry, but I'm not going to sell them to you right now." He loosened the ends of the bags in the air with another loud flapping sound before setting them beneath the counter.

What? She cocked her head. "You're not?"

"Instead of shopping today, would you give me the honor of allowing me to take you out for a bit of fun this afternoon then to an early dinner?"

Her eyes widened.

"You can shop any day, but an adventure is necessary on one's birthday."

"How did you know?"

"That will forever remain my secret, but with strings pulled in a short period of time—not to mention a bit of bribery," he said exchanging glances with a smiling Emma and Marie, "an afternoon with a birthday girl has been planned—if she wishes to go with me."

Claire's cheeks burned. "Oh, I do. I'd love to!"

"I'll meet you at the cottage in 15 minutes. Wear comfortable shoes."

Chapter Fifty-five

As they traveled along a twisting secondary road, Claire rubbed her sweaty palms. She wrestled between trusting Philip and desiring to be with him. They had spoken only sporadically since they discovered the other wasn't marrying a Hollenbeck.

He's not like them. She checked off the many differences between him and Daniel and Parker. But Daniel and Parker had been nice at first too. "*Not all men are the same,*" Grace had said.

Lord, please help me relax. If he's trustworthy, please help me trust him.

Philip's light conversation centered on and included her, something the other two had rarely done, and soon her anxiety calmed.

Philip parked his jeep in the parking lot of a state park, and when they got out, he led her to a wide, well-traveled path. "This path follows the water, and the scenery is grand. I hope you don't mind hiking."

"I haven't hiked since last summer. This will be fabulous!"

As they began their hike, he asked, "So, what do you normally do on your birthday? What did your parents do to make your day special?"

Dear Philip! He knew she would miss her parents today. "Because I was an only child they spoiled me terribly. When I was young, they would create a scavenger hunt for me with a present waiting at the end of the hunt."

"That sounds like fun!"

"It was! In recent years instead of a scavenger hunt they took me to a DU."

"A 'DU'?"

"A destination unknown. We'd jump in the car and drive someplace I had never been to before or where I would learn about some fascinating new place or thing."

"Hmm. Sounds intriguing."

"Oh, I miss them today, Philip, but I'm so glad to be with you."

Layers of pine needles softened their steps while the ocean curled beside them below whipped-frosting clouds. Claire drew deep breaths of balsam-scented, briny air into her lungs. Bending over some bushes, Philip plucked some newly-ripened blueberries and dropped them into her hand. She lifted the little crowned orbs to her lips to release tangy bursts of sweetness into her mouth.

Philip asked her questions of her childhood, her hobbies, and her favorite things. She in turn learned about the amazing man beside her as she asked him similar questions. The afternoon flew by.

"I'm famished," he announced when they returned to the parking lot. "Are you ready for our early dinner?"

"Yes!"

Philip drove the SUV down a finger of land that narrowed as it pointed into the ocean. He pulled into the driveway beside two other cars of a small diner-style restaurant with red-and-white striped awnings.

They jumped out of the jeep, and when Philip opened the glass door for Claire to enter, the smell of fresh fish and newly baked yeast rolls greeted them.

"Well, look who's here!" A woman in her late 60s with the name "Susie" on her nametag greeted them. "Now, where have you been, Philip? We haven't seen you in ages."

"Has it been that long?" Philip teased.

Though half his size, she whapped him in the arm before peering around him. "And you have someone with you today."

"This is my friend, Claire." Claire brightened at having graduated from tenant to friend.

"Welcome! A friend of Philip's is a friend of ours," she said to Claire before looking back at Philip and wiggling her eyebrows.

"It's her birthday today, and I couldn't think of a finer place to take her for dinner."

"You just know you won't get a better halibut dinner anywhere but here," she said as she led them through the restaurant's pine-walled dining room. She directed them to a table covered with a red and white gingham oilcloth. Philip seated Claire before himself.

Claire pored over her menu, but Philip didn't open his. "I highly recommend the halibut dinner."

"Umm…"

"Have you ever heard of halibut?"

"No. Some kind of fish I assume."

"It's a mild-tasting, cold-water fish with white, flaky meat. They give you a nice thick piece here," he said demonstrating with his forefinger and thumb. "It's delicious, but, please, get whatever you want," he said pointing to the menu.

Claire studied the menu one last time but knew she would order the halibut if for no other reason because Philip had left the choice up to her.

The convivial atmosphere continued with their waiter, Gus—Susie's son and Philip's boyhood friend—demanding his tip before he would serve them their glasses of water.

After placing their order, Philip, still chuckling, excused himself. Claire gazed out the large window by their table. Positioned on a cove and sitting at an angle to the road, the restaurant provided customers with a sweeping view of massive slabs of rock that stretched from the road to the ocean.

Philip returned grinning and placed in front of her a package wrapped in brown paper and tied with string. "Happy birthday."

"You didn't have to get me anything. Taking me out and spending time with me has been enough of a gift."

"Go ahead, open it."

Excited nonetheless, she fiddled with the string's knot but couldn't undo it. He fished the jackknife out of his pocket and handed it to her. "You have problems with knots, don't you?"

She laughed. "And you seem to know when someone needs a jackknife.

Do you always have this with you?"

"My grandfather gave it to me when I was nine. He said a *real* man carries a sharp pocketknife at all times, and I've carried it with me ever since."

She slipped the blade through the string and handed the knife back to him before pulling a leather-covered book from the paper. "A Bible!" She ran her fingers lightly over the smooth surface.

"It's not new, but it's in good condition. I mean, hey, I only knew today was your birthday less than a half hour before you came into the store. I kept this Bible there for whenever I needed it. That antique one you bring to church is too delicate to use on a regular basis."

"You're right. A few pages have already come loose from the binding." What a difference between Philip and Parker! Such simple yet acute attentiveness went into everything he did. She loved that about him. "Thank you. I'll cherish it always—and read it too."

The meal came, thanks was given, and they began to eat.

"Hey, Gus!" Philip twiddled the salt shaker. "What kind of place are you running around here?" Like a child, he clunked the shaker up and down on the tabletop. "This seems to have lost its mate, and my potato won't be happy without pepper!"

"Oh, you would need pepper! What a nuisance you are! We filled the shakers up this morning and purposely didn't return yours because we knew you'd be sitting there. Your potato will just have to suffer," Gus said as he grabbed a pepper shaker from another table and thunked it beside Philip. "I'm adding pepper to your bill," he mumbled before hustling to the kitchen.

Claire stopped chewing the delicious halibut and stared at the shaker. Philip roared with laughter and shook pepper on his potato before glancing up at Claire. "Claire," he said still laughing, shaker midair, "it's okay. We're just kidding!"

She resumed chewing and swallowed the lump of food. "It's not that. It's what you said—the salt and its mate."

"Ahh..."

"I didn't think of pepper."

Philip raised an eyebrow. "I'm not following you."

"Do you know anything about blue granite in the area?"

"No. Okay, wait. What does pepper have to do with granite?"

As they ate, Claire explained about being led to Hydeport by the riddle and its accompanying chunk of granite. She told him about the button she bought at the festival and the granite Parker found on Dovetail Beach. She revealed what he had said about her cousins and a granite deposit on the night he proposed. "I didn't even know exactly what I was looking for until he told me, but I need help solving the riddle."

"I'm not at all good with riddles," Philip said, "but can I write it down and think about it for a while?" Claire nodded. Philip asked Gus for a pen—who gave him one with a huge plastic lobster taped to the end of it—and jotted it on a napkin as she requoted it. He stuffed the napkin into his pocket. "Who else knows about this other than you, me, Parker, and the Wycoff brothers?"

"Other than Grace, who has sworn to secrecy, I don't know."

"There is only one person I can think of who could help with this."

They said simultaneously, "Mr. Soames."

"Usually now through most of August he and Mrs. Soames visit their daughter on Prince Edward Island in Canada. If they've already left, we'll have to wait until he gets back to ask him about this. But, just as soon as he returns, would you like to pay him a visit?"

"Absolutely!"

Their dinner done, they rose to leave. After paying the bill, Philip said, "I have one more place to take you, but it isn't far." They left the restaurant, and Claire put the Bible in the jeep. Philip led her around the outside of the building to the large slabs of rock. "This is your 'destination unknown.'"

"Really?" Claire clapped her hands together with delight.

"It isn't overly amazing, but it's the best I can think of on such short notice. Let's see if you can find something I don't think you've ever seen before."

They walked about on the slabs. Claire scanned the horizon but saw nothing unusual. "Can you give me a hint?"

"You'll know when you find it." He did not follow as she stepped across the rocks and kicked at seaweed. She looked to the waves then back at the rocks again before returning to where he stood.

"Can I have another hint?"

His eyes lowered to his feet.

"Is that it?" she asked, pointing to a thin strip of turquoise in the drab rock. She dropped to her hands and knees for a better look.

"You found it!" he said as he sat beside her.

She fingered a vein of square, milky, opaque crystals. "This is pretty! What is it?"

"It's amazonite."

"I've never heard of it before. Wouldn't it be lovely in a mosaic?"

"There are other veins scattered about the state, but this—see how it runs the length of this slab?—is one of the prettiest representations. It's protected, though, and we'd get into trouble if we took any."

While touching an area dense with crystals she said, "You seem to always know exactly what I like."

"I'm glad you're pleased, but I wish it were the blue granite you're seeking."

Sitting beside him, she continued to admire the amazonite. Philip checked his watch. "We have to go soon. I promised Marie I'd close for her tomorrow if she stayed today until 6:00, and Emma is working on her scheduled day off."

Claire held her face to the sun and closed her eyes. "Oh, I don't want this day to end."

"Neither do I."

"Thank you so much for making today happy, Philip. You've made me feel special."

"That's because you *are*." Philip cleared his throat. "May I ask you something before we go—something that's been nagging me?"

"Of course!"

He stared at the ocean. "Did you—or do you still—love Parker? I was told you are quite in love with him."

"At one point I thought I was. Someone gave me advice regarding him, but I foolishly disregarded it. I kept getting caught up in his flatteries and in my selfish desires for the experiences and opportunities he offered me. Then, over time, I realized what kind of man he really was. The night he proposed I intended to tell him I never wanted to see him again."

"I see."

Should I say it? She hesitated. "It's funny. Whenever I was with him, I always compared him with someone."

"Oh?"

"And each time Parker fell far short of that other person." *I've gone this far. I have to say the rest.* She rubbed her finger back and forth over a piece of amazonite. Its coldness warmed under the intense friction. "I always compared him to you."

Philip sat motionless.

Her hope dangled on the tenuous string of silence strung between them. She busied herself tracing the lines of a large, smooth crystal.

"So…" Philip swallowed. "Does that mean you wouldn't mind if we saw more of each other and got to know each other better?"

"Not just as friends?" she dared ask.

"Not just as friends."

"I'd like that more than anything."

A corner of his mouth turned up. "So would I. We'll have to be discreet, you know. Our living arrangements may cause people to talk. We have to be very public when we're together."

"I understand."

Philip looked at his watch again and sighed. "This is one of the few times I wish I weren't responsible for a shop, but we really must go. I don't even think we're going to make it there by 6:00."

"Can I tag along with you? I can sweep or straighten things or do whatever you'd like me to do until closing."

"Only if you let me take you out for an ice cream afterwards."

She smiled. "For a fudge sundae with extra whipped cream and nuts?"

"You bet."

"That's a deal."

Chapter Fifty-six

Claire hefted the last box onto the table then plopped onto the loveseat. She pulled her feet out of her sandals and propped them up. Contented she leaned against the cushions and wiggled her toes.

"Of course you can share my booth!" Sasha had said. Though she sold only a few pieces, Claire counted her first experience as a vendor a success. The fun she had laughing with Sasha, meeting customers, and watching for Philip far outshined all the work she put into her small mosaics.

Philip had stopped by the booth often throughout the day. "So this is what you've been working on the past month," he had said. It pleased her that he took special note of the sign she had made that read "Claire As Glass," a mosaic of tile and sea glass with the glass fleur-de-lis he gave her replacing the "i" in her name.

"Not you again!" Sasha had whined the eighth time Philip stopped by the booth. "How come you never came by my booth this often in the past?" Failing to stifle a smile, Philip had replied, "You never had anything at your booth quite so interesting before." He had winked at Claire who burst out laughing as Sasha shooed him from the booth. "Get out of here!"

The past four weeks had been some of the happiest in Claire's life. She spent hours at the shop learning and helping, then after closing, she and Philip would lick ice cream cones by the harbor. They had early-morning picnics on area beaches before the shop opened and looked for sea glass after they ate. They sat together in church and discussed the message afterwards when not helping customers. They talked and laughed, sharing their opinions and goals and dreams.

Claire knew by the way Philip looked at her and how he talked with her and treated her that he loved her, but she sensed he had reservations regarding her. Was it the way he watched her? Was it how he held onto her every word during some of their conversations? Was there something he didn't like about her?

The day she had been waiting for had come. She showered quickly and met Philip at 8:10. As the sun descended before them, they followed the beach to the Soames' property where Mr. Soames waited for them on his bench.

"Philip! Miss Claire! It's good to see you. Come sit by me." His eyes twinkled as he looked from Philip to Claire then back to Philip again. "I see a lot has happened in my absence."

They caught up on the latest news, and he told them about his visit to Prince Edward Island. "Now, let's get down to business. Claire, Philip told me you need assistance regarding something of utmost importance."

Claire told him about the riddle and its accompanying piece of granite.

Mr. Soames chortled. "I wondered how long it would take you to come to me about this."

Claire's eyes widened. "You already know?"

"Shortly after I met you, I figured you were a Wycoff. Your roots run deep in this area, you know. You're Sam's daughter aren't you?"

"Why, yes!"

"You have Sam's eyes and his wide smile. You also have that Wycoff spirit. I knew it was only a matter of time before the real reason why you came to the Cove surfaced and had hoped you would come to me."

"So you already knew about the riddle and the blue granite?" Claire said pulling from her pocket a copy of the riddle and the chunk of granite. She handed him the rock.

"Ah, the elusive and beautiful blue granite!" He rolled it in his hands before handing it back. "Your great-grandfather bought and worked a quarry north of town. I assume you've been by there?"

Claire nodded.

"When he died, he left it to his only child, your grandfather, Bryce. Bry was several years older than I, but we were good friends."

"Bry? Of course! My grandfather must have been Briny Bry!"

Philip and Mr. Soames exchanged glances.

"When I was little, Dad told me bedtime stories about the adventures of an old sailor named Briny Bry."

Mr. Soames chuckled. "Briny Bry, aye? The name sure fits. Your grandfather was an avid sailor who must have filled your father's mind with his many adventures."

Claire warmed at the thought.

"Bry was a clever, highly-driven businessman and continually searched the region for other deposits to invest in. Though he wouldn't tell me where, he told me he had found some blue granite of exceptional quality and beauty. He said its location would make extraction difficult, but the potential for wealth would be well worth the effort and expense.

"When he tried to purchase the land, however, he ran into difficulties over a clear title to the deed. He told his two sons—your father, Sam, and Garry— he would purchase the land as soon as he could but refused to divulge its whereabouts.

"Always competing fiercely, those boys searched high and low for that deposit knowing only it was slightly exposed and somewhere in the area. Driven like their father but very greedy, each thought if he were able to find the deposit himself he could somehow buy the land before his father or brother could."

Claire stared at Mr. Soames.

"Tension in the family escalated. At one point Garry became convinced his father had purchased the land and was somehow quarrying the granite and funneling the profits away from the family. He suggested to Sam they murder their father and make it look like an accident so that they could inherit the land and be privy to its location."

Claire gasped. "Murder?"

"Garry had it planned to the last detail. Appalled and even fearing for his own life, Sam told your grandfather Garry's scheme."

"I can't believe anyone would murder for this!"

"You'd be amazed what people do for money," Philip said.

"I suppose." Claire knew all too well about that. "But murder?"

Mr. Soames shrugged. "I'm just telling you what your grandfather told me. He, of course, didn't believe Sam despite Sam's affirmation. You see, Garry was your grandfather's favorite son, so he could do no wrong. Your grandfather's disbelief infuriated Sam, and one day he left the Cove never to return or be heard from again that I know of. Your grandmother was devastated because Sam was *her* favorite son, and she died shortly after he left.

"Bry eventually gave the quarry north of town to Garry and those two scoundrels of his—Hugh and Jake. Near the end of Bry's life he finally obtained a clear title and purchased the land but was too old to extract the granite. He told me he had a—how did he say it?—'fair and simple' plan for his sons so that whichever son used his head the best could have the land. I assume upon Bry's death his attorney was instructed to find Sam and give him and Garry the riddle you spoke of."

He pointed to the paper in her hands.

"Garry's troublemaker sons, Hugh and Jake, no doubt knew something about the granite, but I wonder if their father kept the riddle from them. A machinery accident at the quarry a few years back crushed Garry to death. Though there's no proof, there's no doubt in anyone's mind those boys murdered him. With no other witnesses, their aggressive and capable attorney, however, got them off the hook on technicalities, and the episode was ruled an accident." Mr. Soames paused and looked at Philip.

Philip's voice quieted. "Their attorney was Parker."

Claire winced. *I really wish I had known some of this sooner.*

"Extraction at the quarry north of town is now complete. Hugh and Jake no doubt possess that riddle, and I bet their thirst for money will drive them to stop at nothing to find the land."

Claire handed Mr. Soames the copy of the riddle. She used to dream of her father's family, romantically depicting them as kind and fun and perhaps even a little aristocratic only to know now her family was a torn, unhappy, and scandalous one. No wonder her father spoke so little about them.

Mr. Soames read the riddle. "Who all knows about this?"

"You and Philip—and Grace Hearst. I had to tell her once, but she has sworn to secrecy."

"Yes, she's one to be trusted," Mr. Soames agreed.

"Hugh and Jake know, of course, and Parker Hollenbeck knows."

Mr. Soames' eyebrows shot up, "Parker knows? That's not good. He's definitely one to be reckoned with, and it wouldn't surprise me if he's using those boys to somehow obtain the land for himself."

Philip glanced over at Claire. She closed her eyes at the painful reminder of Parker's proposal.

"Tell me what you've figured out so far."

"All I've come up with is the location is somewhere around Hydeport; there's some sort of connection with salt and pepper; and *'pieces'* may be referring to a flat area or even perhaps a mosaic."

"Do you think we're looking for the land or the actual deed? It sounds to me like the riddle could be alluding to both," Philip said.

"Mmm, I'm not sure. It does sound like both, though, doesn't it?" Mr. Soames waved the paper in the air. "If it's okay with you, I'll keep this, Claire, and will let you know if I can think of anything else."

"Oh, I almost forgot. Along with the granite and riddle was this." She pulled the little key out from under her shirt and showed Philip and Mr. Soames.

"Interesting. I'm sure Parker has already done this, Claire, but check with the Registry of Deeds not only in this county but also in the others counties within a reasonable radius of Hydeport in case your grandfather registered the deed."

"Okay, I can do that."

"Go to the library and research towns, villages—oh, I don't know, I would even check islands if I were you—that may have a connection with the words or some of your solutions to the riddle. The reference area at the library here in town would have that information, but when you research, keep in mind the names of some places have changed over the years."

"I'll do that," she said.

"I'll help you all I can to find Bry's granite. I'd much rather you find it than Parker or those boys. Be careful, Claire, and watch your back. They can't be trusted, and there's no telling what they might do in order to find that deed or the deposit before you do."

Chapter Fifty-seven

Now the middle of September, the atmosphere of the Cove slowed. Fewer cars passed through town, and shops kept shorter hours.

Late Saturday morning Claire stepped into the post office to mail two completed mosaics commissioned during the festival. Lorna handed a customer his change and receipt as Claire stepped behind him to wait her turn. Others straggled in behind her.

"Yup, the sheriff's office was there Friday. It's a shame to mar that pretty old floor. What is it with these floors getting torn up everywhere?"

Not another vandalized location! I wonder where it is. The customer mumbled something then shrugged as he left.

"Hello," Lorna said.

Claire placed the two boxes on the counter. "Good morning, Lorna."

"You and Philip England have been seen a lot around town," she said as she weighed the first box. "First it's Parker then Philip. It doesn't take you long to get around to all the eligible bachelors in town. Are you dating both at the same time?"

A customer behind Claire snickered.

She clenched her purse. "I'm only seeing Philip."

Lorna glanced at the customers over Claire's shoulder then stuck the postage on the first box before grabbing the other one. "Must be convenient for you two being such close neighbors and all. I remember when you told me about Philip and some blonde—"

"Lorna," Claire cut in, "you know, I was wrong for speaking about Philip and her. At the time I didn't know who she was and had insinuated something inappropriate was going on. Of course, that blonde was Philip's sister, Julie. I never should have gossiped about it, and I apologize for that."

Lorna twisted her lips to one side as she weighed the second box.

"As far as living on the English Rose Estate, I live in the cottage and stay in the cottage. Philip lives in the house and stays in the house."

"You need anything else today?"

Claire shook her head. "Before God and this community, neither of us has set foot in each other's house since I have lived there, and I know—"

"That's going to be $12.39."

Claire handed her a twenty-dollar bill. "—you will stop any rumors to the contrary because you now know the truth." She accepted the change and receipt Lorna handed her. "Thank you, Lorna. Good day to you." When Claire turned around, everyone in line stared at her wide-eyed and silent.

<center>~~~</center>

Claire placed her purse and paper-stuffed notebook on the counter as Grace rang up her bill. "Are you ready for the picnic tomorrow?" Grace asked.

"I still need to make a potato salad, but I can do that tonight. I'm really looking forward to it."

"It's always a lot of fun. I confess I'm eager for an afternoon off too, although it always feels strange not opening the tearoom after church on Church Picnic Sunday."

"The crowds sure are down, so you shouldn't lose a lot of business being closed for the day. I know Emma and Marie have been complaining how slow it's been."

Grace waved her hand toward the empty tearoom. "Yeah, the weekends are slow now, which is why we have the picnic in September." She chuckled. "Even though we've nearly frozen some years, too many of us depend on tourism to have the picnic during the summer."

Claire put the change in her purse.

Grace leaned on the counter. "When does Philip get back?"

"The show was supposed to end around noon today, so he should be here sometime this evening. It's only been a few days, but I've missed him terribly."

It had been such fun watching Philip and Claire's love flourish. Grace's voice hushed. "You really like him don't you?"

"I'm crazy about him, Grace. I didn't know it was possible to be so happy and to feel loved and protected without being controlled."

Claire had made such progress since July. "I'm glad for you, Claire. I'm glad for both of you."

"You know something, though? I truly believe he loves me, but sometimes I feel like—How do I say this?— he's reticent about expressing his feelings for some reason. It's almost as if he's waiting for me to say or do something that will cause him to change his mind about me. It worries me."

Grace bit her lip. *I was afraid this would happen.* "You should ask him about it. Tell him what you just told me. Remember it's always best to get questions out in the air as soon as they arise no matter what the answers may lead to."

"You're right. I'll do that."

Grace stood and pointed to the notebook "You going to do some writing today?"

"I'm heading to the library to do a little research."

"Oh, speaking of the library, did you know a vandal broke in there Thursday night and tore up a section, the only decorative section, of the entryway floor? I suspect it's the same person who vandalized the church— probably some kid." She shook her head. "Such a shame people are so destructive."

"I heard about it at the post office but didn't know where it took place. I'll check it out when I go over."

~~~

Claire climbed the wide, granite steps of the library's rounded portico. After noting the library's five-o'clock closing time, she opened one of the heavy wooden doors and stepped onto oversized pink granite tiles that stopped abruptly at a line of yellow police tape. She skirted the taped perimeter where piles of broken mortar and bits of tile still lay. She stopped at the front desk.

"This is terrible!" Claire commented to the young woman behind the desk.

"It was my favorite part of the library too," she said.

"Why is that?"

"Have you not been here before?"

"I haven't."

"Though it wasn't detailed, it was a map of the coastline pieced with granite."

A map. Granite. "Under pieces on a level plane." Claire wondered if her cousins were the culprits. *If it were them, though, why would they burglarize too?*

The young woman continued. "The Cove was marked with a brass star, and it had a brass compass in that corner," she said pointing to the corner farthest from them. "The compass and star are gone."

"That's a shame," Claire said before asking her the whereabouts of the library's reference materials.

Dust danced in sunbeams streaming through the floor-to-ceiling windows as the young woman led Claire through the library. Wooden sailboats, pottery, and handmade baskets dotted the tops of the book-laden shelves. Why had these items not been stolen?

The women descended a central staircase made of more pink granite to a lower level lit with dim, fluorescent lights. Portraits hung on the walls between sections of shelving. The young woman directed Claire to the reference area, a hushed musty-smelling room. After thanking the woman, Claire set her notebook on a short wooden table and clicked on a green banker's lamp.

She gathered volumes and land maps and registries and piled them on the table. Her surroundings faded into the background as she engrossed herself in the history of Maine's coastal granite industry taking special note of the mentions of the Wycoff quarry. She studied land maps within a hundred-mile radius of Hydeport and carefully studied the area around Dovetail Beach. Nothing coincided with the words in the riddle.

Upon reading about deposits excavated on islands and following Mr. Soames' suggestion, she scanned nautical maps. *There are so many islands!*

After surveying the island charts north and just south of the Cove, she glanced up at the clock. It read 4:20. She had time to look over one last chart—the one of the islands outside Hydeport. She would have to study the islands south of Hydeport another time.

She recognized the Spice Chest islands, and her memory of being on the schooner with Parker sent a quiver up her back. *Focus! I need to put him out of my mind.*

She swept her finger side to side across the map and read each island's name. She searched for Salt Island or Pepper Island but found neither.

One island on the edge of the Spice Chest grouping caught her attention. Shaped like a croissant it bore the name Temple Island. *Temple Island?* With islands surrounding it named Clove Island and Rosemary Isle, Temple did not fit the Spice Chest theme. Temple Island—*"Place of old design and date".* Could it be?

Remembering Mr. Soames' words, she hurried to the archival section and grabbed an oversized book containing pre-1900 navigational charts. Her hands shook as she turned the pages to the section illustrating the Spice Chest area.

She drew in a quick breath.

Instead of the name Temple Island written above the croissant-shaped piece of land she read a different name—Peppercorn Island.

Chapter Fifty-eight

Claire's head shifted back and forth between the two charts as the riddle replayed in her mind. Did her father suspect the granite was on an island and some of Briny Bry's treasure-seeking stories were actually *his* adventures looking for the deposit? Could Parker or her cousins have figured this out yet?

She eyed the clock, then scanned the room as she grabbed her wallet, picked up the charts, and searched for a photocopier. Finding one on a far, outside wall, she flipped the cover, pressed the older chart on the glass, and sent a coin chinking down the chute. After punching the start button, the copier whirred to life. As she waited, she looked at the wall above her.

Two portraits hung—one of a man with thick, white hair and an unsmiling mouth and the other of a woman whose gray bun rested at the nape of her neck. The man's aqua-blue eyes, the only color on his portrait, skewered the woman whose unintimidated steel-gray eyes stared back from her dour countenance. The only color on the woman rested on her finger.

Claire's eyes widened with recognition.

She squinted to read the names on the tiny brass plates below the portraits. *My great-grandparents!*

She slid another coin into the slot, and exchanged the old map for the newer one. After sending the copier into another whir, she looked up at the portraits again. At the same instant, the smell of stale cigarettes overcame her. Her skin prickled.

"She was an ugly old bird wasn't she?" a voice whispered behind her. "I wish I knew where that tourmaline ring went."

Claire grabbed the book off the glass and spun around. Aqua-blue eyes mirroring hers fastened onto the portraits. *Jake Wycoff!*

"They donated the granite for this library. Except for the pink tiles, all the granite in this building came from our quarry—*my* quarry." He dropped his cold gaze onto her.

Claire reached behind her and snatched the two photocopies from the tray and slid them between the chart book and her body.

"You've been busy this afternoon. You were oblivious to me sitting there watching you all this time, weren't you?" He nodded at the book she held. "Discovered something important, didn't you? I know what books you looked in, and, based on your candid reactions, approximately where. It won't take long to figure out what you found when the library opens again."

She twisted and grabbed the other book and, with shaking hands, clutched them both to her heaving chest. "You just try. I won't be intimidated by you or your brother or Parker for that matter. I have plenty of resources and friends to help me."

The lights dimmed to half-power, the signal the library would close. Jake leaned within inches of her face. The stench of cigarettes on his clothes and breath nauseated her. "I warn you, *cousin.*" His voice seethed. "You may think you can just blow into town and take over, but you're no match for us."

She struggled to breathe and leaned back against the photocopier for support.

"The blue granite is *ours,* and we'll find it and take it no matter who's in our way." He turned around and swaggered up the stairs.

◡◡◡

Sitting on his top step and leaning an elbow on his knee, Philip rested his chin on a finger as he studied the charts in his other hand. "I really think you're on to something. Do you think Jake knows for sure which books you were looking in? I mean they all probably look similar, and it might be easy to confuse them."

"He could be bluffing, but I'm not sure. I was focused on what I was doing and didn't pay attention to anyone around me. Who knows how long he had been watching me and what he actually saw."

"I suppose," he nodded. "Well, it's definitely worth going out to Temple Island for a look, and the sooner the better. I'm just not sure when we can go. We can't go out tomorrow, and it's supposed to rain all week." He handed her the copy of the old chart. "Is it okay if I keep this one?" he asked holding up the other photocopy.

"I guess so. I mean—I don't see why not."

He pulled his eyes from the chart and adjusted his glasses. "Claire, I have no intention of finding this granite for myself or by myself. Please trust me."

"I know. I'm sorry. I'm just anxious about it, that's all. You've always been open and honest, and there's no reason not to trust you. I *need* to trust you— and I do."

Philip didn't look convinced.

"Also, in case this thought has entered that pretty head of yours," he said gently tapping the side of her head, "if the granite is never found and you never become wealthy, it will not change how I feel about you. I don't want you to ever think that my—my deep regard for you has anything to do with money. All right?"

But I'm already wealthy. He must not realize that yet! She hadn't been sure if he knew. His words endeared him to her even more. "All right."

"Be careful of those guys. They're not to be trusted. I'll try to keep an eye on you—a task I certainly don't mind doing," he said with a grin, "but we're not always together. Avoid them, especially if you're by yourself. I'm glad I don't have another show until the end of October. Perhaps by then we'll have some solid answers, and they'll leave you alone once and for all."

"I'll be careful."

Chapter Fifty-nine

"Where did the sun go?" Claire asked as she hopped onto the front seat of Philip's jeep.

"Yeah, it's too bad, but we won't let a few clouds stop us from having a good time at the church picnic."

Claire set her bowl of potato salad on the seat between them before slamming the door and buckling her seatbelt.

"Mmm! What did you make?"

"Peanut butter potato salad."

"You can't be serious. Does such a salad even exist?"

"It does. I saw a recipe for it this week. Are you going to try some?"

He gulped. "Maybe a bite—a small bite—and only because you made it."

Claire laughed. "Well, you're in luck because I happened to leave the peanut butter out this time."

"You're in trouble, girl!" he shot back with a grin as he threw the jeep into gear and headed toward the highway.

They journeyed past Hydeport before turning at a sign reading "Macintosh Point." The hilly road curved around rocky spruce forests juxtaposed with fiery early-turning maples.

"Macintosh Point is at the end of this peninsula," Philip said. "Many ships on their way in or out of Hydeport have met their demise against a mass of rock lying just above the water line off the point. Hundreds of lives have been lost there."

"Shipwrecks! Drowning sounds like such a terrible way to go."

"The government purchased the end of the peninsula from a Scotsman named Ainsley Macintosh and erected a lighthouse. They named the point Macintosh Point and the lighthouse Macintosh Light in his honor."

The trees opened, and the road ended abruptly at a small parking lot. Between them and the ocean stood a watchful, white-brick lighthouse brushed with a wide red stripe below a window-lined room. A small room at the base joined the lighthouse to a simple, white house with two brick chimneys.

Claire giggled.

"What?"

"I expected to see a red lighthouse with a green top—you know, like a Macintosh apple."

"I'm sure you're not the first to think that," Philip said as he parked. With his hands still on the steering wheel he hunched and looked up at the lighthouse. His voice softened. "It's one of my favorite places along the coast, but…" He stared at the top.

"But what?"

"Oh…nothing." He turned the ignition off. "I haven't been here for a while."

"I'd think it would be hard to stay away from such a fascinating place."

They unbuckled their seatbelts. "You can walk up to the top—to the lantern room—you know. Do you see the people?"

She opened the door and got out for a better look. "Why, yes, I do! Anyone can go up there?"

"Yes. It's even free."

"I bet the view is grand. Let's go up before we leave."

Philip got out and shut his door. "Hey, there's Pastor Tim and the Harrimans."

To the left of the lighthouse, a grassy lawn scattered with picnic tables stretched to the ocean. Philip strode to Pastor Tim and the Harrimans to assist with moving tables.

Bowl in hand, Claire walked straight to the edge of the grassy lawn. Below her feet long slanting bands of rock sloped until they disappeared beneath shooting sprays of frothy turquoise water. Out farther, the steel-grey and dark-green water churned over an extensive area of rock just off the point.

Claire's heart raced. With no light to warn them, Claire pictured a ship speeding toward the rocks on a moonless night. Unaware of their fate, she imagined the men's excitement mounting as the lights of Hydeport glittered on the horizon and their families grew closer.

She pulled at her collar. *So close to the warmth and safety of Hydeport only to drown after the ship splintered in the unrelenting deep!*

A loud squeal from a playing child jolted her from her rumination. *No! I can't dwell on these dark thoughts.*

She turned around and pinpointed Grace organizing food by herself at two abutting picnic tables. She hurried over.

"Hey! Glad you came over. I could use a little help here."

Claire placed her potato salad on the table before lifting and sliding its lid under the bowl.

"Do you mind taking all the lids off and putting serving spoons and forks in them? We'll be ready to eat soon."

Thankful for the diversion, Claire grabbed the closest condiment jar and twisted its lid.

"Can I assume you're going with Philip to the gala at the Soames' house this Saturday?"

"Yes, he told me about it last week. It sounds elegant!"

"The Soames' galas are top-notch. Did Philip tell you it's formal—fancy dresses and tuxedos?"

"Yes. In fact, I'm going shopping in Hydeport tomorrow for a dress."

"Good! I wanted to make sure you knew what to wear. Sometimes guys forget to mention important details like that." Her tone turned serious. "You do realize Parker will undoubtedly be there."

Ugh! Parker! Claire stabbed a fork into a jar of pickles. "But I understood this gala was for shop owners—to celebrate the end of the season."

"It is."

"But Parker doesn't own a shop."

"I know, but since Mr. Soames owns most of the Cove he can ask anyone he wants to attend." She tore open a potato chip bag. "And every year we shopkeepers get to endure an evening hobnobbing with the wealthy and influential members of the community."

Mustard spurted on the table as Claire broke the bottle's seal.

"I assume you haven't seen him since he proposed."

"No I haven't, and I don't want to either." She twisted the cap to a soda bottle, sending its vapors whirling into the breeze.

"Don't worry about it. You'll be close to Philip and us and others you know all evening. You'll be safe with your friends around you."

"Thanks, Grace. You're a dear friend." She knifed the mayonnaise. "I won't let him ruin my evening or anything else in my life. I'm still going to look forward to the gala and especially to being on Philip's arm all night."

"What's this about Philip's arm?" a deep voice asked.

Claire spun around and met Philip's wide grin. "It's strong and secure, and I'm looking forward to being on it on Saturday."

Jason and Sasha Harriman and Jason's brother Carl came up behind Philip as she said this. Carl rolled his eyes. "Oh, whatever! Can't we just eat?"

Most of the church had come to the picnic, and over the course of the afternoon during eating, games, and races, Claire built and solidified friendships. Laughter shredded the brooding thoughts of shipwrecks and Parker, and joy filled her heart. Like a family, these people had accepted and befriended her and had filled the void. She had come to the Cove broken and lonely, and now she felt loved and wanted and blessed.

Philip doted on her, and when games or people separated them, they exchanged winks and smiles and from time to time crazy faces, sending the recipient into stitches of laughter. How she loved him!

The afternoon now spent, cool drizzle coated everyone with tiny beads of moisture. Many had gone home. Jason, Sasha, Carl, and Pastor Tim sat on one side of a picnic table while Philip sat across from Jason then Claire and finally Grace. Worn from the games, they nibbled on cookies and sipped one last steaming cup of coffee or tea from the large thermoses Grace brought.

Jason's voice boomed to an attentive Philip. "So, I figured if the engine on the *BMG* was okay, then it had to be something else."

"Of course it wasn't the engine!" Carl broke in. "I had already told you that."

Ignoring his brother's comment, Jason continued, "We had had the engines serviced on both the *BMG* and the *Squabble* last spring, so a problem with the engine was pretty unlikely."

Claire shifted from one brawny-bearded brother to the other as they bantered back and forth about—what exactly were they talking about?

"Wait!" she cut in. "What's a *BMG* and a *Squabble*? Are they cars?"

Poised to speak, Carl snapped his mouth closed. All eyes shifted to Claire. Sasha laughed. "I suppose you'd have no idea what they're talking about," she said.

"They're boats," Carl said. "Our boats."

"They are the *names* of their lobster boats," Sasha explained. "Go ahead, Jason, tell her what *BMG* is and how you got it."

Changing the course of the discussion, Jason complied. "The *BMG*— that's the *Buoy Meets Girl*—is the name of my boat."

"That's B-O-U-Y not B-O-Y," Carl clarified.

"Now tell her how you chose it, Jason. Tell her the story." Sasha turned to Claire. "I just love this part!"

"Okay, to make a long story short, one day while out lobstering I got my wrist caught on a nylon rope attached to a buoy. The rope cut a gash right here." He pointed to a large scar on his wrist. "So I had to go to the ER for stitches where I was helped by the prettiest little nurse in Maine." He winked at Sasha.

"Oh, please!" Carl moaned, rolling his eyes.

"And his boat is the *Squabble Magnet*," Jason retorted.

"A squabble is a group of seagulls," Philip said. "You always see seagulls flying over lobster boats, and for some reason Carl seems to attract an unusual number of them."

"How clever!" Claire said. "What would you name a boat if you had one, Philip?"

Jason guffawed. "Yeah, *if* he had one. Let's see. What would he name a boat *if* he had one?"

"*If* he had one, he'd name it…" Carl began.

"…I'd name it *The Rust Bucket*," Philip answered narrowing his eyes at him.

"*The Rust Bucket?*" Claire laughed as her eyes darted among the three men. "I see. There must be some private joke going on here."

"Oh, yeah. It's a joke all right!" Carl said.

"Do you have a boat, Pastor Tim?" Claire asked.

"No, but if I did I'd name it *Fishers of Men* or *Fishing for Men*. Seems appropriate, don't you think?"

Grace piped up. "Yeah, it sounds impressive, but you'd probably be doing more fishing for fish than fishing for men if you had a boat." Everyone roared.

"Hey, I could use a boat for the ministry! You know, invite men out for a day of fishing and…" He trailed off as the men at the table agreed with him. Grace just shook her head.

"Okay, Claire, what would you name a boat if you had one?" Philip asked.

Her voice softened. "I'd name mine *From Shards to Sea Glass*."

Philip cocked his head.

Carl spoke. "Umm, I'm not getting it."

"It's not funny or clever, but it does have meaning, like yours," she said, nodding toward Jason. "When I arrived at the Cove, my heart and emotions like shards of glass were broken and—and ugly and useless. I've been through a lot of tumbling, so to speak, this past year dealing with my parents' deaths and becoming a Christian and…" She blinked repeatedly. "…other experiences. I know my sharp edges aren't smooth yet, but eventually I hope my life will become something useful and—and beautiful like a piece of roughed-up sea glass."

A hush fell over the table.

Chapter Sixty

All eyes riveted on Claire. Her cheeks blazed crimson, and her eyes dropped to her cup of tea.

Pastor Tim spoke. "So then, Claire, you were serious last May when you became a Christian? You didn't do it or say you were one just to be accepted?"

Her head sprung up. "Oh, no! I hope no one thinks that! Believe me, I know what it's like to be deceived. I would never be untruthful about such a thing."

Pastor Tim's eyebrows shot above his mist-dotted glasses. Everyone cast expectant glances at Philip whose bent head hung over the empty cup in his hands. The ocean's thunderous roar echoed off the lighthouse as Sasha and Grace exchanged insightful nods.

Grace patted Claire's arm. "Well, I never doubted for a moment your decision was real." Sasha bobbed her head up and down. "This drizzle is getting heavier. Do you think we should pack up and head home before the rain moves in?"

Everyone spoke at once as they rose from the table.

つてつてつて

Claire placed her empty bowl in the jeep then jogged to the Hearst's car. Pastor Tim cracked his window. "Do you know where Philip is?" she asked. She had seen little of him as everyone rushed in the rain to pick up trash and reposition the tables.

"You may want to try up there," he said, pointing to the top of the lighthouse.

"Ah, I bet you're right! Thanks!"

They waved their goodbyes, and Claire dashed to the tiny structure separating the lighthouse from the main house and opened the screen door. A woman appearing to be in her early 70s sat on a stool. "You won't have to fight the crowds today. The light keeper's house is still open," she said motioning to her left, "as is the lighthouse." She glanced at her watch. "But you have only about fifteen minutes before we close."

"Guess I'll have to save the house for another day," Claire said as she stepped into the tower.

She mounted the black ornate steps of the coiling iron staircase, pausing only for a moment at each of the two small windows along the way. With labored breathing, she clambered the iron ladder at the top, and at the final rung, two familiar hands reached for hers and pulled her through a generous hole in the floor.

"There you are," she said before looking about the small room. He released her hands and leaned against a window, watching her.

Below the black metal-capped top, large windows lined each wall. On a platform at the center of the room sat the magnificent lens. Slanting beveled prisms, tapering in concentric layers, radiated from the middle, the thick glass distorting the view of the lamp behind it.

Mesmerized, Claire brushed her fingers over the beveled glass.

"Impressive isn't it?" Philip asked.

"It's exquisite."

"What do you think of the view? I wish the weather were better. On a clear day you can see for miles and miles."

Silently she walked around the lamp room, captivated by the panoramic view. The turbulent ocean stretched like a drab lacy-edged blanket until it disappeared into the misty, gray horizon. Philip stood close by her side. He smelled of the fresh early-fall air.

"This place is enchanting," she whispered before turning to face him, "and there's no one I'd rather be here with than you." His glasses could not mask the moss color of his eyes. Warmth rose from her toes to her cheeks. "Philip, I love you."

How he'd longed to hear those words! With his uncertainties now resolved, he knew when he drew her into the lantern room he had finally overcome all the barriers of the past.

"Claire, I am more—*much* more—than deeply fond of you. I love you fiercely."

An idea entered his mind, warming his rain-dampened body. A film crept across his lenses. He drummed his fingers against the sides of his legs while speaking his thoughts aloud. "I shouldn't do this. Not here."

She stood on her toes and pushed his glasses to the top of his head. Her hands slid slowly down his cheeks and she clasped her fingers in front of her chest. "Shouldn't do what?"

"Well, I didn't prepare."

"Prepare?"

Rain danced on the metal above them. He brushed his hands against her soft flushed cheeks before threading them through the damp corkscrews of hair.

I shouldn't do this. I'm not thinking rationally.

I should wait.

He knew he couldn't.

He grasped her hands and enclosed them in his. His heart battered his chest. "Will you—I beg of you—will you please be my wife?"

Her mouth fell open. "Are you sure?"

"Am I *sure?*"

"You don't have...doubts? Reservations?"

Had it been that obvious? He rubbed his thumbs over her hands. "No doubts. No reservations."

Her aqua eyes flitted across his face as if they searched for further confirmation.

He held his breath.

Oh no! She's trying to find an excuse. He swallowed. *Heavenly Father, I never imagined she'd say no.* The rain tapped impatient fingers against the windowpane beside them *...but I'm so certain she's the one You chose for me. Did I...*

Claire's lips curved into a smile. "Then, yes—yes!"

Philip released an audible breath. "I was worried there for a minute."

Her eyes sparkled. "You have nothing to worry about. I'd love nothing more than to spend the rest of my life with you as your wife."

Thank you, Lord! He caressed her hands then his gaze fell to her lips. "May I kiss you?"

"Yes," she whispered before lifting her lips toward his.

Bending down, he slid his hands around her shoulders and cradled her as if she could break. He pressed his lips onto her soft, sweet mouth. The sound of the rain faded as he savored the moment he had thought about so many times.

⟿⟿⟿

Having passed that fleeting moment when her trust waivered, she closed her eyes and melted in his loving and protective embrace. Such gentleness! Her heart pounded as she returned his eager but tender kiss.

"Five minutes!" a voice rang from the bottom of the tower, breaking their kiss.

Philip stroked the side of her face with his thumb. "What kind of proposal is this?"

"What do you mean? It's the best! I could burst with joy."

"I don't even have a ring to put on your finger."

"A ring isn't important. Our love for each other is. Besides, I can't think of a better place for you to propose. How many others could say they've gotten engaged here?"

Philip's hands dropped to her shoulders. He stared at her as the rain pelted the window beside them. "What do you think about keeping this a secret?"

She furrowed her brow for only a second. "A secret? That we're engaged? I'm so ecstatic I don't know if I can!"

"Well, not necessarily that we're engaged but that we got engaged *here*."

"What's wrong with here?"

Philip swung his glassed down to his nose and blinked repeatedly. "How about this? Let's…"

"We close in three minutes!" the voice from the bottom of the tower called.

"…let's keep the fact that we're engaged a secret too. I'll check with Mr. and Mrs. Soames, but I'm sure they'll let us make our official announcement on Saturday at the gala. I'll even be better prepared and have a ring for your finger Saturday night. What do you think? Would you like that?"

"In front of everyone?" Her mind raced.

Philip nodded before running his hands over her cheeks and into her hair.

"It'll be hard to keep quiet all week, but if that's what you…"

He tilted her head toward him and pressed his warm lips to hers.

I'll do whatever you want, Philip, no matter how crazy it sounds.

Chapter Sixty-one

Claire skittered the tiny key across her gold chain as she studied the notes and maps pinned to the corkboard one last time. After spending an antsy week waiting for the relentless rain to stop, a stiff breeze finally arrived, drying the precipitation and dispersing the clouds.

Concerned about the remnants of a hurricane barreling up the eastern seaboard, Philip wanted to take advantage of tomorrow morning's narrow window of clear skies and calm seas and had sent her home to prepare for their early-morning departure. With October just around the corner, the opportunities to safely get to and investigate the island would dwindle.

She walked to the kitchen table and picked up a piece of purple sea glass with ruffled edges. Earlier, beneath her umbrella, she had scoured a nearby beach while waiting for the boutique in Hydeport to open.

She replaced the ruffled piece, then stood in front of the two dresses hanging from the casing of the French doors.

"I'd like a semi-formal to formal dress that would go with a ring I own. It has a graduating pink to green stone in it, and I believe it's called a tourmaline," she had said to the lady at the boutique last Monday.

"Ah, that sounds like a watermelon tourmaline. I have just the dress for you."

Claire ran her hand over the dupioni silk as it played off the cottage's lights and shimmered from rosy pink to light green. Folds of silk crossed the waist before cascading from the gather at the hip down the calf-length skirt.

Then she looked at the other dress. Delicate floral lace covered the white, knee-length confection. She fingered the short lacy bell sleeves and rounded neckline.

She had not yet told Philip that she had found the perfect wedding dress.

During the slow days at the shop this past week, they had planned. They would have a small wedding at the end of October, inviting only their closest friends and Philip's immediate family. On New Year's Eve, they would host a grand celebration at their estate, then honeymoon in the Caribbean in January when the Compass Rose would be closed for the month.

She could hardly wait.

～✍✍～

As Claire walked up her driveway, the dark sky sparkled as if strewn with diamond dust. Moisture weighted the chilly, motionless air.

"Good morning, handsome!"

"Morning, sweetheart!" The dome light lit Philip's smile as he tossed a backpack onto the back seat of his jeep. "I sure like saying that."

"In a month you can say it every morning when we first wake up..." She stood on her toes and kissed him. "...which I hope will always be later than 4:00."

He laughed. "I agree!"

She handed him their lunch and a thermos of hot chocolate.

He scanned her from head to toe. "Looks like you have on plenty of layers."

"Here's a knit hat and gloves too like you said."

"Good. It'll be pretty cool out there today. Go ahead and jump in. I just have to get one more thing, and we'll be on our way."

Passing few cars on their way to Hydeport, Claire chatted about their upcoming adventure, excitement filling her. Philip pulled into a parking place, and, after gathering their things, they walked under bright amber lights to the dimly-lit docks. "How are we getting to the island anyway?"

"You'll see."

They descended a ramp before Philip stopped in front of a small boat bobbing in a boat slip. He set the items on the dock and peeled back the boat's protective tarp.

Claire stood stock-still and stared.

With navy-painted bottom and shiny-wooden deck, the boat looked like it belonged in a vintage advertisement. A long blue leather seat sat behind a high windshield protecting a slender steering wheel and wooden dashboard containing a few simple dials.

"How do you like it?"

"Umm…" She gulped.

"C'mon now. A schooner it isn't, but it's all I have."

"You actually go out on the ocean in this?"

Philip stopped folding the tarp. "Of course."

"But how does it work? It doesn't have any masts and…" Her eyes shifted to the back of the boat. "…it doesn't even have a motor."

He stepped onto the deck and stuffed the tarp into a storage hold. "*The Rust Bucket* has an inboard motor…" He rapped a large box at its center with his knuckle. "…right here."

"*The Rust Bucket?* You really do have a boat named *The Rust Bucket!*" She bit her lip. "The name doesn't give me a lot of confidence."

"Please hand me those things," he said, pointing to the items she hugged in her arms. "The Harriman brothers give me a hard time about it living up to its name and not being real compared to their lobster boats, but trust me. It's quite seaworthy."

She handed him the backpack. "But, *The Rust Bucket?*"

"I bought it for two hundred dollars when I was fifteen. What teenage guy doesn't want a fast boat to impress people with? It was in terrible shape, and restoring it took more time and money than I had expected. My father referred to it as the 'old rust bucket' in the backyard, so that's what I named it."

She gave him the lunch sack and thermos.

"I didn't finish it until the summer before my senior year in college, after which I became more interested in kayaks. I share this with my sisters, who use it more often than I do, so I keep it here in Hydeport."

He leaned over the edge and extended his hand toward her. The inky water sloshed between them.

She didn't move.

"What's the matter?"

She looked at his hand before glancing up at him. "I'm—I'm afraid of the water. Oh, I don't want to be, but it's so dark and deep! And I can't swim. And this boat is so—so small." Tremors wiggled up her back.

He dropped his hand and stood for a moment, looking at her as if contemplating what do to next. He jumped onto the dock, sending the boat pitching back and forth. The small lamps at their feet reflected off the bottoms of his glasses. "I didn't know you were afraid of the water."

"I'm afraid of drowning. Oh, don't be cross with me," she pleaded. She could hear her pulse in her ears.

"Cross? Why would I be cross? We all have fears."

"I'm so tired of being fearful. Just when I think I've conquered fear it comes back and haunts me."

"Fear can be mastered, Claire, with help and time and prayer."

"I know." She sighed. "Until we got here I didn't think much about actually getting to the island—just about being there. Oh, what do I do?"

He brushed his hand against her cheek. "Do you want me to go alone? I would much rather have you along but am willing to go and look around for you."

"But I want to be there too."

"You're trembling. Are you sure?"

She swallowed hard. "I need to face this, don't I? If I'm going to live by the ocean, I don't want fear controlling me and keeping me from doing things with you."

"You don't have to tackle it alone, you know."

She nodded. *I can't do this without you, Lord.*

"This will help." He stepped onto the boat and plucked a fluorescent lifejacket from a storage compartment. He helped her push her arms through the armholes. The smell of gasoline and motor oil fought with the strong scent of the lifejacket's plastic coating. She lifted her head to breathe fresh air.

"I wouldn't take you out if it were unsafe. Yeah, late this afternoon and tomorrow it will be too rough but not now." He lined up and clicked the buckles, then tugged the nylon belts.

"I assure you my boat has no holes and no rust despite its name." He kissed her forehead. "I'll be beside you the entire time. Okay?"

"Okay."

Philip helped her board and settle onto her seat. Before starting the engine, he grasped her cold, clammy hand and bowed his head. "Heavenly Father, please keep us safe this morning. If it's Your will, help us find what we're looking for in a timely manner. And please, give Claire victory over her fears and give her peace today while we're on the water. In Jesus' name, Amen."

He gave her an assuring look before sending the engine roaring to life in the sleepy harbor. As they putted between the boats then into the bay, a yellow glow hinted at the horizon. Despite her cumbersome lifejacket and its overwhelming scent, she snuggled close to Philip and gripped the seat, praying she wouldn't fall overboard.

Chapter Sixty-two

The windshield offered limited protection from the cold wind, and with one gloved hand, Claire readjusted her knit hat. Philip's hair looked like porcupine quills sticking out of the center of his thermal headband, and Claire laughed at the sight.

As Philip shot across the water, she repeated the riddle in her mind while watching the sunrise paint the horizon. She paced her breathing and filled her mind with pleasant things—tomorrow's engagement, their wedding, honeymooning in the Caribbean. She focused on living.

Philip tapped her arm and pointed to a rock-edged, crescent-shaped island thick with bristling evergreens. Temple Island!

She had not expected it to be so big! It didn't look that big on the map. *How can we possibly search this? We don't even know what we're looking for.*

Philip propelled the boat to the right and slowed the engine as they hugged the back of the island.

"It's going to take us forever to search this," she called.

"Not if we use our heads." He reached by his feet and handed her a pair of binoculars. "Let's circle around first. If we don't see any exposed blue granite, we can go ashore and hike around to find some sort of '*level plane*' to investigate. Keep your eyes open!"

Following the southern coastline, Philip pointed to a tiny seaweed-edged beach. "That might be a good place to put in."

When they rounded the northern edge, Claire lowered the binoculars and handed them to Philip. "Look!" She pointed. "Right there!"

A small outcropping of bright-blue rock jutted beneath a spruce forest. Keeping a hand on the wheel, he held the binoculars to his glasses. "We need to check that out."

With no place to land by the outcropping, they followed the shoreline. A wide, gravelly beach formed the inside curve of the island's crescent, but Philip sped to the little beach they had seen earlier.

He cut the motor and, grabbing some ropes, sprung from the boat as it glided up to the beach. He pulled it in the best he could before securing it and helping Claire.

"Hooray! Land!" she said as she stepped over the fishy-smelling seaweed and unbuckled the clasps on her life jacket. "Why here and not on that other beach?" She took the jacket off and tossed it on the ground. "It looked closer to the outcropping and an easier place to land."

"For some reason I feel safer here."

Leaving the life jacket and their lunch above the tide line, they followed the edge of the island, trekking over rocks and pushing through thick underbrush toward the outcropping. They topped a granite hill surrounded by spruce trees and blotched by green lichen.

"Look!" Claire said.

Both scooched and ran their hands over a section of bright-blue granite sprinkled with black mica and sparkling quartz.

"It's beautiful!" Claire exclaimed.

Philip stood and looked about them. "'*Blue surrounds*' could mean being surrounded by blue ocean, but I'm not sure what '*blue releases*' means."

"Maybe it releases a person from poverty? I don't know. The first part makes sense—about the surrounding ocean. If we could only figure out what '*under pieces on a level plane*' means."

The granite stopped at a mossy rise of small trees and brush. Philip parted the vegetation and disappeared. Claire looked back at the granite then out at the ocean. *Blue releases…Blue releases.*

"Claire, come quickly!"

She jounced through the bushes.

He knelt on a blue-granite slab so flat it looked as if it had been rolled out. A section about fifteen inches long by five inches wide had been inset with three gray stone tiles.

She knelt beside him. "Can it be?" Unable to move the tiles, Philip fished his jackknife from his pocket and handed it to her. She wedged the knife into the cracks and lifted the tiles. Below them in a chiseled recess lay a long brass tube with an ornate fastener and tiny brass padlock.

"'*Under pieces on a level plane*,'" she quoted, elation permeating her words.

She sat cross-legged and withdrew the key from beneath her shirt. Philip sat beside her as she pushed the key into the keyhole and popped the padlock open. After pulling the padlock from the staple, she lifted the hasp. Inside the brass cylinder nestled a glass tube with a metal, screw-on cap. She unscrewed the cap and pulled out a single piece of paper.

Her hands shook as she unfurled it. "'Gift Deed,'" she read aloud. With Philip watching over her shoulder, she read the deed. "So this is an actual deed?"

"I believe it is, but we should check with an attorney."

She tapped the paper. "It looks like all it takes is for someone to fill his name in here, file it, and the island would be his. Anyone could have happened upon this."

"I suppose you're right, but I think it would have been pretty unlikely for someone to just happen upon this spot without the riddle."

"That's true." Claire scrolled the paper, tucked it back into its glass tube, and screwed the lid. "I can't believe I'm holding the much-sought-after deed!" She inserted the tube into the brass cylinder and clicked the padlock closed.

After they stood and brushed dirt off their pants, Claire threw her arms around Philip. "Thank you for helping me. I never could have done it without you."

He bent to kiss her but stiffened as if a ramrod had been shoved down his back. His eyes searched the trees and brush beyond her.

She looked over her shoulder then back to him. "What?"

He put his finger on her lips.

She sniffed.

Cigarettes!

"Quick!" he whispered.

Swift and silent, they retraced their steps to the boat, stopping often to listen and look around them. Back on the beach, the boat strained against its ropes. Their things lay untouched.

"You don't think our minds were fooling with us, do you?" Claire asked.

"It sure smelled like cigarette smoke. I had hoped we could have lunch here, but I think we should get going."

When Philip revved the engine, Claire admired the brass tube one last time before stuffing it between the life jacket and her chest. They rounded the island, and as they sped away, Claire looked back.

Inside the crescent, a tethered boat bobbed in the water.

Chapter Sixty-three

A gust of wind shook the cottage so severely, Claire expected shingles to fly past the window. White-tipped waves surged toward the beach beneath a cloud-striped sky.

A knock sounded at her door. "Who is it?" she called, her hand suspended over the latch.

"It's Philip."

Surprised, she opened the door to a rush of air. "You're home?"

Philip held a box in both hands. "Only for a minute. I got thinking about a few things and decided to scoot back. First...," he handed her the box, "...here's a lantern, a flashlight, and some utility candles. I'm sorry I don't have a generator for the cottage, but at least with these you won't be in the dark if the electricity goes out."

She grabbed the box. "Thanks."

"Also, I really think you should let me put the deed in the safe at the Compass Rose. I don't trust Hollenbeck and your cousins. If that boat at the island belonged to them, and they saw us leave or came across the empty cavity, who knows what their next step will be."

"I'd really rather keep it here—close to where I can put my hand on it."

"I don't think that's a good idea. You should give it to me."

As if out of darkness, distrust shot into her mind. "Okay, but let me sign it first."

"No! Whatever you do, don't do that!"

"But why?"

"You should sign it in front of an attorney to make sure your right to the island isn't compromised. This is too important, Claire. I'll make an appointment with my attorney first thing Monday morning, and we can get in to see her as soon as possible."

"Oh, but at least let me keep the deed here. Monday is only the day after tomorrow, and—"

"No, Claire. It would be unwise to leave the deed, the tubes, or even the padlock and key here where they could be stolen."

His uncharacteristic insistence unsettled her. "I can hide it. I know of a good place where—"

"Claire."

"Oh, all right. I'll be right back."

After closing the door behind her, she placed the box on the table and picked up the brass cylinder. For a brief moment she considered giving him an empty tube. *No, that would be deceitful.*

She returned and reluctantly handed Philip the locked tube and key.

He lifted her chin drawing her eyes to his. "Hey, everything will work out fine. Just wait and see."

She nodded.

"I'll pick you up after I close. Let's make it 7:25. The Soames know we'll be a little late." He stroked her cheek with his thumb. "I love you."

"I love you too, Philip."

～～～

Claire reached to the nape of her neck and fastened the dress's hook onto its eye. Tonight Philip would publicly declare his love for her and his intention to marry her. This should be one of the happiest evenings of her life.

Yet, since Philip's brief visit, anxiety had built within her—waiting and watching for the right time to overtake her.

She pushed a bobby pin into her loose bun.

It must be because so many eyes would be on her—the outsider who stole Philip's heart. Surely people would see how much she adored him. Hopefully her love would outshine the flicker of distrust she had been unable to extinguish over the course of the afternoon.

She slipped into her low-heeled, flesh-colored shoes.

Then there was Parker. If only something—anything—could prevent him from being there tonight. *Focus. Focus on being beside Philip all evening.*

She added the final touch to her right hand—the watermelon tourmaline ring. She looked at her empty left hand. How he would announce their engagement, Philip had told her, was a secret he could barely contain, and only Mr. and Mrs. Soames knew of last Sunday's proposal and of his plans.

After sweeping lipstick over her lips, determination crossed the face in the reflection before her. *I love Philip with my whole heart, and I know he loves me.* She poked in another bobby pin. *I'm not going to doubt him.*

She sucked in a deep breath and released it slowly. *No, anxiety, I won't let you best me tonight.* She straightened her neck. *Doubts and fears, you won't overtake me.* She rolled her shoulders and straightened her back.

This will *be one of the happiest nights of my life.*

Chapter Sixty-four

Tall and handsome in his tuxedo, Philip looked her up and down and whistled.

"You're pleased then?"

"Pleased? I'm besotted!"

Claire beamed. "Let me get my coat."

"You won't need anything heavy. The air riding with this hurricane is pretty warm."

She returned with a sweater, and, locking arms, they walked against the wind to the jeep—no beach or wooded path tonight!

When they arrived, Mr. and Mrs. Soames greeted them in the foyer. "There's the happy couple!" Mr. Soames said.

Claire handed her sweater to the hired help while Philip started polite conversation with Mrs. Soames.

Mr. Soames took Claire's hand between his and whispered, "You look beautiful, Miss Claire. No wonder Philip wants to marry you! I knew you two were meant for each other the evening I met you. Good thing I helped put you two together."

Claire couldn't help but go along with his self-proclaimed achievement. "What would we have done without you?" she whispered back. "I'm very much in love with him."

"I can tell, my dear." He looked over at Mrs. Soames and lowered his voice further. "Philip tells me you have other news—about the blue granite."

"He didn't tell you?"

"No. He said you should. Perhaps later tonight we can speak privately about it."

"Absolutely!"

He winked and patted her hand before letting go.

Mr. Soames turned to Philip. "After you've introduced Claire to those who don't know her, will you check the generator with me?"

"Are you having problems again?"

"I tested it last week, and it worked fine. On a whim I tried again just before everyone came, and it wouldn't start."

"Do you want to look at it now?"

"No, not yet." He looked at his watch. "We're expecting one more couple, and I really do want you to take Claire around first."

"Okay. If it's the same problem you had before, it'll be an easy fix."

"Good! Then we should be able to slip away and return before anyone notices. With these strong gusts, I want to make sure it'll run just in case."

"Yeah, especially with a house full of people."

Claire noticed her hair in a silver-framed mirror. "Speaking of the wind, it's wreaked havoc with my hair. Is there somewhere I can freshen up?"

Mrs. Soames pointed to the hallway opposite her. "Turn right at the end of this hall, and you'll see two lit rooms. You may use either of them."

"Thank you, Mrs. Soames."

"I'll wait for you here," Philip said.

After following Mrs. Soames' directions, Claire found herself in a muffled hallway, its walls hung with sconces cupping lighted candles. Beyond her she saw yet another labyrinthine passageway extending to the left and out of sight. Hearing voices in the first lit room, she chose the second where the smell of melting wax mingled with the scent of fresh sweet-smelling roses.

She settled into a peach boudoir chair before a large well-lit mirror. She pulled bobby pins from her disheveled hair and stuck them between her lips. With elbows straight, she smoothed her wayward curls and pulled her ponytail high above her head. While recoiling the ponytail back into a bun, movement in the mirror distracted her.

She noticed the silver high-heeled shoes first, then the tight black dress glittering with each slithering motion.

No! Not tonight!

The door clicked shut.

Chapter Sixty-five

"Hello, Claire." Vanessa slinked across the room and sat beside her. "Need any help?"

"No," Claire muttered through the bobby pins.

Vanessa leaned to sniff a white rose in the arrangement between them. "Mrs. Soames always has the most impressive displays when she entertains." She brushed her nose atop another rose. "But, of course, you wouldn't know that."

Claire's bun did not go together right. After grabbing the bobby pins from her mouth and dropping them onto her lap, she unwound her hair to try again.

"There are a lot of things you don't know, Claire." Vanessa preened in the mirror before withdrawing a brush from her purse.

Once again, Claire smoothed her hair and methodically coiled the ponytail into a bun. *I will not let her irritate me.*

Using her left hand, Vanessa glided the brush through her glossy hair with exaggerated strokes. A diamond ring the size and shape of a small postage stamp sparkled on her ring finger. "Do you like my ring?"

"It's lovely."

"Philip gave me this. He wanted to give me some dinky family ring, but I wanted this one."

A weight dropped on Claire's heart, and she forced a breath to calm herself before reaching for a bobby pin and over-focusing on its placement.

"You mean he didn't tell you?" She stuffed the brush back into her purse. "I hear he's supposed to announce his engagement to you tonight?"

Claire scowled. "How do you know that?"

Vanessa curled her red lips into a smug smile. "Let's just say Mrs. Soames and I have a good relationship—thanks to Philip, of course—and she told me you two were secretly engaged last Sunday. She didn't tell me where Philip proposed because she didn't know."

Vanessa wiggled her long fingers sending the diamond into a flurry of shimmers. "But if I were to guess—let's see—I bet he proposed to you at the top of Macintosh Light."

Claire's eyes widened. "But how did you know?"

"I know because it's the same place Philip proposed to me."

Claire's pulse quickened. "I don't believe you."

"He gave me this ring," she said, flitting her fingers in front of Claire, "and he held me in his arms and promised me his love as he kissed me over and over and—"

"Stop! I don't want to hear it!" The vivid, mental picture throbbed in her mind. "I refuse to believe you!"

Vanessa snickered. "You had better believe me, Claire, because it's true. When he was up there with you last Sunday, I know him well enough to know he was remembering the enchanted evening when he proposed to *me*."

"How could you say such a thing?"

"I know him far better than you do. Despite your forcing your way between us, I still have his ring and still consider us engaged."

Claire's hand shook as she struggled to push a bobby pin into her hair. "Philip told me it would never work between you and him and assured me he did not love you."

"Nonsense! He will always love me, and I can draw him under my spell at any time."

"What's that supposed to mean?"

"We have always made a perfect couple, and we always will." She flipped her long hair over her shoulder. "So Philip didn't tell you we had been engaged? If you were to ask him, he'd have to admit it. I dare you to ask him."

Anger swelled within Claire as she reached for a bobby pin that had slid onto the floor.

"I suppose he wouldn't have told you then that he canceled our wedding two weeks before the ceremony." She sighed. "Everything was planned. We had almost finished moving my things into his house. We had set up my studio in the cottage—the one you have taken over."

I must stay composed. "Taken over? I signed a contract. I'm renting it."

"To think he backed out of our wedding over a minor misunderstanding. No doubt you too will experience a 'misunderstanding' with him." She smirked. "He'll back out on you too. Just wait and see. Then he'll come to his senses and run back to me—the one he truly loves."

"You're just hoping he will. He's not going to do that, Vanessa, and you need to get over it."

"Oh, and the painting of the cottage you bought from Barbara…"

"I bought that anonymously!"

"Has Philip talked to you about that?"

"He doesn't know I have it."

"Oh, yes he does, but he hasn't said anything about it, has he? Do you know why? I'll tell you why."

Claire jammed the last bobby pin in.

"He hasn't dared tell you because it's a painting of me! I'm the model for all of Barbara's paintings. I'm the woman entering the cottage." Bitterness pricked her words. "That painting was my wedding gift to Philip, but he returned it after our misunderstanding."

"I'm not going to take any more from you." Claire rose upon shaking legs and grabbed the chair for support. "You are cruel and—"

"—Truthful!"

"I don't trust you to be truthful with me." The confidence she portrayed conflicted with the despondency that gripped her heart.

"You forget, outsider, I've been Philip's girlfriend for a long time. No one knows him or understands him better than I, so I'm the only one suited to marry him. Besides, he told me how hard it is for him to trust you."

"What? When did he tell you that?"

"Not that long ago."

"But, I've been nothing but—"

"Think about it, Claire," she cut in. "Has he demanded honesty from you?"

"He's *asked* me to be honest and truthful with him."

"Ah! Yet from what he conveniently hasn't told you he obviously doesn't think he needs to be honest and truthful with you."

Betrayal boiled within her. "I just can't believe we're talking about the same man."

"You seem to have a problem believing things, Claire, especially when it hurts."

The possibility of Vanessa's words being the truth pierced her heart like a poisonous dart.

Vanessa's voice quieted. "I'm guessing he plans to marry you for your money, and then once he has his hands on it, he'll discard the girl without a family." She twisted the diamond in the light. "But that's okay. I'll wait for him."

Tears filled Claire's eyes as she pictured Philip signing his name to the deed. She imagined him taking her on a ride in his boat...

Yanking at the collar of her dress and gulping for air, she ran from the room.

Chapter Sixty-Six

Philip looked at his watch. *Where is she?*

The Soames had given up on the arrival of the last couple and had joined their guests beyond the foyer's grand paneled doors.

He could hardly wait to show Claire off. He glanced down the hall where she had disappeared fifteen minutes earlier.

For the umpteenth time, he rubbed his hand across his pocket and tapped the circle of his maternal grandmother's Edwardian engagement ring. He rehearsed once more the words he would say.

His beautiful Claire came running toward him.

Running?

"Philip!" she said wild-eyed and panting. Tears glistened on her cheeks.

"What happened?"

"We need to talk!"

"What's the matter?"

"Please, we have to talk now."

He creased his brow. "Okay."

Motion beyond her distracted him. Vanessa rounded the far corner of the hallway and sashayed toward them. She narrowed alluring eyes before puckering her lips and blowing a kiss. Philip glowered at her.

"We need to go somewhere—somewhere private."

"Let's go this way," he said pointing down the opposite hall.

He scowled once more at a smug Vanessa before leading Claire to a room with its door ajar. Coatracks with neatly-hung coats and sweaters lined the walls. Philip closed the door behind them.

"Is it true?" Claire choked. "Were you once engaged to Vanessa?"

He averted his eyes. "Yes."

"She said you called off the wedding, but—but you two are still engaged. How can you propose to me if you're still engaged?"

"We're not engaged. I told you—"

"But she still wears her engagement ring."

Philip put his hands on her shoulders. She trembled beneath his touch. "She may wear the engagement ring, but—"

She jerked away from his hands. "Did you propose to her at Macintosh Light?"

He swallowed. "Yes."

She shut her eyes and grimaced as if in pain. "Why, Philip? Why did you propose to me there?"

"I can explain."

"Explain? Explain what? That I'm a second-string replacement for her?"

Philip concentrated on controlling his mounting agitation and answered her as calmly as he could. "That is definitely *not* the case."

"You can't tell me that—that when you held me and kissed me up there you didn't think of holding Vanessa in your arms and kissing her."

"Claire, that's not fair."

The chandelier above them flickered.

"Fair? Now I understand why you didn't want anyone to know about our engagement. You knew you shouldn't have proposed there and wanted to cover it up."

"Claire, I love you and only you."

"Yeah! You promised your love to Vanessa too—promised. Now I'm to believe you love me?"

"I assure you no one was at the forefront of my mind last Sunday night but you."

"Forefront? So Vanessa was in your thoughts lingering in the background, and she always will be. I've even—I've even been sleeping under her wedding gift to you. Is it true you knew I had it?" She rubbed her knuckles across her cheeks.

"Yes," he whispered.

"And you didn't tell me? If I had known—"

"Philip! Are you around here?" Mr. Soames called, passing the door.

Claire rubbed her hands up and down her crossed arms. "Here you've wanted me to be truthful and honest with you when you haven't been with me. You've wanted me to trust you when you don't trust me."

The overhead light dimmed.

"Claire, I'm sorry. I'm so sorry…."

The room went black.

"Philip, where are you!" Mr. Soames called again.

"In here!" Philip yelled before lowering his voice. "I never should have proposed to you—"

"Philip, I need you urgently!" Mr. Soames voice, sounding panicked, cut in.

Philip groped for the doorknob. Finding it, he twisted it and opened the door washing the room with dim candlelight from the sconces across the hall. "I'm in here, Mr. Soames!"

"You mean—you mean—" Claire coughed on her words.

"Oh, there you are, Philip, finally. I've been looking all over for you. Quick! Let's get to the generator."

"Go ahead. I'm right behind you."

"Please hurry!" Mr. Soames said.

Philip turned back to Claire. Her watery eyes glinted in the candlelight. "Claire, please—please wait here. I can set things right." He glanced at the door. "I'll be right back and will clarify everything."

Empty eyes stared back at him. Fresh tears dribbled down her cheeks.

"I wouldn't leave you unless I had to. I'll be right back."

As he dashed from the room, he knew she wouldn't be there when he returned.

Chapter Sixty-Seven

He regrets proposing to me!

Claire lowered her arms over the unmerciful knots twisting her abdomen. The coats crowded around her sucking air from the room. If only she could breathe!

She stepped into the empty hall. The candles flittered finger-like shadows up the walls.

How could she look for Grace? How could she face the crowd beyond the doors? What if she saw Vanessa again—or worse, Parker?

With no other choice, she knew what to do.

Run and hide.

Disregarding her sweater, she slipped out the front door into the untamed wind. Oblivious to her plight, clouds played tag across the moon—one second cloaking her surroundings in terrifying blackness and the next offering her illuminated respite.

If I can just get home.

Her dress billowed as she stumbled to the stone wall and, running her hand along its rough coping, allowed it to guide her to the path between the properties.

At the break in the wall, she looked back at the house where candles and flashlights floated behind the windows. To her right, the ocean roared fiercer than she had ever heard before. In front of her the path at her feet led to the black, gaping mouth of the woods. If only she had a light—any light—to get through it.

I'll be safe at the cottage. It's just over there. I can do this.

As if sympathetic to her need, the clouds parted over the silvery moon. She gulped and stepped onto the path. With breaths bursting from her lungs, she ran through the woods until her shoes depressed the grass of Philip's back lawn.

I made it. I'm almost home!

Taking advantage of the moon's glow, she hastened around the garage and along the driveway. As she ran down the incline, the moon disappeared.

She stopped.

A beam of light speared the darkness through the cottage's back window.

She crept along the side for a peek and gasped.

Shafts of light held by gloved hands shined on ransacked pieces of her life. Jake poked through her father's coin collection strewn across the kitchen table. Parker dumped a storage box of sea glass onto the floor.

The fetor of cigarettes touched her nose before two arms encircled her. She screamed. A gloved hand rose and covered her mouth while the other arm lifted her from the ground. She kicked with all her might.

"Hey, look who I found!" Hugh yelled as he dragged her through the French doors.

"Oh, this does complicate things," Parker said pointing his flashlight at her face. "Hello, darling. You look a little windblown but lovely as always. Aren't you supposed to be at a gala?"

Hugh set her on the floor and dropped his hand from her mouth but kept his arms tightly about her. The acrid stench of cigarettes in the cottage and on his clothes sickened her.

"What have you done?" she cried looking at the disarray. "What are you doing?"

"*Tsk, tsk.*" Parker shifted the beam away from her eyes. "Too many questions. *We* will be asking the questions here."

"Yeah!" Hugh said.

"Where is it, Claire?" Jake demanded, pointing his flashlight at her.

"Where's what?"

Hugh crushed her in his grip and said through clenched teeth, "Don't get smart with us, *cousin.*"

"Ouch! Let me go!"

Parker nodded at Hugh before saying, "Very well, as long as you cooperate." Hugh released her to Parker who grabbed her arm and pushed her onto a kitchen chair. He leveled his cold dark eyes to hers. How could she have ever been attracted to this man?

He snapped his finger at Jake and pointed to the table. Jake tossed him her piece of granite. Parker caught it in his fingertips and held it between their faces. "So this is what brought you to Maine, huh? Thankfully these boys lent me the chunk found in their father's possessions. My 'finding' theirs on Dovetail Beach helped confirm we were working toward the same goal—solving the riddle."

He lobbed it over his shoulder, sending glass chinking to the floor.

"You really should have married me, Claire. We could have found the deed together on a romantic excursion to Temple Island."

A tremor shimmied through her body.

He sighed. "Instead you had to go with England." He shined the flashlight in her eyes again. "You did find the deed, didn't you? Something was in that empty cavity."

Claire lifted a shaking arm to shield her eyes. *I have to get out of here.* She glanced at the open French doors then jumped and bolted toward them.

Parker dropped the flashlight into his pocket and seized her arm. "You're not cooperating!" He jerked her around and shoved her back onto the chair. "Answer me!"

"Yes, yes," she cried, rubbing her arm, "we found the deed."

"Ah, I thought so. Where is it then?"

"Yeah, where did you hide it?" Jake repeated.

"What if I don't tell you?" she asked, choking on the lump in her throat.

Parker's upturned flashlight cast ghoulish shadows across his face. He clutched her shoulders and bent to within inches of her face. His sandalwood cologne wafted toward her. "You *will* tell me; otherwise, I'll compel you with more persuasive means."

He lifted a finger and traced it slowly down the side of her left cheek. Her eyes drifted to the long scars highlighted by the weak light. "Ah, yes," he whispered. "We haven't forgotten that night, have we?"

Her eyes widened.

Parker stood. "Tell me where it is, Claire." He withdrew the flashlight from his pocket and crossed his arms sending the beam bouncing off the ceiling.

A blast of wind whammed one of the French doors against her worktable. Her parents' torn wedding picture rocked on the floor beside her crumpled wedding dress. Her eyes darted from Parker to Jake to Hugh.

Mr. Soames' voice repeated one word over and over in her mind.

Murder.

Chapter Sixty-eight

Oh, Lord… Why hadn't she thought to pray earlier? *…what do I do?*

She vacillated as her breaths hitched in her chest.

It's not worth it—it's just not worth it. At least she'd always have the satisfaction that she, Sam's daughter, found the deed. Parker and her slimy cousins could now grapple with Philip over it.

She calmed. "Philip has it."

"Ugh! Do we have to search his house now?" Hugh whined.

"It's in the safe at the Compass Rose."

Jake said, "C'mon! Let's go get it!"

Parker patted her arm. "That's a girl! I knew you'd come through."

"Yeah, but what are we going to do with her?" Hugh asked. "We can't just leave her here. She'll blow everything."

Resting his elbow on his fist, Parker tapped his lower lip and stared at her.

"I—I've told you what you want to know. Just let me go."

"Well?" Jake asked.

"Hmm. If I remember correctly Claire is an expert swimmer and loves being close to the ocean."

No! Not the water!

Parker turned to Jake. "When was low tide?"

"About a half hour ago—hour at the most."

"You boys have any rope and a couple pairs of knee boots in your truck?"

"Yeah, why?" questioned Jake.

"Quickly! Run and get them. Meet us on the beach."

Jake darted through the open doors.

Fear shimmied through Claire's body. "You know everything. What more could you possibly want from me?"

Parker ignored her and pulled Hugh aside. With their backs turned, the men whispered.

Claire eyed the new telephone on her worktable. No, it would take too long to dial. Besides, the lines might be down. She slipped her shoes off then glanced back at the men. *This is my chance, Lord. Please help me.*

She bolted through the doors into the darkness.

"Get back here!" Hugh yelled.

Heavy footsteps pounded behind her. Arms reached around her chest. "Help! Help me! Help!"

The same gloved hand covered her mouth. She screamed into it, kicking her feet.

"Bring her back in here!" Parker growled.

Hugh strengthened his grip and pulled her back into the cottage. "You're a little fighter aren't you?"

"Yes, she is—just like a wildcat." Parker scowled. "And I don't like cats."

Hugh threw her onto the chair.

"We can't have any more outbursts like that," Parker said grabbing two flour-sack towels from the sink. He tossed one to Hugh who tied her hands behind her back while he gagged her with the other. "Come on! Let's go. No more flashlights."

After they darkened their beams, Hugh yanked Claire by the towel and pushed her behind Parker to the edge of the path leading to the beach.

Clouds covered the moon, and light, horizontal rain veiled the Cove's radiance. Dark, angry waves charged up the beach. The wind sent her dress and hair into a riotous flurry.

While zigzagging down the path, Claire slipped on the slick dirt and toppled to the sand. She screamed as her body sandwiched her ankle against a rock. Pain shot up her leg.

"Oh, come on," Hugh said, pulling her up.

The gag muffled her anguished cry as her ankle buckled, sending her to her knees.

"Quiet!" Parker said. "Just drag her."

Hugh wrapped an arm across her chest and dragged her sideways, jostling her ankle against the ground. Through night-adjusted, tear-filled eyes, Claire stared at the waves as they clawed to devour what little beach remained.

At the far end, Hugh dropped her on the sand, summoning another painful cry. She scooted to the cliff and leaned against it. Hugh and Parker stood over her.

"I sure could use a smoke!" Hugh said. "I should've taken Jake's cigarettes and lighter."

"I think you'll find Claire has an aversion to smoking. Don't you, darling?"

She whimpered.

"That so?"

"Did you know, Hugh, Claire's parents died because of a cigarette?"

"How can someone die from a cigarette?"

"Her father was a plumber, you see, and it's believed while working on a gas line in their house one morning, he unknowingly punctured it. While Claire and her parents worked all day, their house filled with gas. That afternoon at the same moment her mother opened the door and they stepped over the threshold, Claire's father lit his cigarette."

Hugh mimicked the sound of an explosion.

Tears spilled from Claire's eyes.

"Yes, the explosion incinerated everything within several hundred feet. Didn't it, darling?"

With white rope looped loosely around his neck, Jake scuttled down the path wearing rubber boots. He handed Hugh a similar pair.

"Well," Parker said, "sorry I can't stay and watch all the fun, but I have a gala to go to and a cute little redhead waiting for me." He scooched beside Claire. "Speaking of redheads, did I tell you I got ahold of your old boyfriend? Daniel's criminal past and his name on your joint account in Chicago helped me find him."

I didn't know he had a criminal past.

"He seemed interested in visiting the Cove."

"No!" she said through the gag.

"Anyway, regarding the deed—if it's where you say it is, we'll try to remember to come back and free you before the water gets too high."

Too high? No! The knots in her stomach tightened.

"If it's not there, I'll make sure Philip gets fingered for whatever happens here." He clutched her chin and shook it. "Remember, Claire. No one makes a fool of me."

He pushed her away and stood. "I'll let you boys do what needs to be done. I'll meet you at 12:30 at the usual place." He strode into the misty darkness.

Jake hooked his arms around Claire's elbows while Hugh grabbed her legs.

No! She wiggled in protest then shrieked as pangs knifed her ankle and leg. Her body slacked in their arms as their feet splashed into the water.

They stood her facing the beach in the frigid water against the third weir pole. Dark swells engulfed her calves as they rolled past. Uncontrollable shivering racked her body. *Oh, Lord, I know You're with me. I know I'm not alone, but I'm so afraid. Please help me.*

Jake said, "You won't need this anymore." He yanked the tourmaline ring off her finger before wrapping rope around her ribs.

"Make sure it's tight enough," Hugh said, binding his length around her thighs tight against the slick seaweed.

She cried out as razor-sharp pricks cut through her dress into her legs and back and arms.

A swell rushed them. Both Hugh and Jake grabbed the pole for support.

"Let's get out of here," Hugh said. He snatched Jake's lighter from his shirt pocket then flicked it in front of Claire and held the flame. "So this is the last thing your father saw before he died, huh?" The fire bowed in the unruly wind. "Here's to your old man."

"Oh, come on," Jake said. "Let's go. I want to get those old coins."

"Leave them. We'll have time to get them later."

They sloshed through the water and disappeared into the drizzle.

The sharp pieces biting into her flesh and the impossibility of putting weight on her ankle hampered every effort to free herself—to reach the safety of the beach. *It's so close!*

A wave hit her legs and lower back and curved around her body. In no time it sucked back, spraying water in her face and soaking her gag with the brackish water. *I'm not alone. I don't have to face this alone.*

Numbness seeped into her body and mind as over and over the waves tormented her, each one higher than the last.

Philip's face flashed in her mind—his green eyes, his deep voice, his gentleness, the love she knew he had for her.

What if he hadn't signed the deed?

What if his explanations were reasonable? *I should have waited. I should have given him a chance. Now it'll be too late. I should have—*

She heard it first—the wave as it battered the rocky protrusion behind her. Her heart pounded. *It's coming!* It swamped her middle back and pulled her from the pole as it railroaded toward the beach. *I'm going to drown!* The deafening wave drew back, slamming her body against the myriad pricks on the pole. *Lord, help me die quickly.* Short, shallow breaths leapt from her lungs. Nausea swirled through her numbness. A blackness darker than the night crowded toward the center of her vision. Her body felt weaker…weaker…

Chapter Sixty-nine

The huge generator finally droned to life, and the lights lit the house. "So much for an easy fix, Mr. Soames."

"Yeah, I'm just going to buy a new one then I won't have to worry about it again. Thanks for helping. You're a lifesaver. Sorry to take you away from Claire."

Philip had already started toward the door.

"Just give me the cue when you're ready, and you can have the floor, Philip."

"Okay." Philip doubted the night would go as he had envisioned—not unless a miracle happened in the next few minutes. Avoiding the crowd, he hurried along familiar hallways to the room where the coats hung.

As he expected—no Claire.

He stepped inside the large room where the guests mingled and scanned the faces. Vanessa locked eyes with him, but he quickly looked beyond her and kept searching. Pastor Tim and Grace stood talking with a man by the fireplace. When Philip walked up to them, Grace turned toward him. "Where have you guys been? We've been waiting for you."

"Have you seen Claire?" Philip whispered.

"No. Why?"

"I can't find her." Embarrassment and shame kept him from expounding. "Can you keep an eye out for her and make sure she stays with you if you see her?"

Concern crossed her face. "Of course."

"I'm going to look around a bit. Don't say anything to anyone about this other than Pastor Tim. I'll be right back."

"Okay."

Philip made another unsuccessful circuit inside before stepping into the wind and encircling the grounds. Calling her name, he walked along the stone wall to the thundering beach. Light rain speckled his glasses, and he swished them with a finger as his eyes adjusted to the darkness.

Could she have gone back to the cottage?

Retracing his steps to the path between the properties, he traversed the forest and walked past the hum of his tiny generator to his back door.

Since he had given Claire his good flashlight, he dashed upstairs to his bedroom for the one on his nightstand. While fumbling for it, he glanced out the window. A small light flickered low over East Beach before disappearing. He squinted through the droplets. Nothing. *Surely she's not on the beach.*

Finding the flashlight, he grabbed it, sprinted down the stairs, and ran through the rain to the cottage. He rapped on the front door. "Claire? It's Philip. Are you in there?" He tried the latch. Locked.

Receiving no answer he rounded the cottage to look through the back windows. A loud repetitious thump sounded above the howl of the wind. He clicked the flashlight as he approached the open French doors.

The hair on the back of his neck stood on end. "Claire?"

He swept the beam over the disarray then silenced the thrashing door. "Are you here?" He frantically searched the cottage pausing only when the shaft of light highlighted the painting above her bed. Fresh regret squeezed his conscience.

While returning to the French doors, the beam crossed Claire's shoes lying on their sides beneath an outward-turned chair. *Lord, what has happened here? Please help me find her.* He went to Claire's worktable and lifted the telephone handset. Silence. He dropped it onto its cradle and hurried outside to survey the yard. Nothing.

Unable to get that flicker out of his mind, he descended the path to the beach. Fresh footprints and drag lines impressed areas not yet erased by the water. Steadying the beam before him, he hugged the cliff and dodged the surging waves until he arrived at the base of the other shoeprint-covered path.

Before ascending the cliff, he paused for one last look. He swung the light above the black waves.

A cold breath blasted down his neck as the light crossed something bulky attached to a weir pole. He rubbed the rain off his glasses then twisted the end of the flashlight to concentrate the ray. *What in the...*

His skin prickled. "No!"

He ran into the water toward Claire's slumped body, timing his pole-to-pole dashes with the ebb and flow of the waves. When he reached her, his heart pummeled his chest as he lifted her lolling head and shined the light on her ashen face. "Claire!" He pulled the gag from her darkened lips. "Oh, Claire. No!"

He clutched the pole for support before jamming the flashlight into his shirt and pulling the jackknife from his pocket. He flicked it open and slashed the gag. A wave rammed into him. His legs bent under the force, and he gripped the pole tighter, shredding his skin against the sharp barnacles.

While wiping the salty drops on his glasses, the flashlight blinked.

He shifted behind Claire and reached into the water, cutting into the ropes around her legs. *I can barely feel this knife, Lord. Please, I can't drop it.* Finally, the rope loosened and fell into the surf.

Another wave pounded him jostling the flashlight into the water. He grabbed for it, but the wave carried it away from his grasp. As it rolled beneath the waves, the light flickered before turning as black as the deep.

Supporting her against the pole with one arm, his other hand followed the rope that secured her chest. With numb, shaking hands he sawed the braided cord until it dropped into the water. When her body collapsed against his arm, Philip dropped his knife and wrapped his arms about her.

With the ocean contending to claim her and drag her body out to sea, he secured her against his chest and fought his way to the beach.

Chapter Seventy

Claire opened her eyes to a white-tiled ceiling. *Where am I?* She licked parched lips with a dry tongue.

"Oh, am I going to be in trouble!"

Claire darted her eyes toward the voice.

Sasha stood and leaned over the railing of the bed. "Philip is *not* going to be happy I shooed him out of here a half hour before you woke up." Her eyes bore into her and her voice quieted. "He so wanted to be here when you did."

Claire lifted a hand, and Sasha grasped it gently.

"How about a sponge for those lips?"

Claire nodded.

Sasha dipped a little sponge into a cup before patting it across her lips. "You're looking better than you did last Saturday. Do you remember being in the ER?"

Claire shook her head.

"I was working when Philip brought you in. You floated in and out of consciousness a few times, but you were mostly out of it."

"Why?" Claire whispered.

"Well..." She dunked the sponge back into the cup before dotting Claire's tongue. "You were treated for hypothermia and exposure, and your ankle—well, let's just say your foot was pointing in a strange direction. The ropes and barnacles did a number on you. In fact, we had to dig barnacles out of your skin, but..." Sasha plopped the sponge into the cup and leaned back over the railing. "…thankfully the frigid water kept you from bleeding to death."

Claire grimaced.

"Do you remember what happened Saturday night?"

Memories of Parker and her cousins and of darkness and fear flooded her mind to the point of physical pain, and she nodded. Her widening eyes swung from Sasha to the door then back to Sasha. Her breathing sped to match her pulse.

Sasha glanced above her bed before pushing the call button by Claire's hand. She bent close to her face and spoke in a soothing voice. "You're safe, Claire. No one will come through those doors who shouldn't."

A nurse arrived and fiddled with the bags on her IV pole.

"Philip saved your life, you know. The police wouldn't have made it in time. With the phone lines down, he brought you here in your car. I can still picture him standing in the ER in his drenched, sand-covered tuxedo carrying you wrapped in a brocade bedspread stained with blood."

Claire could barely keep her eyes open. *If only I had stayed at the gala.* Her eyes closed. *If only I had trusted him. If only…*

Chapter Seventy-one

Waking to a brighter room, Claire turned her head toward the source. The sun wrapped around Philip as he leaned on the windowsill with his head hanging and his wide, athletic back to her.

She licked her lips. "Philip," she whispered.

He spun around. "Claire!" After striding to her side, he stroked her hair while worried eyes skimmed her face. "Claire, I'm so…" He swallowed and looked away.

Claire's eyes burned as tears fell down her temples. "I'm sorry."

He swiped a tear from his cheek and shook his head. "Sorry? There's nothing to be sorry about. I'm the one who should be apologizing." He pushed aside the hair on her forehead. "I'm just so grateful you're okay. When I saw you tied to…" He looked away again before pressing his lips together and wiping another tear. "I was so sure you were dead, and the thought of having lost you was…" He gulped.

"If only I hadn't—"

He touched a finger to her lips. "I'm to blame. If I had been forthright, this would never have happened."

She licked her lips again and pointed to a cup on her table. "Please."

He poured a little water into the cup and handed it to her. "Do you remember what happened?"

She grabbed the cup with shaky hands and sipped the water. "I remember leaving the cottage with Parker and Hugh and falling and hurting my ankle.

The rest is sketchy, but I remember darkness and water…and being cold. So very cold. Do you know the rest? Will you tell me?"

"Are you sure you want to know?"

She nodded and took another sip.

He dragged over a chair, and, leaning on the bed, held her hand and gently told her about leaving the Soames' house, seeing a flicker of light from his bedroom window, searching the ransacked cottage, and finding her while searching the beach. "Then out of desperation I checked, and there it was— a weak pulse. Shocked but filled with hope, I rushed you here praying you wouldn't die."

"Thank you for not giving up on me." She closed her eyes, then fluttered them open again. "It's so strange. A flame caused my parents' deaths but saved my life."

"Uncanny."

"You know how they died?"

"Yes. I'm so sorry, Claire. Why didn't you ever tell me?"

"I couldn't."

"Knowing how they died explains a lot now and gives me understanding how to help and comfort you."

"I don't know if I'll ever feel safe again, though."

He rubbed his thumb across her hand. "Well, Parker and your cousins are in jail with a very long list of charges against them. I had installed a new security system after that theft last summer, and Hugh and Jake tripped the silent alarm on their way to my safe. A deputy discovered your tourmaline ring in Jake's pocket while patting him down."

"My ring!"

"Yes, it's still in evidence but is safe. After further questioning, they admitted to tying you up and trying to steal the deed. They even admitted to vandalizing mosaics up and down the coast and burgling when they had the time."

"They *are* the ones!"

"Apparently they thought '*Under pieces on a level plane*' meant under a floor mosaic. Whenever they stole, they carted the goods down the path through my property to their boat waiting off East Beach."

"And left behind their cigarette butts."

"Yup! Following a tip, the police kept combing the shore between the Cove and Hydeport but couldn't catch them or find evidence."

"The men in the orange-striped boat."

"Likely. Hugh and Jake accused Parker of blackmailing them and masterminding everything from destroying mosaics to your attempted murder. I have a feeling Parker is going to have a hard time finagling out of this. When Daniel came to town looking for him…"

Claire's jaw dropped. "Daniel?"

He patted her hand. "Parker found him and invited him to town."

"Yes…I now remember Parker telling me that." *Oh, no! It was true.*

"Shhh. Listen." He rubbed her hand and gave it a light squeeze." Pastor Tim was at the post office on Monday and overheard Lorna talking to a lady about a Daniel Smith asking for Parker and wanting to know where you lived. For once in her life, Lorna did something right and didn't give him any information."

Claire sighed in relief.

"Pastor Tim told Grace who explained about Daniel. Pastor Tim, his off-duty deputy friend, the Harriman brothers, and I paid Daniel a visit at his motel."

Claire glanced at Philip's bandage-wrapped hand. "Did you rough him up?"

"This is because of the barnacles that shredded my palm," he said, glancing at his hand. "No, we didn't beat him up, but trust me it was all I could do not to after hearing how he treated you. All we did was tell him Parker was in jail for trying to murder you, remind you had every right to charge him in Illinois for what he did to you, and inform him if he ever tried to contact you in any way, we would pay him another visit. Then Carl and Jason 'helped' him pack his car, and he left."

She couldn't help but smile. "What would I do without you guys?" She took a last sip of water and handed him the cup. "Thank you for taking care of me. I don't deserve you, Philip, especially after being so irrational and unfair and—and untrusting."

"After Daniel and Parker, I can understand why." He returned the cup to the table. "Oh, and just so you know, I took the deed to my attorney, and when you're up to it, you can sign it. She'll file it for you, and the island will be yours."

How could I have doubted him?

"As far as Vanessa goes…" He hesitated. "Is it okay to talk about her?"

Dread filled her. "Okay," she whispered.

He took a deep breath. "I wanted to tell you about her at our impromptu picnic after the gallery night."

"I remember, and I told you I didn't want to know."

"I should have insisted on telling you anyway." He cleared his throat. "Vanessa and I grew up together and dated for years. I overlooked her many flaws because she was rich and talented and attractive.

"I would—and still do—buy fresh lobster from the Harriman brothers. They would always talk about God and my need for Him. Eventually, I became a Christian and changed into a completely different man. When I told Vanessa, she was furious. We started to drift apart from the rift until one day out of the blue she decided to become a Christian as well. I was thrilled!

"Soon afterwards we got engaged. The date was set. She moved most of her things into my house and set up her studio in the cottage. Two weeks before our wedding, I overheard her telling a friend she was only pretending to be a Christian—by going to church and talking about God and the Bible—because she loved me and didn't want to lose me. She said after we were married she would do whatever she could to get me away from church and the 'foolishness' of serving God.

"I was shocked! When I confronted her, we had a huge argument. Losing all trust in her, I broke off the engagement and wanted nothing more to do with her. Ironically, I had seen very little of her since we broke up until you came to town." He shook his head. "Her divisive half-truths and actions toward you have been deplorable."

She fought against the exhaustion that pressed upon her. "And Macintosh Light?"

"Yes, I proposed to her there."

Claire pulled away from his touch and smoothed the waffled blanket lying across her legs.

"I knew at the time I should have waited and regret proposing to you there. I certainly hadn't planned on it."

"But at the Soames' last Saturday you said you never should have proposed to me at all."

"Claire, I'm sorry. That's definitely not what I meant. Of course I want you to be my wife—now more than ever. I love you very, very much. Believe me, during that spontaneous proposal I knew exactly who I was asking to be my wife and who I was holding in my arms and kissing."

She rubbed her eye, then reached back and threaded her fingers through his.

"Last May when I saw you standing in my shop after seeing you in Chicago, I just knew you were the one God chose for me, only to be confused later when you told me you weren't a Christian. When you *did* become one, I had a hard time trusting the genuineness of your decision because of my experience with Vanessa. But, after you explained your boat name and answered Pastor Tim's question, my doubts vanished. Overwhelmed by my love for you in that light room, I couldn't help but propose."

"I understand now." Hot tears filled her eyes as fatigue weighted her eyelids. "You have no idea how much I understand. I have to tell you...about the deception...between my parents, but I'm so tired right now."

He stood and kissed her forehead. "Sleep then. I'll be here when you wake up."

She closed her eyes and whispered, "I love you, Philip. It will be such a...such a privilege to be your...wife."

Chapter Seventy-two

Claire ran her finger over the date before clicking the Bible's clasp and replacing it beneath the heady cluster of pink roses. When Philip turned the jeep at the dangling sign, the crutches in the back seat clinked and toppled to the floor.

As rocks popped beneath the tires, Claire clapped her hand on top of the new jackknife in his pants pocket. "Wait!"

He braked and rested a warm, tender hand over hers. "Do you want me to turn around?"

She blew a slow breath through her pursed lips.

"We don't have to come here today, Claire."

"No—no, I know, but I want to—I need to."

He wrapped his fingers around hers. "Do you want to close your eyes?"

"Good idea—yes." She closed her lids tightly. "Okay. Go ahead."

At the end of the driveway, Philip parked and got out. The cool air bit when he opened her door, but she warmed when he covered her with a soft blanket that smelled like balsam. He lifted her and walked toward the gentle rhythmic slosh of the waves. After placing her on a cold flat rock and tucking the blanket about her, he sat and pulled her close. She snuggled into his arms and drank in his musk-scented cologne.

He nuzzled her hair and kissed her. "I know you can do this. I'm right here for you."

Seagulls squawked as they flew overhead, and a boat's engine chugged in the distance.

She opened her eyes but, knowing where he had placed her, cast them downward while she summoned her courage. The colorful plaid blanket contrasted with the drab rock beside her. Wedged in a crack by her thigh, a glint of red blazed in the sinking sun.

"Look!" She freed her arm from the blanket and pried the small sugared glass from the crevice. "I finally found one!"

Philip plucked it from her outstretched palm, inspected it, and returned it. "It's a beauty."

"Did you…?"

He chuckled and bopped her nose with the tip of his finger. "No, I didn't plant it there."

She withdrew her other arm from the blanket and turned the piece over. "It's so rounded and pitted and scarred. I can't imagine the tumbling—the storms—this must have gone through."

Philip ran his fingertips over the red welts and healing cuts marring her hands, wrists, and arms. His voice softened. "But if its journey hadn't been arduous, it wouldn't be as treasured."

"Yes—yes, I suppose you're right." She examined it for a few moments longer before gripping it and letting out a deep breath.

She lifted her head. "They're gone!"

He gave her a light hug. "Mr. Soames was horrified when he heard of your ordeal and pulled strings as only he could to remove the poles as soon as the storm passed."

"I—I just didn't expect them to be gone."

Philip drew her closer. "I know you didn't. Their absence is the only reason why I agreed to bring you here today."

"It looks so different now."

"It does but definitely for the better."

She stared at the beach. "I'm not ready to go down there yet."

"There's no hurry."

She glanced at the cottage and bit her lip.

"When they weren't taking care of you, the ladies of the church took turns moving your things out and cleaning."

"And the painting?"

"We'll never see it again."

She nodded. "I'm not ready to go in there either."

"That's okay. When you are, we'll go in together."

"I'd like that."

"So…" He cupped her chin and turned her face toward him. He ran his thumb over her lips. "I guess that means you have to come home with me then. Is that okay, Mrs. England?"

She answered him with a long, eager kiss. "I confess when I first moved here I daydreamed about living in your house—about waking each morning in that corner top room to a grand view of the ocean."

Philip pressed his lips onto hers before standing and scooping her into his arms. "Then daydream no more."

While he carried her to the house, Claire leaned her head on his shoulder and nestled into his warm embrace.

He kissed the top of her head. "You know what?"

"What?"

"Of all the amazing and beautiful treasures I've picked up off these beaches, you're by far my most precious find."

She fingered her piece of sea glass as a tear of joy splashed onto her cheek and a wave of serenity washed over her heart.

ACKNOWLEDGMENTS

First of all, though Lone Spruce Cove and Macintosh Light are fictitious, they were both inspired by two of my favorite places—Camden, Maine and Pemaquid Point Light. If you ever have the chance to visit either location, I feel confident you will find them beautiful and well worth the visit.

Thank you to my husband, Brian, for his endless patience while I talked about this book and its progress from beginning to end.

Thank you to Everett and Jessica for taking notes for me when ideas came to mind while driving and for not complaining while I wrote. Everett, thank you for your hands for the front cover, and, Jessica, for your sketches.

I'm grateful to Brandy for setting me on the right path, for Renee for her great ideas and endless encouragement, for Dana (madebythewaves on Ebay) for her big pieces of red beach glass for the front cover, for Abigayle Claire for her expertise in proofreading and editing my manuscript, and for Dave for putting together my website.

Many thanks too to Mom for her input, support, and ideas. I appreciate the many hours she took to help me make this book what it is. Also, while some of the sea glass on the front is mine, many pieces are hers. It was great fun going through her stash and being able to write her pieces into my story. May they inspire you to find a beach and search for your own beautiful treasures. You never know…you just might find a red one.

Made in the USA
Middletown, DE
27 November 2018